THE THURSDAY NIGHT MEN

Tonino Benacquista

THE THURSDAY
NIGHT MEN

*Translated from the French
by Alison Anderson*

Europa
editions

Europa Editions
214 West 29th Street
New York, N.Y. 10001
www.europaeditions.com
info@europaeditions.com

Copyright © 2011 by Editions Gallimard, Paris
First Publication 2012 by Europa Editions

Translation by Alison Anderson
Original title: *Homo erectus*
Translation copyright © 2012 by Europa Editions

Library of Congress Cataloging in Publication Data is available
ISBN 978-1-60945-079-3

Benacquista, Tonino
The Thursday Night Men

Book design by Emanuele Ragnisco
www.mekkanografici.com

Cover illustration by Luca Laurenti

Prepress by Grafica Punto Print – Rome

Printed in the USA

To all the women in my life

THE THURSDAY NIGHT MEN

1

For some of them, it was an opportunity to meet on their own, among men, to talk about women. Others were in need of solidarity, and this was their last refuge, where the deep wounds from the never-ending battle would have time to heal. For everyone, no matter where they were from or what they had experienced, it was first and foremost a place to tell a story. Or, to make a clean breast of it, not trying to convince anyone or thinking of it as therapy, not hoping for anything in return other than to have their words strike a chord with those anonymous listeners who'd come in search of an answer. Each participant was the sole judge of his story's validity and had any number of reasons to share it. Perhaps he wanted to get it off his chest once and for all, or to give it the false veneer of a fable, transforming it into an epic memory. He could also share his story in order to help others, to keep them from wallowing in a similar torment. Or perhaps his motive was the chance, in the presence of others, to go back over the many choices he had had to make, the twists of fate he had managed to avoid. And, if his misadventure had turned to tragedy, by sharing it here he would find consolation that he had not suffered in vain.

The regular participants kept quiet about the existence of these sessions. If they had to mention them, they would resort to neutral expressions, calling it their *Thursday group*. Lodge, club, coterie, brotherhood: the fact that each member could use the term of his choice to designate the assembly prevented any temptation to turn it into a ritual or let it become a secret society, with the requisite laws and exclusions. Still, only sincere individuals were tolerated, men who had no malicious intent. Anyone else never came back, or only in an emergency, for no one, in these matters, was safe from a stroke of fate.

There were no written records regarding the brotherhood, and no one knew how it had come about. Poets and storytellers claimed it had been around since time immemorial, a place for men to gather in a forum and try to understand the infinite workings of the random events that governed their destiny. Some maintained that the tradition had been born with the despair of the Sabines as they mourned their women, whom the Romans, bent on founding families for their Empire, had abducted. Others supported the idea that the tradition had been imported from North America, the offshoot of an ancient Indian custom where warriors sang their joy, or their distress, at having met, or failed to meet, the mother of their children. Another theory posited that it had been formed during the post-war reconstruction, to allow survivors to evoke the idylls incited by the dark years, in each of the camps. Others, finally, claimed that they had attended the very first sessions in the late 1960s, in Paris, a time when social movements and the sexual revolution were giving rise to all sorts of committees— some of which, like this one, had survived, even though there'd been no proselytizing.

Nowadays the sessions were held on Thursdays at seven P.M., including holidays, summer and winter alike—there was no season, no respite, for a meeting like this. The number of participants did not vary greatly, and that was a real mystery. Given the diversity of those attending—some were just passing by, some disappeared once they'd shared their testimony, others waited for months before they could bring themselves to speak; some were regulars, some showed up again at a scheduled date—an odd law seemed to hold that their numbers always balanced out at roughly a hundred, give or take a few. The mystics among them saw this as a magic number, but the more pragmatic attendees could see no rational explanation. In spite of the absence of by-laws, there *was* one law that seemed irrevocable: a participant could have his say only once. Even if there were unexpected repercussions, out of respect for the audience, a speaker was not allowed to go back over his testimony at a later date, once it had been voiced. Tough luck for those who hadn't known how to express what was in their hearts: others were waiting their turn.

While the day for the meeting never varied, the venue changed regularly: empty, anonymous apartments, private rooms in bistros, cellars that were barely furnished, abandoned theatres and cinemas, derelict buildings scheduled for demolition. No matter where the men met, and despite their great discretion, they always ended up making the landlords, managers, or neighbors suspicious: they had no idea what these occult meetings were about, so they imagined all sorts of conspiracies or twisted intrigues, and eventually asked them to get the hell out. So everyone came up with new suggestions, even the most off the wall sorts of places, and more often than not a new venue was found.

It was early spring then, and the sessions were being held not far from the Place de la Nation in the prefabricated premises of a technical high school that had burned down ten years earlier. Before those temporary classrooms were demolished to make room for a permanent construction, the guidance counselor took advantage of the headmistress's tolerance in order to lend out one of them. When she asked, *What sort of meetings?* the counselor replied, *It's a non-profit organization that studies contemporary society and mores.*

There were some new faces that Thursday. A tall, dark-haired fellow in his early forties slipped into the back of the room. Yves Lehaleur, in his black jeans and motorcycle jacket, had a casual air about him, as if he were just a visitor—he'd even prepared his answer in case anyone asked, *I'm just visiting*, but no one ever asked any questions, even inadvertently. Being back in a classroom made him think of the few exams he'd taken in his life—back in the days when someone had checked the *working life* box on his report card, and his parents, who had worked all their lives, had not protested. Before walking into the room Yves had been obliged to set aside a sort of hereditary complex that made him feel he did not belong there, particularly if it meant having to get up and speak. The friend who had told him about the brotherhood had reassured him on that score.

"As long as you don't disrupt the flow of the meeting, and don't leave the room while someone is speaking, you don't have to say a thing."

This final argument was what persuaded him in the end. The anger he felt inside and his need to vent it took care of the rest.

A first speaker—over seventy, probably the oldest one there—raised his hand, saw that no one else had raised his, and headed up to the teacher's podium, where he stood next to a leatherette armchair spilling its yellow foam guts. He had attended the three previous sessions before deciding, this evening, to take the plunge.

After a few weeks of palliative care at the Hôpital de Villejuif, his wife had died in his arms. He related the events as if he'd gone through a sort of reverse adolescence, that time in life when everything happens for "the first time": the first cigarette, the first love letter, the first kiss. In that sterile hospital room, he and his wife had just had their sweet, beautiful last times together—their last laugh, their last glass of alcohol, their last kiss. He had read her an entire novel by an author she liked: the very last book in a long life of ardent reading.

"She left like that, in a breath, her eyes wide open."

Then he spoke about his life to come, because he would have a life to come. The final days of the woman he had loved so dearly were not his final days, and while he might not come right out and say it, it was a confession all the same. Infinitely tender, she had told him, *Don't stay by yourself.* He had replied, *Don't be silly,* but there was nothing silly about it. This evening he was saying as much, and with a hundred people as his witnesses. Other than to an audience like this, to whom did an old man have the right to say that he still had enough life left in him to fall in love? That all those first times could come once again?

There were some who were convinced they would die alone the way they had lived alone, and therefore his story did not touch them. Others did not rule out the possibility that some day they might ask themselves the same questions as this newly-widowed participant. Custom had it that no one must react to any of the stories; it was a tacit but essential rule for all those who, like Yves Lehaleur, feared any confrontation. Every individual was entitled to speak without fear of counterpoint, question, or commentary, no matter how kindly. Neither distress nor joy was a cause for debate. There had been such rich, fervent silence; any everyday platitude would have ruined it in an instant. But nothing prevented a participant from going up to someone at the end of a session to exchange a few words, go back over a detail, offer or ask for clarification. It was not unusual to see little groups form, prolonging the meeting with a conversation at a bistro, but that was no longer a matter for the brotherhood, and it happened elsewhere.

Others came up to the podium; the length of their talks varied. One of them related how he had fallen in love at first sight, in very particular circumstances: a week earlier, at the bottle bank, he had met a young woman who, like him, was recycling her empty bottles.

"It's the sort of situation where you would rather there

weren't any witnesses. Whether you're holding a bottle of Benedictine or a jar of ratatouille you always feel a bit ridiculous."

But the girl was dispatching her chore with the majestic flourish of a queen granting clemency to an unfortunate wretch. She honored every label with a final gaze, as if saying goodbye, and yet it was the very same wine that the speaker preferred over all others: a Puligny-Montrachet, a white Burgundy. He had appropriated it, labeled it his favorite, had become its greatest advocate, so much so that when he described it, he was describing himself: a wine that was neither modest nor pretentious, a wine that was elegant yet accessible, a wine that needed neither feast nor ceremony to come into its own. On the contrary, this wine was never more eloquent than when accompanying the complicitous inebriation of a romantic rendezvous. And the beautiful stranger he'd met on the street corner seemed to drink nothing else.

"Yet there were more surprises in store. The last bottle was the *coup de grâce*: a *Petrus Boonekamp*."

A name that would mean nothing to those present, who were hardly amateurs of bitter liqueurs.

"It's Dutch, black as gall, and it tastes like it too. I always have some at home."

He had never met anyone who shared his penchant for that thick bile, meant to be drunk like a shot of sheer nastiness. More than once he had tried to convert a friend, but they had all spat it back out like a spurt of ink. And while he hadn't dared react as the empties of Puligny-Montrachet were flashing before his eyes, this unhoped-for appearance of the Petrus Boonekamp provided him with an opportunity to speak to the astonishing young woman. They debated the relative merits of Hungarian Unicum, German Jägermeister, and Italian Fernet-Branca, but nothing, in their opinion, nothing could equal the Petrus Boonekamp. The uninitiated—everyone else, in other words—were not worthy of such an elixir, or of its benefits, or of its mysterious ingredients, or of its closely kept recipe. They went even further: if you could handle that much bitterness, it was proof of an intense inner life.

There was a moment of awkwardness at the end of their exchange: they became two strangers standing next to a gutter. She said, *No fruit juice, not a single water bottle, just booze, I'm ashamed.* And as if to confirm her single status: *The worst of it is that I don't even share it with anyone.*

It had been terribly unwise of him to let her get away. Ever since, he had been feeling bankrupt, ashamed he hadn't been able to hold onto the only woman whom fate had so clearly earmarked for him.

"If two people can get along because they think the same, then this was the woman for me."

As the weeks went by he waited, hoped, even kept a lookout for her. She must live only a stone's throw from his own place, and the only link he could count on from then on was the bottle bank. He went there as often as he could, knowing full well that chance, like lightning, would never strike twice in the same place, but nearby—at a local shop, in one of the adjacent streets, in the nearest park, and at the most unexpected time.

Those in the audience who had fallen in love in unusual circumstances silently wished him luck. He went back to his seat, and another man came to lean against the blackboard; he took a deep breath then launched into a confusing story, told all out of order, mingling objective information and personal points of view. He described himself as physically unattractive, rather gauche and irascible—something his listeners saw as the typical pose of a person who wants to produce the opposite effect. He said it was beyond his ability to avoid quarrels or power struggles, principally with women. Until the day he had met a certain Nadine, a sort of alter ego who, similarly, described herself as *ugly and not very cultured.*

"We're not in love, we won't grow old together, but together we are irresistible."

He made a comparison with two chemical components that are harmless on their own but explosive the moment they are mixed together. If anyone didn't understand what he meant, he was referring to the mathematic principle whereby the sum of two negatives is a positive: *minus* plus *minus* equals *plus.* Driven by their bitterness and frustration, and a thirst for revenge, they formed a couple not so much to nurture one another as to devour everything around them. And as they were not fated to stay together in a relationship, and had nothing to build, they remained separate individuals, without any fear of revealing their shadow sides. She laughed at his fits of anger, he couldn't care less if she was dishonest, and when they did happen to spend the night together, they would betray the secrets of their own sex while going on and on about the opposite sex. But that was not their favorite pastime. Left to their own devices, they turned into formidable predators. In public, this meant provoking, acting debauched and, if either one of them was attracted to someone else, the other partner would give instructions on how to proceed. Their victims were fascinated by the strange game this extravagant couple played, and fell all too easily into the trap.

Yves Lehaleur studied the speakers for inspiration, for the day he would feel ready. But how could you find inspiration among such atypical cases, when their logic, while it deserved to be exposed, only seemed valid to the interested party? Two seats over from him sat another newcomer, Denis Benitez, head waiter at a renowned Paris brasserie, a bachelor like so many others and then some. One evening when he was complaining about living alone, his brigade's maître d' hinted covertly at the existence of a *circle* he used to frequent, where *guys who have a story to tell* would get together, regardless of the nature of their confession, banal or extravagant. The maître d' had since remarried, and no longer felt the need to attend, but he still felt a certain affection for those who'd been a part of it. Denis had decided to take the plunge, and now he was about to speak out, unafraid of being ridiculed—unlike Yves Lehaleur, after twenty years working at a brasserie he had no difficulty at all speaking to complete strangers. And God knows that what he had to say was irrational, and might seem like vain, absurd, disproportionate navel-gazing, or even just terribly naïve, to any other assembly. Except this one.

"Maybe everyone else here has a story to tell, but not me: I don't have a story. I've been living without a woman for years now, which wouldn't be anything out of the ordinary if I hadn't managed to figure out the reason why—and the reason *is* out of the ordinary."

Denis had grown up to be a typical young man with a determination to enjoy life before he thought of settling down. He had fallen in love dozens of times, and he had charming memories of the many young women he had lured into his bed. But by the time he turned thirty, and finally felt ready for a lasting relationship, the women had begun to flee.

"At first I put it down to bad luck, since I'd been attracted to women who were married or engaged, or women who were in love and happy in their relationship and made that dead clear to me. I was careful from then on to avoid that kind of obstacle, but there were others barring the way. Right from the first date the woman would announce that she'd love to have me as the friend she'd never had, or she'd hand me her résumé as a barmaid, or she'd make it clear that *she didn't want to get involved for the time being.* The list started to get long."

After numerous attempts he came to realize that the range of excuses was infinite—as if simply suggesting to a stranger that he'd like to see her again had become the most unnatural gesture on earth. What had happened to make women so evasive, to the point where they would give him a wrong number or never return his calls?

"And God only knows, as a waiter, I have the odds on my side. I would say that on average, fifty to eighty times a day, I ask my customers, on their own or in a group, *What would make you happy today?*"

From his very first day on the job, he had entertained countless women with his joking manner, or flattered them with his attention. Very often, when clearing the tables, he found napkins scribbled with flirtatious messages: *Denis, I've got your number, here's mine,* or *I'm coming back for dinner on Tuesday, alone this time*, or even, in English, *What a waiter!* He would share them with his brigade, then toss them out, and he never tried to contact any of their authors; a minimum of professional ethics held him back. Over time, his success faded, for no reason, as if he had lost some of his presence and charisma.

"So you try and persuade yourself that there are periods, places, opportunities that are more favorable for meeting people than others. I let my coworkers drag me along to bars and nightclubs because I was convinced that that's what those places were for. But I suppose I was not as well cut out to be a hunter as some are . . . "

That was precisely what a little man, scowling as he leaned against the radiator in the back of the room, was thinking. For Philippe Saint-Jean, like Denis Benitez and Yves Lehaleur, this was also the first session, and he was not at all certain that there would be a second one. To justify his presence there he had come up with several clever alibis, and he was almost disappointed when no one was interested in hearing them. He would have pleaded intellectual curiosity, he'd gotten wind of these mysterious secret meetings from his small circle of fellow thinkers. Even so, he had nearly turned around and left when he was at the door to the room for fear of exposing himself to others' gazes: he was well known. Or at least so he thought, adding with a hint of modesty: he was *relatively* well known.

After his brilliant studies at university, he had obtained a

PhD in sociology, then he'd ventured into ethnological research. His byline appeared frequently first in professional journals then in national dailies, but it was when he published his first book—*The Memory-Mirror, or the Dream of a Collective Consciousness*—that he carved out an excellent position for himself in the milieu of intellectuals. Judging from the number of laudatory reviews, he had graduated mysteriously from the rank of a sociologist to that of a *philosopher.* And what was more, he was an accessible philosopher, the kind a mainstream audience could understand, which meant he was a regular guest on literary forums or panel discussions requiring a seal of moral legitimacy or the type of palaver that even the lowest common denominator would be able to make sense of.

For the time being, he was trying to make sense of Denis Benitez's confession, as someone who knows how to read into the speech of those who do not know how to speak. Philippe was impressed by the completely spontaneous way the fellow had of putting his solitude down to a conspiracy on the part of a rival clan. But Denis was adamant, he was sincere, at a complete loss, yet very rigorous as he enumerated the stages of his gradual exclusion from the realm of universal female desire.

"Then I began to rely on the people around me. I could bank on the simple notion that everyone must have a female friend who needs a companion, since I was her male equivalent."

So Denis had publicized the erring ways of his celibacy, and he turned to his friends, who thought it might be amusing to make one couple out of two lonely hearts. And while he had not forgotten a single one of the women he met at their arranged dinner parties, what he remembered above all were the awkward moments when he could see he had failed the test, before they'd even started on dessert. There'd been the divorcée who, three days earlier, *had just met someone.* There'd been the embassy secretary, who'd come halfway round the world, determined to go back there *for good*. And the medical assistant, whose ex had just called to make up, now that she'd finally gotten over her broken heart.

As he listened, Yves Lehaleur was also wondering about this series of unfortunate coincidences, but he didn't doubt them: he was a firm believer in adversity. Philippe Saint-Jean, on the other hand, saw them as so much equivocation on the part of a Manichean mind that lapsed on occasion into misogyny. Was such an image of The Woman really necessary in order to imagine a coalition of all of them?

"In the months that followed, I re-evaluated my selection criteria. I didn't have the impression I was leaning toward a certain type of women, but I was ready to extend the field of possibilities, to waive any distinction on the grounds of age, looks, culture, social class or skin color. In fact, I was ready to envisage *all* women, absolutely all of them, but it still wasn't enough."

Given the utter absence of women in his life, Denis would turn around to look at any skirt that walked by, and this had become a habitual reflex, a pretext to find multiple opportunities to make himself miserable. Philippe Saint-Jean knew that there was no need to have read the Romantics or the behavioralists, it was simply a matter of common sense: the more one desires, the more the object of desire recedes; the first lesson you teach any languishing adolescent. The guy at the blackboard was making the fundamental error of trying to pin a specific nature on women, to lump them all into one category and view them as symmetrical at best and contrary at worst. So Philippe was waiting for Denis to stop blaming his bad fortune and start questioning his own behavior.

"The problem was with me, *that* I could see, but what was the problem? Had I changed so radically once I passed thirty?"

He had been careful to keep in shape, to watch his weight

and his appearance, and only rarely did he not find time to run or swim, or to ride around Paris on his bike. Moreover, he asked the chef at the brasserie to cook up some healthy meals for him. It had even become a joke with the entire staff, *Denis and his fussy food*—fish, vegetables, tea, and it wasn't just some dietary obsession but a real preference. If anything, he had become more handsome with the years, and would reach his prime at the age of fifty.

"Had I become so boring that there wasn't a single woman crazy enough to spend an evening or a night or a lifetime by my side?"

It must be that the rites of seduction had changed over time and he had not noticed. There was no shame anymore in *putting yourself on the market*, promoting yourself like a product, a consumer good, dependable, and available. Once he'd summed up his basic self in a few clicks, he signed up with a few online dating sites, eager to try this new means of communication that only a year earlier had seemed pathetic. He hid nothing, did not invent any qualities he did not have, and he eventually met a few candidates who had been drawn to his scrupulously defined profile.

Philippe Saint-Jean suspected that another series of fiascos lay ahead; if the fellow had only known how to see them coming, he could have spared himself many a lonely moment.

"They'd seen my photo, they knew about my job, how much I earn, whether I believe in God or not, whether I was up for a *long-term relationship* or not: how could there be any nasty surprises?"

While Yves Lehaleur was still wondering why the man seemed to labor under such a strange curse, Philippe Saint-Jean saw beyond the specific case to the syndrome of a more universal disarray among men. It had even become the bread and butter of a few essayists he knew: rampant cynicism affected even love relationships, modern men had lost their bearings, women had legitimately reclaimed their rights after millennia of servitude. What Philippe found fascinating about Denis Benitez's account was the totally indecent way he described his ordeal, as if he were some veritable Christ figure on the path of the cross, already doomed to be crucified.

"One evening when I felt I'd really touched bottom I called all my exes one after the other."

It was a ludicrous effort, bound to fail, nothing short of a bad joke, and yet he took out his old notebook and picked up the receiver, and didn't miss out a single one of the girls he'd slept with. After all, he and Véronique had split on good terms. And Hélène must have forgotten about their quarrels by now. Mona had surely forgiven him. Maybe Nadège wasn't married after all, or maybe she was already bored. Not to mention a few more, further back in time but who, with a bit of luck, might be going through the same rough patch as he was. In hopes of a minor miracle, he'd come up with a very simple opening line: *Hey, it's Denis, Denis Benitez, remember me?* And he hoped to conclude with: *Hey, why don't you come have lunch one day at my brasserie?* Alas, not a single one took him up on his offer, and some of them explained why, not without irony. Ever since that sad visit to the land of his lost loves—who were determined to remain lost—his speculations about women had become charged with anger and bitterness.

"And then you reach a point where your doubt begins to gnaw away at you. You go from one certainty to the next, and every idea and its contrary is just as good as the next one, so in the end you can't even understand how you can function. One morning I was convinced I was being too direct and too offhand. I wasn't giving them time to feel their desire, as if every gesture I made, every word I said was in order to get them into bed or, worse yet, into city hall. So it made me think: how would anyone *not* run away from a guy like me? Then just the opposite, that very same evening, I saw myself as incurably indecisive, lost in some procrastinating behavior from a bygone era, when you know that women like men who are enterprising and forthright. So again I had to think: how would anyone *not* run away from a guy like me?"

The very next morning, still more doubts came to banish the earlier ones, and so on down the line, until they all disappeared in the light of his utter dejection. Denis could see the specter of resignation looming, and he decided to ask for help.

"I went and saw a therapist. Someone had to help me get things in perspective, and maybe they could give me a key."

Yves Lehaleur shrugged at the word "therapist." Anything that began with the prefix *psy* inspired instinctive mistrust. In his opinion, why should one person be more gifted than the next guy at reading into another man's soul? All those *psy* people were just charlatans who'd figured out that offering an attentive ear to another person's woes was a rare commodity you could charge a lot for here on earth. When he had told his entourage that he needed a divorce, and quick, some of them had urged him to *speak to a specialist* before making such a drastic decision. Yves had told them to mind their own business: if someone needed a therapist it was his bitch of a wife, not him.

Philippe Saint-Jean, on the other hand, thought that Denis was rather courageous. Having gone through it himself many years earlier, he knew how difficult it could be to ring at a therapist's door and entrust a stranger with one's dysfunctional self. In his milieu, it was almost a rite of passage for anyone who presumed to penetrate the mysteries of the human mind and its hidden meanings. To avoid psychoanalysis would have been tantamount to professional misconduct. Nowadays, his friends who were in treatment far outnumbered those who weren't.

"He listened patiently, then offered to help me *get the wheels of seduction rolling again.* Three sessions later I was surprised to find myself telling him a childhood memory, the exact moment when I realized just how fallible my parents were, after they . . . forgot me at a friend's house one boozy evening. I dug deep in my memory and was able to describe the event as if it were straight out of a horror film: the distraught mother, the guilt-stricken father promising me a miniature car if I stopped crying right that minute. I could hear myself telling the shrink, *I even remember the model! A Dinky Toys Facel Vega, gray with a hard top, they brought it out in 1960,* and I wondered if this were the right way to get my *wheels of seduction* going again."

Denis struggled to find his words, and for a moment everyone thought he had finished. In fact, this part of his testimony seemed less pertinent to him than the conclusion; as if this were an official announcement, there was something he had told neither friend nor brother nor psychoanalyst and which he was about to share with a hundred strangers.

"After five years of drifting and humiliation, where I was incapable of understanding why the entire female gender had deserted me, I had to accept the explanation I would have preferred to avoid: a conspiracy theory. As unlikely as it may seem, *they* have decided to assuage their age-old desire for revenge on *me.*"

A ripple of astonishment went through the audience; those who had been attending the Thursday meetings for a long time had heard all sorts of fantasies, but they always bore in mind that new ones could surface at any time. Yves Lehaleur, with his neophyte's gaze, looked around him and met the eyes of his nearest neighbor, Philippe Saint-Jean, as much a neophyte as he was.

"Every time one of you, gentlemen, commits a crime of sexism, discrimination, loutishness, harassment, misogyny, domestic tyranny, or brutality, I'm the one who has to take the consequences."

It was not enough for *those women* to ignore him, *they* had to have their revenge as well. Denis was being made to pay for all *they* had suffered at the hands of men since the dawn of time. To make sure he understood that he needed *them* more than *they* needed him, *they* had spread the word, and he could take his fine virility and stick it wherever he liked.

"I feel certain I have been chosen to inform you, this very evening, and to warn you: you will be next."

Philippe Saint-Jean had already diagnosed a subtle form of paranoia, but he hadn't been expecting this theory of a martyr sacrificed on the altar of deposed masculinity. With prototypes like this one among the brotherhood, there was a good chance he would be a frequent visitor. As for Yves Lehaleur, he would rethink his rejection of psychoanalysis, if it were to prove useful to someone like Denis Benitez.

Denis went to sit back down in the last row, where he was greeted with a discreet smile from his neighbors, Yves Lehaleur and Philippe Saint-Jean, both of whom were astonished by his performance, admiring not only his nerve but above all his outrageous imagination. Their expressions told him they had heard what he had to say.

Yves was tempted to climb up on the podium and come out with everything he had on his mind, too—if guys like Denis were allowed in, there was no reason why he, Yves, should have any hang-ups about telling his story. But it was getting late and he would have to keep his anger for another week. As for Philippe Saint-Jean, he would need another session before he could make up his mind about something he now viewed as a social phenomenon. He was curious about this group therapy without a therapist, this astonishing all-male confessional, this occult congregation you could adhere to without any co-optation or initiation rites or preliminary enquiry. He had come there fully prepared to pass judgment or share some savory sarcasm with his entourage. But in fact he had just witnessed a rare moment of tolerance, of the kind you could not label in any way, or subject to even the most woolly dogma. What he did not yet know was the real reason for his presence here. His intellectual curiosity had been satisfied, and it probably wouldn't take long for his true motivation to surface, one of these Thursday evenings. Philippe was inhabited by absence, and nothing could explain away the pain—and he was someone who was greatly in need of meaningful explanations.

Before they all left the room, they were informed that the next meeting would be held in the same place. Some of them would not come back. Others would. Between now and then, life could go on.

2

Some men like to undress a woman with a single gaze; Denis Benitez indulged in a far more presumptuous pastime. He could wrench the hidden truth from every woman who passed him in the street. Since in their eyes he no longer existed, since he was no longer a physical presence in their world, he had discovered that he had a talent for invisibility which allowed him to brush by women like a ghost, to spy on them and steal their secrets.

Crossing a median strip on the edge of the Place de la Nation, a female figure suddenly appeared: *white flowered dress, her expression that of a mother for whom it has all gone too fast.*

Another woman climbing into a taxi: *blonde, thirtysomething, slightly, but disarmingly cross-eyed, ready to proclaim her independence to whoever will listen.*

With experience he had reached a point where not a single woman in his path was spared, and he only took their age, looks, or clothing into consideration if they provided a serious clue.

A jogger, all in a sweat, resting on a bench: *very dark eyes, slightly plump, full of a tenderness that no one returns.*

In her newspaper kiosk: *thirty-five-year-old adolescent, displaying her breasts like medals.*

Or that one, in thigh boots and suede: *straight, slow, blasé shadows under her eyes, she dreams more of laughter than of sex.*

The saleswoman smoking outside her boutique: *haughty, classy, no one knows the operating instructions, not even she herself.*

The girl climbing onto her scooter: *badly dressed, strict eyeglasses, ready to fall in love with a man as if he were the last one on earth.*

And that one, standing next to her fiancé, who's as arrogant as she is: *very modern, ready to elbow her way, and later she'll say to her grandchildren, If only I'd known.*

Or that one: *pregnant, lovely smooth skin, she knows who she can share her joy with, but not her fears.*

Or that one: *tourist from the north, husband walking way ahead, she's sorry she isn't out exploring Paris with her girlfriends.*

And that tall girl: *innocent, thirty-odd, looks self-conscious in her matronly blouse, burdened by complexes that will cause her to waste twenty years.*

As he weaned himself off women, Denis discovered in himself an extraordinary male intuition. But this activity—obsessive, dangerous—was wearing him out, and to no good purpose; it merely fueled his bitterness. Just before seven o'clock he hurried toward the gate of the lycée that had been left open, found the same classroom as the week before, and nodded to Yves Lehaleur and Philippe Saint-Jean in the last row.

Yves had seen enough the previous week to feel confident: tonight was the night. He waited for the audience to fall silent, raised his hand, then headed up to the blackboard like the good pupil he'd never had the time to become.

"I'll probably babble and repeat myself, so I'd like to apologize in advance. I will begin by telling you about my life the way it used to be. To be exact, my life before the fourth of November of last year."

Judging by his opening words, Philippe Saint-Jean was afraid that his story would be interminable, so he allowed his gaze to wander out into the darkening schoolyard.

"For five whole years, I was a married man. Her name was Pauline and she worked for a real estate agency run by Alain, who was a childhood friend of mine. He had introduced her to me because she needed some double glazing—that's my job, I install windows for a major company—so I went over to her place for an estimate."

A woman like Pauline, single? That was a minor miracle that surely would not last, unless he were to outrun her other admirers. Their early years living together were just Bohemian enough for them to acquire some precious memories. But their work came before everything, because they were both working very hard to fulfill their dreams. They decided to start a family—two kids, no more, but no less—so they needed to find a little house in a quiet suburb, and that was Pauline's job. In order to obtain a loan at the bank, Yves used his 87,000 euros of life insurance as collateral—everything he had saved since obtaining his vocational training certificate, plus a little early inheritance from his parents—and Pauline would borrow the equivalent of a third of her salary over twenty years.

Yves did not spare his audience a single detail: even the financial ones, which were insignificant at first glance, had acquired a symbolic value that was a source of relentless torment to him.

"With Pauline in charge, everything was bound to work out fine."

She was a petite little woman, bursting with energy, always smiling, and she never gave the impression that her heart was not in her job, or that she was going through a rough patch. Running a household, fighting with the administration to obtain what was owed them, negotiating with banks and carefully filing away every single credit card receipt, she managed everything as if it were a breeze. Nor had it kept her, after hours, from unearthing their Xanadu—in Champigny, on the banks of the Marne river, a stone house that had been restored. It had an open plan ground floor with a gigantic fireplace, no fewer than four upstairs bedrooms, a garden that was well-protected from outside gazes, and all of it less than fifteen minutes from the Porte de Vincennes. Happiness had an address.

"We had an appointment to sign the sales agreement and the move was set for January. After that, Pauline planned to stop taking the pill so she'd get pregnant."

Philippe Saint-Jean couldn't really see why all these details were necessary. His own fear of talking too much sometimes hampered his ability to listen. He did, however, find it interesting to listen to a story that so painstakingly described the sort of aspirations that were the opposite of his own. When was the last time he'd met a man who dreamt of starting a family in the suburbs? Ten years ago? Twenty? Had he ever even met one? The great dream of the majority, the one that went to make up a country and contributed to the durability of its values: a family and a roof.

Philippe felt neither pride nor regret: he knew he was an exception, and it was pointless to turn to him to contribute to the survival of the species or to take part in a national endeavor. He wasn't antisocial or a maverick, he wasn't even rich, and yet everything that preoccupied his compatriots was of so little concern to him—inflation, public housing or transport strikes; none of it had any bearing on his lifestyle. Starting a family in the suburbs? He himself was a product of that very enterprise, his parents had never called it into question, at the time it was neither a choice nor a dream but a necessary passage in life. Nowadays, Philippe lived in a three-room apartment in the Latin Quarter, right at the heart of the Paris intellectual movement, a stone's throw from the Sorbonne and the publishing houses. At the age of forty-one he somewhat pompously decreed he would never have children, now; the only woman who had ever made him want a child had vanished from his life as if he had woken too soon from a wonderful dream.

"And everything would have been so very different if there hadn't been that party on November fourth."

The agency that Alain ran was part of the biggest real estate company in the country, and to celebrate their annual results, management were inviting a thousand of their employees, selected on the basis of their performance. For the first time, Alain, Pauline, and their coworkers were going to be rewarded.

"My wife called me at around one in the morning to tell me she was having the greatest time of her life. She'd been congratulated on her results, she'd been introduced to the company's second-in-command, and she was drinking champagne in a sidewalk café on the Champs-Elysées. In short, she was in no hurry to come home. I congratulated her too and begged her to be careful if she'd been drinking. She told me that she was going to follow the crowd she was with, they would probably go on partying at a nightclub, and I could sleep easy, she wouldn't take the car. Since I knew that my buddy Alain would have an eye on her, I fell asleep, reassured, and proud of my wife. When I woke up at around nine in the morning there was a text message that said, *Dead drunk. Sleeping at Fanny's. C U tomorrow. Love U.*

She came home at around noon, eyes half-closed, face puffy, struggling against the worst hangover in her life, and she rushed over to a tube of aspirin, then to her bed, without even looking at Yves. He let her sleep it off until evening, when she emerged to take a shower and drink some tea, until she regained the power of speech and was able to give Yves a rough outline of her evening: the nightclub, the vodka tonics, so many she'd lost count, until she could hardly stand on her feet and Fanny took her home with her at around five in the morning.

"I remember thinking the whole episode was really 'healthy,'" said Yves. All her hard work in the ranks, recognized at last, that was healthy, and the fact she'd met the big company bosses, that was healthy, too. And so was partying, and without me even more so. Let her get completely wasted for once in her life: that was healthy, too."

Yves was bringing out all the details he'd filed away in order, then examined, and commented on, and brooded over ad nauseum.

"Monday morning life went back to normal. Until Alain called me at the end of the afternoon: *Yves, I have to talk to you, but not on the phone.*"

At the neighborhood bistro Alain, his voice lugubrious, wondered whether he had the right to do what he was about to do. *I adore Pauline, you're my best friend, but either way I'll be betraying one of you.* That famous Saturday evening had started so well. Pauline, in her lovely gown, a cocktail in her hand, the Champs-Elysées sparkling at her feet. The big boss for the whole Île-de-France region had said to her, "So you're the famous Pauline Lehaleur?" When the first guests had left, Fanny suggested they go to a trendy club on the Rue de Ponthieu, a short distance from there. To thank his team in person, Alain had decided it would be his treat. The kind of place you only ever see in movies: gold, silver, red satin, perfect lighting, several dance floors, music to set the place on fire, staff straight out of the pages of a glossy magazine and, above all, a stage with pole dancers.

"Strippers who curl around a bar," explained Yves to the hundred men hanging on his every word. "A show every fifteen minutes, the guys are blown away, the girls think it's funny. But every third show the situation is reversed: it's a guy who gets undressed. A go-go dancer. In less than a minute all he has left is a towel around his waist, and he goes down into the audience to wiggle his hips between the legs of young women who are squealing hysterically."

None of the women in their little group had been ignored, but the dancer lingered by Pauline, who was both surprised and amused to see a male specimen of the sort wiggling his ath-

letic body not four inches from her face. The man had perfected his performance, and like any good professional he went
off to the other patrons just before any kind of awkwardness
had time to set in. Pauline had not made a show of it, she'd just
played along in the presence of her colleagues and denied
she'd had any sort of special treatment. To recover from her
emotion, she drank her umpteenth vodka tonic, determined to
go on with the party: tomorrow would never come. She started
dancing, euphoric, as if to fill herself with light and energy
before the winter came, until she herself was incandescent.
Until all of a sudden, the eyes of all the women turned to see a
young guy appear out of nowhere on the dance floor, a young
guy wearing a pair of frayed jeans and a white shirt open on his
chest. Pauline hadn't recognized the go-go dancer straight off
in his street clothes, now that he was once again a customer
like any other—but then again, was he? He had a break for an
hour, and sometimes he would start up a conversation, hand
over his business card, and describe his private services, which
covered part of his income: bachelorette parties, hen nights,
birthday parties where he was the living present. Tonight, however, he was happy just to be dancing with a glass in his hand,
making far less of a show of it than during his professional
crawling number. He exchanged a few smiles with Pauline,
then a few words, amidst the infernal racket. Then they started
up another conversation, silently this time, and far more sen-
sually, in the middle of the dance floor.

Alain was discovering a Pauline he'd never seen, yielding
euphorically to her own frenzy. He was worn out by all the
craziness, and offered to take her home, but she refused outright: *I'll get a cab! See you Monday!* Alain walked back to his
car, unsure what to make of what he'd just seen. Was she just
a young woman enjoying an exceptional night out, or the wife
of his best friend, dead drunk, trying to hit on a semi-gigolo?
Should I leave her there? Or should I go back and keep an eye

on her? Insist on driving her home? I did not know what to do, Yves, please believe me. On the one hand I figured she probably didn't know what she was doing, and that she'd thank me the next day for intervening. On the other hand I thought, well, she is an adult after all, and it's none of my business what she does.

At the beginning of the evening Yves had said to him, jokingly, *She's in your hands!* and now those five little words weighed heavily on his conscience. Alain turned back, determined now to persuade her to leave, even if he had to be abrupt about it, but it was already too late: the go-go dancer's car had just flashed by, and Pauline was in the passenger seat, reaching over to turn up the volume on the radio.

Denis Benitez was enthralled by Yves Lehaleur's story, as was everyone else, and he knew that in this brotherhood he had found what he was looking for. His own story seemed anecdotal, and for the time being the only one that mattered was this stranger's, so radically different from his own.

"So that was where my friend Alain's story left off; he was still there, though, with his elbows on the bar counter and a drained expression, and he knew he had jeopardized our friendship. *If I had kept quiet I would never have been able to look you in the eye again.* He insisted, mortified: *Can you forgive me?* His need for absolution seemed ridiculous in comparison with the shock I'd just had. I was astonished to hear myself say, *Me, forgive you? If in twenty years you've given me a single true proof of friendship, then this is it. You did what you had to do, and I'll be in your debt for life.*"

Before leaving, Alain warned him against misinterpreting things. What he had seen might not have been as bad as it looked, and it was easy to imagine other far less traumatizing outcomes to the episode. But were any of them even credible?

"I went home—already it no longer felt quite like home any more—and poured a full glass of whisky and drank it as if it were spring water, while I waited for Pauline. That's where my horror film began, with that image of her leaving the club in that guy's car, the film I've been watching over and over for months now, and which still comes back to haunt me."

Of all those in the audience, Philippe Saint-Jean was probably more intrigued than anyone by the way in which this man was describing his wife's infidelity, the terms he used to retrace the mechanisms of suspicion and, more to the point, the details he chose to tick off, or not. A long time ago Philippe had developed an entire theory about adultery among the working classes, a form of adultery that was far trickier and more complex than in the other classes. In culturally powerful milieus like his own, adultery was seen to be inherent in a relationship, a sort of inevitable derivative, a subject for debate, which one could relativize; you encountered the likes of Emma Bovary and Don Juan, and literature was often relied upon to lend legitimacy to a secret liaison. The *grands bourgeois* viewed adultery as a necessary evil, to be filed away in the same drawer as venereal disease: sooner or later you got it, but there was a cure. But for those who had no recourse to luxury or romanticism, there were complications, practical difficulties—how to find a place to harbor one's lovemaking, how to juggle with a schedule that was often regimented down to the quarter of an hour. It was more than just adultery, too, it was cuckoldry, bringing with it shame and betrayal. Afternoon trysts became borderline Greek tragedy; lasting affairs, a crime of bigamy. Philippe Saint-Jean had always wondered why the phenomenon carried such a dramatic charge, when it was such an insignificant event.

"Pauline thought I was very quiet, there with my glass in my hand, and she said, *You're having a before-dinner drink at a time like this?* Then she added, *Yuk, I'll never have another strong drink in my life.*"

Racked by doubt, Yves went straight to the crux of the matter: *You didn't sleep over at Fanny's—where were you?* Pauline acted the girl who is completely taken aback, but with so little conviction, and so fearful of discovery, that she gave herself away. *What on earth have people been saying . . .* And Yves, unflappably, dousing his inner flames with great gulps of Cutty Sark, put her on the trail without the slightest irony: *Dead drunk in a stripper's car at five o'clock in the morning, I'd love to hear what happened next.* She tried everything—indignation, anger, her utter disgust with malicious gossip, particularly when that gossip came from people you were close to; it was so pernicious. Yves did not relent, but asked the same question over and over, indefatigably, so calmly it could only portend the worst. An hour later she cracked and confessed to her only crime: *Yes, I was drunk, yes he asked me to go with him for another drink, yes I told Fanny to cover for me, yes, yes, yes, but I didn't sleep with him, I beg you, believe me!* How could she dare to think that the man she'd spent the last five years of her life with would be satisfied with so little? *Another drink . . .* Shouts replaced sobs, but Pauline didn't give anything else away, if anything the opposite: how could this man she loved, her husband, refuse to believe her? All the more so when she had just confessed to such a petty crime! She'd had a stupid drink with a stranger, who'd gotten it into his head that he'd take her home with him, but despite her drunkenness she'd stood her ground. Besides, she didn't even fancy him, that studmuffin with his muscles bursting out of his shirt, what a caricature!

"She was so convincing, so precise, that for a second I had my doubts. She described the ridiculous way he had of hitting on her, and the place they'd ended up, an '*after*' she called it, in English, a bar that opens when all the others are closing, she even described the guy's mates they'd run into, and all those cool dudes into their good-natured boozing until noon. To be honest, I would have preferred to let that scenario keep playing. But Pauline had lied to me once already, why should I believe her this time around?"

There would be no time for a second confession that Thursday. An hour had already gone by, but no one had looked at their watch. Those who had planned to speak would just have to come again the following week.

In spite of his ultimatum, Yves did not manage to get the true version of how the night ended: Pauline would not change a word of her version from then on. In deathly silence, he put on his parka and slipped the bottle of Cutty Sark into his pocket. Almost nauseous, he left the apartment without even looking at her and went off to a little hotel on the Rue de Tolbiac, where he locked himself in and, with his glass in his hand, lay on the double bed and stared at the cracks in the ceiling. *His Pauline* had become *that bitch Pauline*; never again would he refer to her in any other way, and soon he would not need to refer to her at all. But before he envisaged the final episode of their life together, there was one thing he had to be sure about.

" . . . I don't know what came over me, at around three o'clock I saw the red numbers flashing on my clock radio on the night table and I told myself that the sooner I was sure, the sooner I could start a new life without that bitch. A stripper, at that time of night, must be hard at work . . . "

Philippe Saint-Jean sat up: would this guy telling his sad story of ordinary jealousy have dared do something that extravagant? Corner the Chippendale who'd slept with his wife? No one, in his milieu, would have ever been able to do such a thing, but they would all have dreamt of it! Yves Lehaleur suddenly rose in his esteem.

"I know it's ridiculous, and ridiculous isn't even the right word, it's the stage beyond ridiculous, like some pathetic farce that is trying to be funny to no avail: Pauline had slept with a stripper, a guy who does bodybuilding, as oily as a chicken on the spit. The woman I'd been living with for five years had walked right into the trap."

In fact, the word he was looking for was "grotesque."

"What sort of fantasy was it? Was he the exact counterpart of some vulgar female stripper with tons of makeup, a real turn-on, the type we men like so much? Was it the same thing? Did Pauline want *that?*"

Even if he did not look like one of the club's usual customers, the bouncer let him in, this guy in his parka, terribly silent and slow and so absent from the world. Yves watched Sabrina and Marcy perform, and then over the mike they announced a show by a certain Bruno.

"I was overwhelmed with hatred the minute I saw him. I so rarely feel like that, it was like a sign of proof: this was him. Pauline had left with him that night."

As he watched the way the stripper moved among the women, Yves imagined how his wife, like the women around him, must have followed the guy's every move. How had she reacted when he grabbed her hands to place them on his butt? When he shoved his crotch into her face? Had she given a silly smile, like the others, or blushed with shame or excitement; had she felt bold or ill at ease, did she want to run away from her unexpected attraction, or let herself be overwhelmed by it? Yves asked to meet Bruno by telling the barman that he was the boss of a club that was seeking to hire talent from the fashionable bars in the capital. Ten minutes later, the artist bounced up to him, hastily dressed, streaming with sweat.

I'm Pauline's husband.

The only thing Bruno heard in the short sentence was the word *husband*, and when you thought about it, what else would a guy wrapped up in his parka in a trendy Mecca of Parisian nightlife look like, other than a husband? *Whose husband . . . ?* Yves refreshed his memory: *The slightly plump little blonde you screwed last Saturday.*

"He thought I'd come to smash his face in. What a pleasure

to see a big guy like him who spends hours at the gym be frightened of a guy like me. I'm anything but a fighter, I hate any form of violence. And yet in the state I was in I could have smashed his nose on the edge of the bar and removed any hope he might have of ever finding his cute little trendy face again. And he sensed it."

What can I say? It was three in the morning . . . She was a consenting adult . . . I didn't think I'd be hurting anyone . . . and I don't think she did, either . . . Bruno recoiled when he saw Yves slip his hand into his inside pocket. And pull out a checkbook.

"Even though I really felt like tearing the place apart, I wasn't there to take revenge but just to make sure. And, above all, to get the details. Without paying I would never have gotten them."

With all these details—which would only make him miserable—he'd be able to add new scenes to the film screening nonstop in his head. These details would hurt, of that he could be sure, but they wouldn't lie—all he needed was one, no matter how cruel, to bring an end to all speculation, misinterpretation, lying, equivocation, false hopes. Bruno was prepared for anything—except to be paid for the story of that night—and no doubt he would have asked the cuckold to leave him alone if he hadn't had the check in his pocket. Yves was offering him the possibility to earn in fifteen minutes what normally took him an entire evening of playing the birthday present from a group of girlfriends to the one who expected it the least.

Bruno came clean, trying to remain as objective as possible. When he skipped something, Yves asked him to go back. *Was she the one, or was it you, who suggested going to your place? What time was it? Did she agree right away?* Bruno's report, cautious and methodical, amounted to a slow enumeration of every grueling detail. He began by noting *the little desert island tattoo at the small of her back.* Pauline and Yves had chosen the motif together. A spot of paradise where he had always been the only Robinson.

Did they do it in the bed? On the floor? On the sofa? Did she do "that?" And "that?" In that position? And did you ask her to do "that" or did she do it spontaneously? Caresses Yves had always taken as gifts from his wife to the man she loved. An intimacy they had spent years forging. A stranger had gotten it all, in one fell swoop, without even needing to give her a clue. When Yves asked him if she had come, Bruno replied, *I don't know*, but without leaving the slightest doubt. When he awoke, Pauline was gone, hadn't left a note or a phone number, and for Bruno it was better that way.

Yves asked him one last question: *Why my wife? You can have women who are much more beautiful, much richer, more stylish, why did you want to sleep with a little woman who must seem so ordinary to you?* Without hesitating he said, *Because it's something you want to try at least once, the housewife who's giving herself a treat.* Then Bruno was called backstage, and he cast a last glance at Yves, neither ironic nor unkind. *I know this won't help, but the women I meet here look at me like some sort of living sex toy. As a rule, they go away again disappointed.*

And indeed, it didn't help, because ever since that night Yves was no longer the man who had filled his wife with dreams, her Prince Charming, her object of desire. He had once again become the little man who does double glazing, who looks just like anyone, no more ambitious than the average Joe, just a good guy who'd make a good little husband and a loving father, someone to grow old with who wouldn't leave her with too many regrets. Passion and fire, that was already someone else's department, a stranger who need only walk on stage to make women scream.

"Unfaithful men who get cheated on in turn just had it coming to them. But what did I do? In five years, I never met a more attractive woman than my own wife, and who knows, it might have lasted a long time after that."

All the years he was married, Yves had never thought about fidelity, about long-term couples, about the erosion of desire. Setting sail in a nutshell that had room for only two passengers, he'd set his course for the open ocean and imagined he could go all the way around the world, come hell or high water. Now he'd stepped ashore from a dream, and he wouldn't head back out to sea for a long time.

"I never saw Pauline again. I don't feel even a pinch of nostalgia for our life together. Even in my worst nightmares, she hardly shows up anymore. I'm forgetting her."

As for Pauline, she'd tried everything to beg him to forgive her, ready to swear to anything, mortified that she had strayed for even one night. To avoid having to speak to her, Yves had entrusted a lawyer with all the material issues and the divorce procedure. But before this bad film finally left him in peace, Yves had to go back over every single sequence to try and identify the one that had caused his marriage to fall apart. An illusory but systematic analysis of every hypothesis, every possible detour in a long series of episodes leading to an ineluctable ending. *And what if that evening . . . ?* And what if that evening they had gone to another bar? What if she'd been drinking whisky instead of vodka? What if that stupid dancer had gone outside to smoke a cigarette during his break? What if Alain had been more persuasive? Could Fanny have acted as an alibi if she didn't live right nearby? And what if even one minute detail had been enough to counter this twist of fate, would Yves have spent the rest of his life with Pauline, surrounded by grandchildren, the two of them with peace in their hearts?

He would never know the answer. But in their way, all these conjectures merely confirmed that tragedy alone knows how to summon destiny in person. Happy endings, never.

"Nowadays I have come to think that this blow from fate

might have been lucky after all. The events are still too recent, but I know that someday I will thank Pauline for having set me free."

Yves left the podium, drained, astonished he'd been able to open up to strangers as much as he had. He hadn't tried to compromise with the truth, they had listened to him openly and generously, and now it was as if his story no longer belonged to him. Philippe Saint-Jean, who generally made it a point of honor not to let anything faze him, was forced to admit that this funny little guy, who said he felt ill at ease in public, had captivated a hundred people for two whole hours; even at the Collège de France, he had never attended a lecture as intense as this one had been. While his story may have been as banal as they come, his experience of it and, above all, the way he had ended it, were not at all common. How could he have been so radical, so merciless with a woman he had loved tenderly until then? So much intransigence seemed unfair, out of all proportion. How could his dark feelings have been so strong that they could destroy such obvious happiness? Philippe could just see her, this Pauline, queen for a night, losing control of her emotions. Was it not obvious that her crime that night was no chance occurrence, but was committed at the very moment when she was about to start a family in her brand new home—an adventure that would pass so quickly that before she knew it middle age would be there to relieve her of her mission. Was it not obvious that the symbolic value of her escapade was far greater than the *frisson*? And that one night's foolish behavior was clearly the last, daring gesture on the part of a young woman on the verge of sacrificing everything, and willingly so, to the daily life of her loved ones? If you loved a woman, how could you not forgive her, when you were prepared to give other far less deserving people the benefit of the doubt? When you granted attenuating circumstances to crimes of passion?

Philippe Saint-Jean and Denis Benitez left the room together and walked along the corridor, reminiscing about primary school. At the main entrance to the building they saw Yves Lehaleur, silhouetted against a streetlamp, opening the lock on his scooter. The three men shook hands, exchanged names and a few pleasantries that had nothing to do with the brotherhood; they no longer knew what to think about it. One of them, on seeing the glow of light from a sidewalk café, suggested they go for a drink.

They became acquainted over their beers as if they'd actually met in more usual circumstances. Philippe was intrigued by Denis, *the man that women avoided like the plague,* and even more so by Yves, *the man who could not forgive.*

If Philippe had had a similar misadventure back in the days when he was living with Juliette, his most recent girlfriend, he would have tried to unravel the truth from the lies, to find a balance between listening and reproaches, to draw both on everyday common sense and psychoanalysis. He would have tried to be more attentive, then virulent, then defenseless, and finally magnanimous, but always there for her and for their life together, in order to make a fresh start. Philippe would have entered into a dialogue with himself, even if it meant getting lost in a spiral of meaning, or he would have confided in a friend who was the author of an essay on jealousy, or he could have gotten in touch with a former therapist for the occasion. Anything except this implacable, irreversible decision, like a blade dropping without leaving the other person even the slightest chance. Philippe still lived in the land of Voltaire and Sartre, the land of words.

As for Yves, he had turned a page that night. As a free man, he did not know what tomorrow would bring, but it hardly mattered; he had paid too dear a price for his future projects with Pauline to come up with any new ones. From now on he was going to leave things up to chance, and if chance decided to bide its time, Yves had already found his time. It was, in a way, the first gift of his brand new freedom: time, time for himself, time for everything, time to lose, blessed time.

While Philippe was ordering their drinks, Denis observed the waitress from head to toe, *pink cheeks and high cheekbones, capable of giving everything she does not have if you know how to ask tactfully.* The knowledge that he was utterly available to every woman on earth suddenly brought his terrible solitude home to him, and in order to stave it off for a few more hours he decided to go back by way of his brasserie for a final drink with his coworkers. Philippe was in no hurry to leave, he'd already decided he'd nod off in front of the rerun of a documentary. And as on every night, once he was back in his big empty bed, Yves would wonder what to do about the only aspect of his single life that bothered him now: the lack of sex.

After Pauline, finding a new partner was not a priority. It took him months to get over the shock and overcome a sort of disgust with any form of human warmth. But since that time, his libido had reminded him of its presence, and was becoming more and more preoccupying by the day. A strange feverishness at nightfall; lingering gazes when a skirt went by; untimely erections. He was going to have to set off in search of new bodies, and in his daydreams he imagined a whole variety of women, as if after five years devoted to a bitch who hadn't deserved his loyalty, the time had come at last to catch up on his interrupted career as a charmer. The loss of the woman he loved had irreversibly modified the chemistry of his sentiments. Never again would Yves—and he insisted on the *never again*—fall into the intimacy trap. While he might not always manage to put words to his emotions, some of those words now filled him with a nauseous reflex, words such as *love* and its parade of synonyms, or *tenderness* and its derivatives, with a special award for *couple,* which was particularly indecent but had no other real equivalent. Other words fared better: *affection* did not conceal anything too sordid, and *attraction* remained sufficiently vague not to take any risks. Oddly enough he had banned the word *seduction* from his vocabulary. Seduce? Big deal. The term implied a whole compulsory ritual, each step more fastidious than the next one. Meet a woman, go up to her, act as brilliant as possible with what you have available, get the telephone number off her, wait the right amount of time before calling, wring a date out of her, remain patient and keep your sense of humor, all this just to end up in bed together—but, don't act too bold, guess her limits without transgressing them. And if peradventure you managed to make your way safely over all those hurdles, the girl who had succumbed must under no circumstances go thinking that she had *met someone.* From now on Yves Lehaleur, his heart drained of courage, would dispense with any romantic scruples.

Philippe, with his glass in his hand—and this was not like him—was talking more than the other two. As a rule, in a conversation he often waited in ambush, ready to reappear whenever one of the speakers went off on a dead-end tangent. That evening, no doubt because he was the only one of the three of them who had not yet spoken out at the session, he was monopolizing the conversation. Denis, amused by the way Philippe thought their barroom gossip had some sort of significance, was happy enough just to keep him going. As for Yves, he was looking for the least vulgar way to talk about sex with two strangers: *and you guys, how do you manage?* If Denis's testimony were to be believed, he hadn't made love in years, and Philippe said he'd only just separated; it was fair to assume that each of them would have something to reply.

But despite Yves's efforts they did not broach the topic that evening. They would learn nothing about Denis Benitez's forced abstinence, the anxiety he felt at the loss of desire, the specter of impotence. Over the years, every form of sensual enjoyment had deserted him, right down to his dreams, that last refuge of unappeased urgings. Denis placed virility at the top of his list of lost causes.

Nor would they learn anything about how Philippe tried to find Juliette in other women's beds. None of them smelled like her, none of them knew how to curve her back the way she did so that they could spoon, none of them moaned with pleasure the way she did, discreetly yet so intensely. He had tried to console himself with the first woman who came along, then the second, and with every embrace he had to imagine Juliette's body in order to bring on his partner's orgasm and to get there himself, which was proof of a kind that faking it was not solely a female preserve. So while he tried to refrain from indulging in any form of nostalgia and stuck to his resolutions and feigned indifference as he reread his classics, life had lost all its charm ever since his woman had left him.

They had met at a seminar where Philippe had publicly lambasted a biography of Spinoza she had written. Not the least bit intimidated, she had stood up to him with such assurance that he had invited her out to dinner and apologized profusely. In the beginning, he had been disconcerted by this woman who was older, taller, and more experienced than he was. She was at least a head taller than anyone around, four years older than he was, and she had raised her children on her own. She'd lived several lives in one lifetime, so she was not afraid of grappling with life, unlike Philippe, who acted as if he were pure spirit, at a total loss where everyday life was concerned. The more he paid tribute to her nimble mind and her independence, the more he admired her beauty, which had remained intact ever since the days when, to pay for her studies in literature, she had posed for any number of painters and sculptors. *Juliette Strehler, six foot one, one hundred and thirty-nine pounds, her full-size statue is on display at the Smithsonian museum.* That was how he introduced her to his friends, who had never known Philippe Saint-Jean so proud to be seen with a woman on his arm. Today, wrapped in his pride, he was not about to admit that, deep down, missing Juliette was what had motivated him to attend the Thursday meetings. If she had left him for someone else, even a go-go dancer, the sentence would have seemed far less cruel. She had left him because of who he had become: a man who had not a trace of self-doubt, and was only too ready to accept the image of the brilliant intellectual he saw reflected in other people's eyes. Philippe Saint-Jean took himself for Philippe Saint-Jean, and only Juliette had noticed.

A conversation on sexual frustration failed to materialize, but that wouldn't alter the response Yves had found to get rid of his frustration, as logically as possible: he would consume, without seducing. Without saying a word. Without even knowing the girl. Without even taking the time to figure out whether he really fancied her. Without running the risk of even the tiniest atom of feeling worming its way in. A married friend had told him, *You know, the advantage of a whore is not so much that she'll do anything you ask, but that she leaves right away when she's done.* That same friend, who seemed to know what he was talking about, had left him the number of a certain Kris.

Yves had never been with any prostitutes, and few of his acquaintances had made use of their services. For him it was a practice belonging to another era, and had nothing to do with his milieu or morals. It was not that for Yves there was a moral dimension, no, it was simply a matter of circumstances: he had never needed to pay. And now that he was all of forty, brutally single, eager to avoid any notion of attachment, he had made up his mind to call this Kris woman; he'd had a vague physical description of her. If a stranger like Philippe or Denis had said to him, *I do, from time to time,* Yves would have felt he belonged to the norm, would have been prepared to concede that sooner or later all men take this path. The girl's number had been languishing in his pocket for over a week, and the need to call her suddenly became imperative. She would come, he would take possession of her body and, once she'd left, he would have done with that good Monsieur Lehaleur once and for all, that exemplary little husband en route for the great family adventure. No Kris, from now on, could ever ask that of him.

Before leaving the bistro, Philippe asked the other two whether they planned on being there the following Thursday. Denis nodded and Yves answered, *Sure thing.* Each of them left with the feeling that their trio would meet again.

3

Most of the time Philippe Saint-Jean got around on foot, living as if he were a surveyor of Paris, a solitary wanderer. His activity allowed him the time, and he put his hours in the street to good use. Besides, owning a car would have been counter-rational, anything but ecological, and downright vulgar. His itineraries might include a detour by way of a park, a church, the banks of the Seine or, like today, a secondhand bookstore. Every time he came to the Bastille quartier he would stop by the dusty shelves of a little shop on the Rue Saint-Antoine and await a chance encounter with a title, a forgotten author, or an irresistible foxed binding. His curiosity and patience had allowed him to unearth unusual little volumes which he would read straight through and mention in the course of his conversations. He leafed through a hardback with a gold and red binding that he had found in a tub of loose books, and it had just enough patina to entice him: *With the Bathwater. A Little Linguistic Misadventure,* by a certain Édouard Gilet. For five euros, this could be the day's acquisition and his little bedtime treat.

He crossed the Place Bastille, headed toward Nation, then stopped, intrigued by a cluster of people outside a luxurious café next to the Opéra; a movie camera on rails, technicians waving their walkie-talkies, projectors, extras seated in front of fluorescent cocktails and, in the middle of all the hustle, an actress's stand-in.

"What are they filming?" asked a voice in the crowd.

"A perfume commercial."

Like many people, Philippe liked to linger in the presence of heavy cinema equipment, hoping to see a familiar face, a director whose work he particularly liked. At the word "commercial" he left the crowd of onlookers, acknowledging his total lack of interest in what some people considered an art form—in his opinion, advertising was the worst avatar of mercantile sublimation. But then he saw the figure everyone was waiting for, draped in an immaculate white which emphasized the golden brown sheen of her skin. The young woman took her seat with a professional ease, aware of how radiant she was, but just blasé enough to discourage any bores. Utterly surprised, Philippe recognized the girl's face and tried to remember her name, something like Mira or Mina, an affected little mewing sound which suited her perfectly. *Mia!* shouted someone, to get the model's attention; she granted a smile. Philippe had met her a year earlier during a society dinner organized by a media mogul who bragged that he had *friends in every sector*—Philippe had found his expression execrable, but he'd gone along anyway. During the dinner he had tried in vain to attract the girl's attention with a great many abstract witticisms. As for Mia, who was used to being the center of everything, she thought this intellectual guy was verbose and pedantic, since he hadn't shown the slightest sign of curiosity about *her.*

It was strange to see her again, here in this cocoon of light and celebrity, so distant. First came a sideways tracking, then she made a knowing gesture, tossing a splash of perfume into the air the way you splash your champagne into the face of an insolent lout. Then she left the café at a run, followed by an agile swoop of the camera which would allow you to see, in the background, the Colonne de Juillet on the square. Philippe would have already been on his way, but something kept him there, in the way of any simple curious bystander fascinated by luxury and pomp—which he wasn't. He would have liked to go up to this Mia person for no other reason than to see if she remembered him the way he had remembered her.

During the sixth take she noticed him at last. Holding the train of her dress, she gave a faint smile, narrowed her eyes, and made a great effort to remember: he reminded her of someone, but who? She waved to an assistant to let Philippe come into the field of the camera.

"You remember? A dinner at Jean-Louis's. A big duplex on the Quai Voltaire."

" . . . The philosopher?"

"Yes."

"Incredible, what a coincidence! Just last week I was shooting in Johannesburg and that evening I switched on TV5 Monde in my hotel room, you know, the international French channel, and there you were! You were talking about your book . . . Something with 'mirror' in the title . . . "

The rebroadcast of a news program where he had tried to promote his essay on collective memory. Mia had seen him and, what's more, halfway around the planet. They exchanged a few pleasantries; he found the absurd situation amusing, while she was being assailed by the makeup girl in the middle of an audience, watching their encounter as if it were part of the script. Neither one of them experienced even the slightest twinge of the thrilling symptoms two individuals feel when under the spell of mutual attraction: their hearts did not beat faster, nor did their pupils dilate, nor were there hot flashes or a rush of adrenaline, and, in spite of everything, without knowing why, neither one of them wanted to put an end to their meeting.

" . . . The director is asking for me."

Philippe would have liked to get her phone number without having to ask for it, and Mia wanted to leave room for the possibility of a future meeting without having to take the initiative. Both of them had long ago left behind that stage of polite awkwardness where one feels obliged to stay in touch without really wanting to.

And yet the moment seemed to go on and on.

"I travel a lot, but I come back to Paris regularly," she said, looking for something to write her number with.

"I never leave Paris," he answered, producing a card where only his email address was printed.

Philippe shook Mia's hand, surprised he hadn't had to hold out his cheek, then left the scene, and its audience, to head down the Rue du Faubourg-Saint-Antoine with the Place de la Nation in his sights. Six–forty P.M., a Thursday.

The classroom, with all its windows open, was already filled with a hundred contemplative men: these were its last days before demolition. An administrative decision had finally been implemented, coming as a surprise to all the hierarchy: the west wing of the building would be demolished in order to build a sports complex. The guidance counselor opened the meeting to inform all those present: they were going to have to find new premises by next week. All kinds of ideas were put forward until the security chief of a small private museum with a projection room offered to host the upcoming meetings. A few weeks, maybe more, would go by before anyone would ask him for an explanation. Everyone voted for this solution.

Denis Benitez and Yves Lehaleur saw Philippe Saint-Jean come in just before the doors closed. Yves whispered the address for the next meeting to him while a fellow charged up to the podium.

"I've been coming for a few weeks and I'm not sure this is really the right place for what I have to say, but I haven't found anywhere else. If this seems off subject to you or inappropriate in any way, I'm asking you to excuse me in advance. I imagine that most of the people here live on their own, which is not the case for me. My life is the kind everyone aspires to, where love is shared."

Philippe had already stopped listening, as he was still troubled by his meeting with the inconceivable Mia, there in the spotlights, dressed in platinum, surrounded by a crowd chanting her name. Nothing fascinating—simply unreal, a cinematic moment. From this experience, Philippe could have drawn the preface to a book on the imaginary world of money, and yet despite his position as a sociologist he had been the involuntary actor in the film.

"First I have to tell you something about Émilie. She starts the day with a smile and goes off to sleep saying something funny. Émilie loves life, life loves her, and I don't know if the word even means anything anymore these days: I think she is happy."

Philippe Saint-Jean had his doubts about just how fascinating someone like Mia could be. Her impeccable beauty had not moved him today any more than it had the first time. When he got home from that wasted evening of a dinner, Juliette had asked him, *Is she as beautiful in real life as in the photos?* And he had launched into a long speech about the only true beauty, which is unconscious. To be sure, she had plenty of assets, but none of them would hold up to two hours of non-conversation with a spoilt child who was convinced her life was far more thrilling than that of ordinary mortals. In response to Juliette's question Philippe had said, *The girl is a monster of symmetry, but that in no way constitutes beauty; what is beauty? You are.*

"And yet there's a cloud on the horizon. Émilie and I don't love each other at the same rhythm. It's not so much a difference in intensity as in style. I am passionate; Émilie is pensive. I anticipate the moments that lie ahead; she enjoys the present moment. I call her ten times a day; she thinks that words become drained through repetition. I like knowing everything she is doing; Émilie never asks me a thing. I want to get to know all her friends; she encourages me to party with my own crowd. I use *never* and *always* all the time; she thinks there's no such thing as an absolute. As the months go by I have begun to wonder if so much disparity is not a sign of something deeper. Won't these differences crystallize over time and creep into our relationship until they begin to contradict everything that brought us together? I was well aware that I was creating the problem just by formulating it, but instead of feeling reassured by Émilie's trust in me, which favors the right to be different, and which knows how to make things relative the way they should be, I began listening for the sour notes, even causing them sometimes in order to prove my conclusions. I reproached her for not being as attentive as I am, for never losing her self-control no matter what, for never letting go. I started getting impatient, irritable, unfair, more and more often. Until one morning when I overdid it and Émilie stopped believing in our future together. You will tell me I got what I deserved . . . "

Slumped on his chair, his fists in his jacket pockets, Denis Benitez was sorry he had come. Ever since he woke up that morning, an unexplained weariness had made him question his every gesture, even the very thought of work. But a guilty nagging feeling made him put on his white shirt and black apron and set untold numbers of plates down in front of diners who were hungry, or not, and for the hundredth time he would explain how the cod had been prepared, and put up with the shouting in the kitchen, and the criticism in the restaurant, and the invectives of the boss. During his three o'clock break he looked up thalassotherapy sites on the internet, convinced his fatigue was a result of burnout, and that a little bit of hot water would do him a world of good. At six thirty he took the métro to Nation and wondered why. After all, he'd already spoken his mind in front of a bunch of strangers—what was the point going back there? To subject himself to the moaning of some guy who dared to complain about his wife's affection?

"The fear I might lose Émilie calmed me right down. No more embraces? No more luxuriating in her scent? No more devouring her like a lamb? No more letting her play the wolf from time to time? Never to know the children we would have? And all because I measure attachment with a double decimeter? For five or six months following her ultimatum, I acted the perfect partner, a model of understanding and tact. At least on the surface, because nothing had changed; other than that; I kept my anxiety to myself from then on, since it was getting more and more severe and unfair. *Why isn't she here with me now, right away? What better things does she have to do? Why doesn't she say she loves me when I ask her? Why is she so cautious when we talk about our plans for the future?* I knew our relationship would not survive a second crisis over such absurd complaints. I had to learn to leave her alone, whatever the price, to let her live and love me the way she saw fit. So I came up with a solution, a terrible solution . . . "

Denis thought this testimony was a disgrace. That guy could leave the room whenever he liked to go and find his Émilie and keep her company and have children with her or fight over the remote, and yet he went on sitting there splitting hairs and quibbling about mindless details in a relationship when there were so many little moments of harmony that had no need to be analyzed or put into perspective.

" . . . A terrible solution, but ever so effective: I am cheating on my wife. I am sleeping with another woman once a week. An act that doesn't mean much in and of itself, only afterwards, when I get back home. I feel pitiful, I am ashamed to have to find a pretext to take a shower the minute I get home, to destroy any trace and to lie about the way I spend my time. That's when I realize I'm living with this wonderful woman who has no idea how base I am. When I take her in my arms, knowing that another woman has just left them, I can evaluate just how unfounded my reproaches truly are, and I stop looking for problems where there aren't any. What I used to take for indifference now seems like trust and respect. I have stopped trying to find out every detail of her time without me, I now know that she needs to find fulfillment on her own, and not live through me, or because of me or for me, and that's the Émilie that I love."

Who the hell is this twisted idiot! thought Yves Lehaleur, exasperated. Since he had begun coming to the Thursday club he had heard some hard cases, but never this hard. Cheat on your wife to keep from harassing her . . . How far does a relationship have to degenerate for you to have to resort to this kind of stratagem? Having seen his own love destroyed by adultery, Yves could not tolerate the idea that it could be a solution for anything whatsoever. In his opinion, complicated psychological intriguing as a response to a rocky love life merely hid other causes of unrest. He had not resorted to any vicious subterfuge in order to cherish Pauline. She had been there, in plain sight, and that had been enough for him.

The witness left the professor's seat and another one replaced him, eager to spit it out and get it over with right from the start: he was impotent. A disgrace he had known *all his adult life*, he said, emphasizing the word adult. At the age when *those who have done it* lorded it over *those who are about to do it*, he waited for his turn, and it seemed it would never come. In spite of his exceptional shyness, which left him absolutely tongue-tied in the presence of a girl, he had sworn he would be cured of his adolescence before he hit twenty. But one summer had followed another, as icy as winter, and his rare efforts—fear in his guts, a flaccid member, evasive glances, confused logorrhea then the silence of the dead—had led to nothing more than early mornings filled with shame, which condemned him to silence—how could he speak of his infirmity when it had become the supreme insult for anyone who wanted to hurt the male of the species? Alcoholics and reformed criminals could assume their botched lives in public, but he could not. What was more, he felt excluded from a universal culture where love in general and sex in particular had the starring roles; he would frequently put down a book when the author started to describe how a man and a woman became acquainted, the cycles of charm, feverishness, and entanglement, just as he would look away whenever, on screen, a passionate lover pushed his partner down onto the table.

Lehaleur also looked away, as he would have gladly turned off the sound if he could have; this testimony was making him feel ill at ease. Imagine yourself deaf? Mute? Both at the same time? A trifle. One-armed, paralyzed? Anything, but not *that*. Like so many men, he could not imagine resigning himself to a handicap that was so much more degrading than any other. That was what he thought already when he was still living with Pauline, and even more so nowadays, at the threshold of a great career of debauchery. But the witness went on, implacably: after revealing what must be the height of misfortune, worse was yet to come. Once he was past thirty he no longer committed the error of judgment of yielding to an attraction to a beautiful young stranger—he imagined she would immediately grasp the meaning of his avoidance behavior, and make herself scarce; nor did he find a bunch of friends to hang out with: sooner or later, they were bound to wonder why he never said anything about his love life, why he did not seem to enjoy talking dirty. In the absence of any effective treatment, and by virtue of never putting the mechanics of desire in gear, his libido had vanished.

A sudden anxiety roused Denis Benitez from his lethargy: every sentence he heard sounded like a foreshadowing of his own future. His life as a shameless rake seemed far in the past, and he too felt a loss of desire which seemed irreversible. To be sure, he could imagine that between a man who has always been impotent and one who is about to become impotent, there must be the same difference as between someone born blind and someone who has lost their sight. But Denis would have been incapable of saying whether nostalgia for a past life gnawed away at one as much as the lack of something one has never known.

"When I turned forty I made a resolution."

He would turn his pathology into destiny: he would no longer be *an impotent man* but a *virgin*. A profession of faith which, traditionally, was better suited to women, but which would allow him to legitimize an entire life of abstinence. Thus, in his virginity he had sought a mystical significance which would transform the agnostic into a believer. But the revelation was a long time coming; no doubt he was not made of that particular cloth.

"So many years spent feeling less than human weren't about to help me find God or the path to a monastery . . . "

When he turned fifty, he gave a different twist to his exceptional status: to be sure, he had never known the pleasures of the flesh or the transcendence of love, but this life of his spent isolated from human passion, exempt of any commerce with his peers, had enabled him to reach a degree of absolute, almost perfect egoism. This never-ending cohabitation with his own self, to the exception of all others, had made an urban hermit of him—civilized, incapable of empathy for others, peaceably inured to the misfortunes of his own kind. He had spent those years as if he were the last individual on earth, full of a silent scorn for all normally functioning men, and all those women whom he had not penetrated.

"I was only sorry that my shell of misanthropy had formed around me so late in life."

And yet, when he reached the year of his fifty-fourth birthday, humanity reminded him of its existence in the person of Emma, a coworker the same age who had been living alone since she had become a widow and her children had left home.

She wasn't the talkative sort, she hugged the walls so to speak, and they must have passed each other a thousand times on the métro platform and in the company corridors and as they pushed their trays along in the cafeteria before they ever spoke. They met again at the theatre, and occasionally on Sundays at outdoor concerts, and over the months their conversations had become more refined, with nothing at stake, joyful for the most part, always serene, yet no doubt it was already too much: what if they became close? The following pages of the script would be as tragic as they were predictable, and in order to forestall the inevitable complications, he launched into a long confession.

"I made up some story about a serious accident that had 'altered my erectile functionality.' I wanted it to sound like a euphemism . . . Since I knew the score by heart, I had no trouble gaining her sympathy. Contrary to all expectation, Emma seemed relieved. Her own libido had vanished along with her husband."

But she was reassured by the idea of spending her old age with a last companion. Retirement was around the corner, and their gentle friendship had evolved into a peaceful life together. Liberated from any pressure, for the first time he was discovering what shared intimacy meant, sleeping with a woman nestled up against his shoulder. Before long the sacrifice of so many years of sensual pleasure seemed far less cruel than having been deprived of these treasures of tenderness.

"Alas, such happiness could not last. And God knows I had waited a long time."

The audience before him had been expecting a happy end to his sad story, but now he looked graver than ever: after a few first nights in their shared bed, he awoke in a frenzy, his cock standing upright against Emma's thigh.

"It was an order from my body, the first it had ever given me with such authority."

Every night his desire for Emma grew, and every night he hid his youthful hard-on, sidestepping the issue ever more resourcefully. To be sure, she would have taken his excitement as a late-blooming compliment, but how could she forgive such a pernicious, diabolically detailed lie—he had described his accident with such precision, recited word for word the doctors' diagnosis, which left no hope that he would ever get hard again; he had even, with the help of a drawing, depicted the absence of blood flow to the cavernous hollows of his cock. This was the man who had said farewell to his virility, and had climbed into Emma's bed claiming to be harmless, and now here he was, destroyed by the brutal self-confidence his member was bestowing on him at last. About to turn sixty, he had to admit as much to his brethren: he had a sexual problem.

Saint-Jean watched him leave the podium to go back to his seat. Without such an astonishing reversal, that man would have taken his secret with him to his grave. Philippe was sorry the man had decided to come and tell his story just at that particular moment in his relationship with Emma, and not just after making love to her: it would have made an ineluctable epilogue, with its promise of unexpected descriptions.

One last participant got up to read at length from the logbook of his relationship, as if he were the captain of an expedition and his wife was first mate. Denis Benitez had respected the protocol by resisting the urge to leave the room before the end of the session. His presence among the brotherhood no longer made sense. It wasn't here that he'd find an answer to the great mystery of female evasiveness. At this point, his struggle against so much indifference had worn him out for good, psychologically but also physically; he needed some rest. He should go away somewhere, into exile, all alone and far away, but above all alone, alone, for Christ's sake, a true solitude, one that he'd chosen and not a constraint, quality solitude, exceptional solitude, well up there among all the great solitudes of

History, an absolute return to the self. Then they'd see, *those women*, all of them, that it was possible to exist without them.

At nine o'clock sharp the men left the place for the very last time. Until the next meeting in the little museum god knows where near the Place des Ternes, Yves, Denis, and Philippe said a hasty goodbye on the street corner—no one suggested going for a drink. Denis disappeared into the métro, Philippe headed for the nearest taxi rank, and Yves hurried off on his scooter for the Place d'Italie. Of the three of them he was surely in the greatest hurry: he had an appointment at his house at ten o'clock, with a stranger.

At nine forty, after he'd tidied the living room and made his bed, Yves put an ice bucket and some bottles on the coffee table. On the phone, Kris had asked him before anything else how he had gotten her number, then she told him her rates. She spoke to him the way he himself spoke to clients, careful to ensure there would be no unpleasant surprises. Their actual meeting, on the other hand, threatened to be more awkward: what do you say to a girl you know nothing about, except that she is blonde with dark eyes, and that *she will do almost everything,* according to a friend. It was something he'd never experienced, but he dreaded the scene of the call girl and her trick, all the clichés you found in the cinema, in literature, in the collective unconscious, and in guy talk in cafés. No matter how he tried to justify the oldest profession in the world, or pay homage to it, a woman was about to show up at his house to open her legs and go away again with 250 euros. Even if he did reject any notion of romance, it made the operation seem all the cruder.

Christelle Marchand, past thirty, had been in the business long enough to know the necessary precautions she must take with a new client. She never had clients at her place, didn't solicit in the street, didn't agree to appointments in suburbs that were too remote, or if she was not sure she could get a taxi home after nine P.M. She recruited on the internet through carefully selected websites, and she'd built up a network of clients who steadily found new ones for her; an average of six a day enabled her to live without fear of failing to making ends meet, or unemployment, or the fallout from economic crises and stock market crashes.

She arrived on time, agreed to a small shot of whisky in a lot of Perrier water, slipped the folded fifty-euro notes from the tabletop into her handbag, and asked Yves if he wanted anything in particular. Surprised, he answered, *No, just the usual thing.* Relaxed, with her glass in her hand, Kris made small talk with her client about the approach of spring. She was wearing a thick black jacket that zipped diagonally, decorated with top-stitching at the shoulders, a skirt that came mid-thigh, and thigh-high boots in black suede. He could see a certain innocence in her features, and a blonde brilliance that hinted at the child she had once been. She headed over to the bed, perfectly relaxed as she removed her clothes and tossed them here and there on the floor. Yves saw she was wearing panties that laced up at the back and a bra made of the same lace; her skin was light and smooth. He undressed like an awkward adolescent, sat down on the edge of the bed, then slid beneath the sheets and embraced the body he had been waiting for for too long, warm with their exhaled breath, a mingling of sweet and sour. He would have liked to take the time for contemplation, for emotion, to enjoy this return to basics, to find in a long embrace everything he had been deprived of, but his urgency to penetrate her betrayed him, and in spite of himself he was already forcing his way between her thighs. She got the condom business over with in a few seconds, and encouraged his too-feverish body to come inside her. Prisoner of her legs, incapable of resisting such an embrace, as if he were being sucked inside her, Yves was lured into a furious in and out, abetted by her hand clinging to his hips. She enhanced the movement even further with violent spasms of her vagina which forced him to come. While he lay on his side, restraining a moan, Kris had already put a knot in the condom which she dropped into a small bowl. Drained, mute, Yves watched her head for the shower, come back out a minute later, and get dressed, validated by her sense of duty fulfilled, ready for her next appointment. He had the unpleasant impression that he'd been robbed of the best part of that sensual pleasure he had so looked forward to. *No need to see me out*, she said, satisfied that she had gotten the job over with in such a short time. *You have my number.*

He was dismayed that his little business had been taken care of so nimbly. He lay in bed, vanquished, his cock drooping, and he already dreaded the terrible solitude to come. *I got laid*, he said out loud, laughing at himself. For a few minutes his body had been hostage to another, and that body, for all its contrived gentleness, had known how to dictate its requirements. Just the thought of it would curtail most of the loneliness that kept him from sleeping.

As he was drifting off he had to admit that he too, at times, had used a woman's body in that way.

That same night, at two ten in the morning, Philippe Saint-Jean lay in bed mechanically turning the pages of a book. He had tried ten times over to get into the little book he had bought that afternoon, and ten times over he had lost the thread, absorbed in the memory of his first meeting with Mia, that dinner at a friend's house, as snobbish as it was boring. For her aperitif she had asked for a mineral water that was totally unknown but *very popular in Switzerland.* All evening long she had involuntarily slipped Anglicisms into her conversation, saying "personalité" when she meant "character" or "insécure" when she meant "hesitant." Convinced she must be an Anglophone, Philippe had asked her where her lovely olive skin came from, and she replied, *Fifty percent Provençal, fifty percent Réunionnaise, and one hundred percent French.* Later he had served her some arugula salad with shavings of parmesan, lovingly describing the countryside of Reggio Emilia where this little masterpiece of six years of age had come from; not even stooping to taste it, Mia had pushed the shavings of cheese to one side of her plate. To finish with a flourish she complained bitterly and at length about the treatment inflicted on a certain species of lemur that lived in the north of Madagascar.

Today she had seemed far less superficial, almost authentic in spite of the circumstances that were anything but. A young woman who, once you removed the makeup and projectors, must be troubled by the same fears and aspirations as anyone. No doubt she was driven by her ego—but then, who wasn't?

Seeing Mia cross his path again like that might be a sign, but of what? He was such a thoroughgoing Cartesian, the resident rationalist, he could go on for hours about the difference between fate and determinism, yet he could not imagine this second meeting had been mere chance. What's more, when he allowed himself to be tempted by a psychoanalytical reading of the minor events that occurred in his life, he gladly conceded that chance did not exist. Mia had not reappeared for no reason. Even if he never saw her again, he had to find the true meaning of what she had called a *coincidence.*

At that same moment Mia climbed into a taxi that would take her back to the Ritz. After her endless day filming she had not been able to get out of a dinner with sponsors who had hired her at a premium. She was leaving first thing the next morning for New York, an initial fitting for a sportswear line that had commissioned the services of some major couturiers. She wouldn't have time to see that intellectual who had made a much better impression on her today than the first time she'd met him. He'd been so overbearing that night, listening to himself talk, beginning all his sentences with *As I am sure you are aware,* lecturing about existentialism as if it were for dummies, zigzagging brilliantly between the theories of Kant and the cinema of Wim Wenders. But what would be the point, after all, of trying to keep a philosopher from reasoning; that was like trying to stop a greyhound from running after a decoy, or a salmon from swimming upstream. Today's meeting had been a change from all those living nullities she met all year round, hollow people who looked good, all a bit cynical and apt to panic the moment they left their luxury hideouts. She was one of them, no doubt about it, but there were times when she tried to fight back. All she had to do was go and see her parents, near Avignon, to remember what a normal person's life was all about.

Her father was still running his trucking company, and her mother looked after the big house, empty now, where Mia and her brothers had had such a happy childhood. Whenever their famous little daughter didn't cancel at the last minute, a family dinner would be organized in her honor. Her mother got cooking, her older brother rushed over with his wife and kids, Mia handed out presents. Afraid of putting on even a hundred grams, she wouldn't touch the Creole pâté, or the pork curry with ginger, or the traditional sweet potato pie; she'd just nibble at a few shrimps wiped clean of their onion salsa. Then she'd be subjected to a thorough interrogation: *I heard you'll be doing the Dior campaign . . . You got in an argument with Naomi? Is that really you on the poster with the handbag, I hardly recognized you . . . You're not with that English guitarist anymore?* Where did they find it all? In magazines, on television, at the hairdresser's? None of it was true, or it had been completely distorted, but there was no way could she say, *I'm still your little Mia.* Her parents had been viewing her as their totem ever since they, too, had been treated like stars in the neighborhood, for having brought into the world a creature whose measurements bordered on mathematical mystery. In the onslaught of questions, the ones Mia dreaded most were the ones about boyfriends. *No, I'm not with So-and-So anymore.* In general, she refrained from adding, *How could I have wasted six months with such a jerk?* An old married American TV network boss, or a Spanish tennis player who was definitely either too tennisy or too Spanish, but the worst of all had been Ronnie—Irish, not English, a bass player, not a guitarist. He couldn't stand the fact that she'd taken the initiative to break up, and he'd had his revenge by declaring to the celebrity press that because she never ate anything, Mia secreted a gastric juice that gave her the breath of a fox terrier. For weeks, people had stood three feet back from her, sometimes with their faces turned to one side. She didn't know how to respond to such bad faith, not even around her parents, who had read the nonsense. This was not the only nonsense they'd read since they'd started seeing photographs of their daughter in every getup imaginable. Gossip, hearsay, but also some direct attacks, like the ones in that prime time program where a columnist had been so tacky as to tell this joke in Mia's presence: *Do you know why models have one neuron more than horses do? It's so they won't shit while they're on the catwalk.* And everyone on the set had laughed their heads off. She'd put a good face on it until she left the studio, and then she'd burst into tears.

She would have given anything that night to be able to seek refuge in a kind person's arms, far away from the cliques and the posers, from fashion and snide remarks. *When are you going to introduce us to someone nice?* her mother asked repeatedly. Someone she wouldn't be ashamed of, someone who wouldn't be driven by his obsession with fame, someone level-headed and thoughtful and who, when he was at her side, would get all those mocking critics to shut up. But it didn't seem likely that Mia would meet *someone nice* at any of her jet-set parties or in the idolatrous circles of the glamour industry.

That someone was not likely to be Philippe Saint-Jean. But how could she be sure if she didn't see him at least one more time?

Late at night, unable to fall asleep despite his exhaustion, Denis Benitez decided to give his companions the slip until further notice. The time to take leave of reality had come. He swallowed three sleeping tablets from a box that had been past its sell-by date for several months now. He wouldn't go to work the next day. With a bit of luck he'd sleep so long that the day would go by and he wouldn't even notice.

He must be headed for some unknown place, lost in the middle of nowhere. But where he'd be alone at last. And never mind if the place turned out to be sad and deserted. Denis was already far too weary to turn back.

4

In the room: a simple bed, a night table, a chair for visitors and overhead, where there used to be a crucifix, a television that was never switched on. The setting wasn't important—nothing was important, Denis slept most of the time. At worst, he drowsed between two visits from the nurse, suspended in weightlessness by medication that changed from one day to the next. On the rare occasions when someone roused him from his lethargy, a blurry image entered his field of vision, most often that of a meal tray, a white uniform, or a handful of tablets in a cup. When a hurried intern announced his presence with a booming *How are we feeling today?* Denis would wonder what was meant by "today." When he was conscious enough to correlate two ideas one after the other, he tried to go back over the cottony sequence of events that had led him to this bare, silent room where he was no longer afraid of collapse. The rest was all forgetfulness, the real thing, the kind that snatches you up. His body felt none of the sensations, whether pleasant or not, that call you back to life, with one exception. When he woke up, Denis would turn his pillow over to feel its coolness against his cheek; the only moment of the day when his nerves flushed his skin.

At the end of that afternoon, a psychiatrist sat by his side for a long time to try and unravel the origins of Denis's depression. His eyes half-closed, his breathing calm, Denis answered the practitioner, who was no doubt a kindly man, but way off track. How could he share with a stranger a message too shameful for confession: living without love, he had gradually lost his faith in humanity. Then, in himself.

They agreed on the word overwork, which avoided the need for any others. As soon as he was alone, Denis glanced at the fading daylight and all he had to do was close his eyes to lose himself in the darkness.

It was Mia who got in touch. Philippe would never have dared take the initiative. The gentlemanly tradition whereby it was up to the man to call upon the woman did not apply in this case. If Mia had been the sort of woman you meet in everyday life, he would have taken the first step, and then all the others. But Mia's image inhabited the streets and dreams of millions of men, her very name sounded like a luxury label, her radiance crossed borders. How on earth could Philippe Saint-Jean, who both questioned and shunned the values of a world sacrificed to appearance, show any interest in a universal object of desire? Just one phone call to the supermodel and he would have been guilty of allegiance. Conversely, it seemed natural to him that the futile, flashy world where Mia lived would be drawn to his own, a world where curiosity in other people remained intact, and answers were far less important than questions.

She suggested they have dinner at a restaurant that was practically a secret, patronized by a handful of initiates in pursuit of anonymity. As was usual for him, Philippe arrived on time, and was instantly sorry—year in year out, his damned punctuality meant he had to wait for careless people. He was led over to a plush corner where red velvet vied with a trendy silver, and did he want still or sparkling, so he made do with sparkling in lieu of the beer he would really have preferred. To strike a pose, he hesitated between reading the menu and jotting down some not really necessary notes in his notebook. He saw some well-known faces at neighboring tables, though he wasn't sure exactly who they were, men and women with perfect figures, as if designed for the setting. In his notebook Philippe wrote, *renew subscription to Paris-Match.* Finally he glanced at the menu, which immediately exasperated him. Philippe was not at all a foodie, and had no real interest in gastronomy, but what he despised more than anything was dietary terrorism, the ultimate hypocrisy of a handful of rich people prepared to pay top dollar for their fear of putting on one ounce. All it took was to read *lightly steamed John Dory on its bed of watercress sprouts €45* for him to want to roast the chef on a spit with an apple in his mouth.

Mia burst into the restaurant like a bullet, planted two quick kisses on Philippe's cheeks, took off her baseball cap and dark glasses, dropped her cell phone on the table and gulped down the entire glass of cold tap water they had just served her.

"So, what will it be, shall we say *tu* to each other?"

"Whatever you like," answered Philippe, still saying *vous,* in order to slow down the pace.

Philippe used the brief moment while she was studying the menu to take a closer look: hardly any makeup, natural, but still watchful—Mia lived constantly with a third eye which kept her on stage. Whether one liked her type of looks or not, she did not go unnoticed. Such harmony between all the features of one human face—mouth, eyes, nose, skin—could not be the result of chance, and its sole purpose was to be admired. Her full lips, narrow at the corners, were not made to speak or eat or kiss, but to smile to men of goodwill. Those enormous eyes glinting with sapphire were not made for her to discover the world but to subjugate crowds, who were always in search of pagan idols. That skin of amber and copper, infinitely glowing, evoked every race in and of itself. Philippe believed in the determinism of nature, that it always tended toward a precise goal: to ensure the enjoyment of the greatest number.

Right from the start they avoided the pitfalls of the previous dinner, which had opposed them on every level, and they risked, rather, going to the opposite extreme: emphatic self-criticism, constant approval of whatever the other one was experiencing. Mia was sorry her life was so constantly frenetic, and she was afraid she might be missing what was truly essential. Philippe emphasized his peace of mind but feared a certain inertia, for he was prisoner of an intellectual comfort that cut him off from contemporary turmoil. In order to find some common ground, they shared their mutual complaints. When Mia evoked the downside of fame, he dwelt on the inevitable risk that came with being *exposed*. When she confessed to a certain confusion between her professional life and her private life, Philippe regretted that his own mental processes never left him alone. When he, in turn, mentioned the handful of detractors who demolished even his most insignificant articles, she invoked the way the media hounded her shamelessly and relentlessly. In the course of the evening their chat reached a certain equilibrium; when one of them ventured a confession, the other would yield a bit more in return. They compared their solitude, fatal for her, necessary for him, trying for both of them. Oh, their dear solitude! Faithful companion, whether one is alone or surrounded. A solitude that returned ever stronger after one had cherished the illusion of being part of a twosome. But before they were to venture into that terrain, they needed to find a more intimate environment: she suggested they go to another one of her hideouts for a drink.

They settled onto the back seat in beige leather of the chauffeur-driven Rover SUV which Mia's agency put at her disposal. After a gray, laborious day, Philippe allowed himself to be drawn into a spiral of luxury without trying to justify it. Tomorrow there would be ample time to put the evening in perspective. No sooner had they arrived at the Carré Blanc than Mia threw herself around the owner's neck as if they had saved each other's lives, something Philippe viewed as some sort of indispensable worldly posturing, a code of recognition, an extreme indicator of notability. They were seated upstairs, in an opulent American bar where impeccable waiters in livery paced back and forth to a background of jazz. Mia ordered a stiff dry Martini, with Tanqueray gin and an olive. Philippe wondered where her panicky fear of calories had vanished to, with all its science of *lite* and *diet*. But maybe these calories were counted differently, because they offered much more than mere energy: calm, or dreams, and one could not do without either.

"There's a club in the basement. We've had some memorable parties there."

The minute she said it she was sorry: *club, parties*, so *not* the image she wanted to give this man. Even her *we* sounded dumb: what could it refer to other than a handful of decadent princes ruining their golden youth? And what's more, it was at that club that she had met that bastard Ronnie, who'd dragged her through the mud the instant they broke up. *Memorable parties*, and at what a cost. Mia swore she'd spare the philosopher any further outbursts of frivolity.

Back in the days when he was just a student of the humanities, Philippe might have viewed Mia as a fabulous subject for a thesis. *Esthetics and Representativeness of the Contemporary Icon.* Enough to assure himself of the jury's congratulations. This evening, as she started on her second dry Martini, he began to view her differently, this famous specimen, situating her at last among her fellow creatures, complex beings as individualistic as they were gregarious, capable of the worst but often of the best as well.

"In my profession, you retire at thirty," she said. "I'm twenty-eight."

"In mine, I still have a ways to reach maturity. I'm forty-one."

Mia's gaze was suddenly drawn to a discreet figure in the half-light, taking his seat at a table not far from theirs.

"It looks like Bryan. What's he doing in Paris?"

"Who?"

"Bryan Ferry. The crooner. You must have heard of him."

Philippe wondered if someone were playing a trick on him.

"He must be here for a concert," she continued, "but I haven't seen any posters. Do you mind if I go over and say hi? I'll only be a sec."

Was it really Bryan Ferry? *The* Bryan Ferry? The Bryan Ferry of his adolescence? When his entire generation was into electronic funk and New Age, Philippe constantly played records by Dylan, Sinatra, and Bryan Ferry, all three of whom were considered dated, borderline uncool. Tonight, in this all-night bar, just when he least expected it, as he gazed at a gentleman of sixty-five or so, with a very British elegance and a voice of pepper and honey, Philippe remembered what it was like to be young.

"He and his wife came up to me to congratulate me after a show for Vivienne Westwood in London, and we hit it off. He's a charming guy, he's got these old-fashioned manners, it's really nice."

Nostalgic for his teenage years, Philippe ordered another cocktail, which he drank down without savoring it, like the adolescent he had become again. What was the point, here and now, in sticking to his theorist's reserve and vigilance? He was drinking dry Martinis with one of the most beautiful women in the world, a few feet away from a personage who had inflamed his youth—why would he need to play the observer? Didn't he have better things to do just now? Such as, for example, live in the present moment?

Mia, all her freshness intact, kept the conversation on course and led Philippe into far less innocent territory. With the skill of a duelist, and without him noticing, she launched into a heated exchange that obliged him to reply:

"In my case it's not an issue: I live alone."

Half an hour later, in a side street off the Avenue George-V, Mia told Philippe her chauffeur could drop him off.

"What about you?"

"I have a room here," she replied, pointing to the Hôtel Prince de Galles. "And I have a shoot early tomorrow morning. Some girls stay out all night and rely on their makeup people to work a miracle. I'd rather rely on nine hours' sleep."

They hugged, then kissed, fervently.

And said goodbye, pleased they'd performed not too badly, considering they'd been sizing each other up.

That night Kris was wearing a long dress, a russet color with an elegant square neckline. Her hair was gathered up into a ponytail, which gave a touch of innocence to her look. Sitting on the sofa with her legs crossed, ready to offer the same services as the previous time, she sipped on her glass of Perrier, looking around for the banknotes on the table. Yves had learned his lesson, and this time he wanted more than a quickie, no matter what it cost him.

"Do you ever stay the whole night?"

"All night long?"

"Yes, all night."

"You have to arrange it in advance."

"You have other appointments after me?"

"I was planning on going home and sleeping until noon."

"I'm not asking you for fancy stuff until dawn. I get up at seven and leave for work at eight. Just tell me your rate."

Convinced that he would bargain with her, she tried €600. He disappeared into the kitchen for a while and took out twelve notes from a thin wad he had withdrawn that very morning at the bank. *How much?* the teller had asked. He would have liked to reply, *Enough for a good eight-hour spree with a pro.*

"Since we've got some time ahead of us, can I get you

another drink, a real one this time? Or maybe you're hungry? I must have some stuff to munch on."

While he was preparing the tray, Yves amused himself by converting €600 into manpower. At the rate of four or five windows installed, he'd earn it in less than a week. Six hundred euros was a lot. With that much, he could go on vacation for a few days or set up a real little home cinema in his living room. He could also lend the money to a coworker who was going through a rough patch. Instead, he was going to treat himself to a woman's body, a woman with all her most secret integrity, but also her kindness, her docility, and her knowledge of masculine pleasure, and he would make her the perfect object of his desire, an instrument of fantasy, a playground, a living toy, a laboratory for his imaginings. Six hundred euros wasn't all that much.

Since his divorce, his relationship with money had completely changed. Released from the obsession with saving, he now had a totally casual attitude toward material issues. What was more, he was not afraid of unemployment, because people would always need windows, and even with that, he felt perfectly capable of changing profession overnight. He had no family to look out for, no expensive tastes, no gold digger to support, no sports car to lavish care on, no modern art collection to keep up to date. So what was he going to do with his stash of €87,000? Keep it for a rainy day? This life insurance was his last relic from his married life: he and Pauline used to talk about it as an entity, "the eighty-seven thou," their major capital, enough to make them creditworthy with the bank and guarantee themselves a housewarming party. With the €87,000, now he'd been able to experiment, find himself, surprise himself and maybe even, in the long run, learn something about who Yves Lehaleur had become. Women in general and sex in particular would play a central role in this quest for himself. What better investment could there be?

The lovely autumn-colored dress eventually slid to the floor. Kris still wore only her stockings before stretching out on her side, her elbow on the pillow. Yves sniffed her from every angle, turned her every which way, explored her, uncovered her secret places, her entries. He suddenly needed to find his way into her, and in a position he'd been dreaming about for far too long, doggie-style. And yet he hesitated: he would never have suggested it to a stranger, it wasn't done, there were women who had made that clear to him. So he resisted the irresistible, and lay on his back, and let her sit astride him. As he watched her come and go above him, he regretted his scruples: *She's a whore, you idiot,* a girl who couldn't care less how you take her. Kris stopped for a moment to pivot on herself then started up again, recreating, from a different angle, the position he had hoped for. Yves tried to resist this unexpected turnaround, but he ejaculated with a rare intensity. Kris knotted the condom and placed it in an ashtray which hadn't been on the night table on her previous visit. Still wearing nothing but her flesh-colored stockings she went back to the coffee table to pour herself a glass of water, while Yves curled up in the sheets, his forehead pearling with sweat. She borrowed a kimono, asked permission to smoke, then leaned against the living room window, her cigarette between her lips. For a moment Yves hesitated to join her, but decided he would rather gaze at her from a distance—her curves draped in satin, her hair loose on her shoulders, the bluish curls of smoke rising in the night.

Kris was wondering what race of man he belonged to. Obviously single, not too bad-looking, not a pervert, or anxious, or violent, or depressed, or condescending; he didn't fit in any of the boxes where she filed her usual clients, and she didn't like that. Men had ceased to surprise her long ago, she could see them coming a mile off and knew her roles off by heart, bitch, confidant or mother, whatever they wanted her to play.

Ill at ease with his nudity, Yves wrapped himself in a sheet, toga-style, and poured himself a glass of bourbon, which he went on to sip in a Roman posture. Kris was the one who felt the need to break the silence.

"What kind of work are you in? I like to find out how people make their living."

"I install windows and shutters. It suits me."

"Install windows?"

"Increase luminosity, or create total darkness, insulate from noise. There are so many people who think they have insomnia because they screwed up their life, when in fact they just have shitty windows."

Kris was surprised to find herself examining the PVC embrasure of the window she was leaning against, then she turned to go and sit with her host. She picked up on the word "noise," complained of being woken by the metal shutter of the bistro across the street from her place, then she rattled off a few stock phrases about urban cacophony. Yves interrupted her to ask her to remove her kimono; she complied, unsurprised. Watching her with her legs crossed and her stockings pulled up her thighs, as she estimated the number of decibels a small child can produce, Yves recalled a day when he had asked Pauline to take her clothes off while she was preparing an olive loaf: she had refused outright. He added a few details about the frequency of the human voice, all the while admiring his guest's superb breasts, her hips, her pubes, the edge of her sex, which he wanted to sniff, and kiss again, so he knelt on the floor. Then he got up, his cock level with Kris's mouth: she would have to pause in her conversation for a moment.

Later that night, Kris's wariness had faded; she wasn't dealing with a hidden sadist but with a guy who hadn't made love in far too long. Counter to all professional ethics, she asked him why he had called a prostitute. Yves had no desire to go through all the various stages that had led to their being together in his bed, so he slanted his reply toward the future and not the past: he wanted to get to know *all* kinds of women. Tall and petite, voluptuous and slight, ladies and chambermaids, semi-virgins and old soldiers, of every origin, every skin color, not to mention all the categories he had yet to discover. How could a man like him, given his life expectancy, his salaried position, and the fact that he rarely traveled anywhere, expect to bring such a project to fruition without resorting to prostitutes?

Kris paused to think then conceded he didn't really have much choice.

He glanced at his watch and decided to doze off at last. For the first time in so long he was going to have the pleasure of waking up next to a woman. Instinctively, he pulled her to him and put his arm around her waist the way he used to with Pauline. She misunderstood and thought she was being conscripted one last time: the client who wanted one for the road, to make sure he'd had his money's worth. To make sure, she in turn had an instinctive gesture, slapping her hand onto his groin to check his erection.

Stunned that his surge of tenderness was met with such a degrading examination, Yves was overcome with a wave of fury: he'd been reduced to a limp sex, to the level of an animal.

He grabbed her by her armpits, lifted her up with all his rage, and thrust her so hard that she collapsed against the wall before sliding to the floor.

Kris sat there on the floor, unmoving, dazed.

In her life as a prostitute she had already been thrown out of bed, but never in quite this way.

Yves slowly regained his composure. Went over to her, holding out his hand.

She understood what had just happened: he had felt the humiliation that she herself had to endure when some lout indulged in the most odious kind of fondling. For once she was the one who'd committed an invasive gesture on someone else's body.

Still trembling, he asked her to forgive him.

No, it was me, she said.

Neither one needed to add anything. They had to let the awkwardness drain away from the moment, for it was a founding moment. A strange complicity had just been born from that brutal embrace; not from sex. Lovemaking was not the quickest way to get to know one another; the quickest way was this lightning war.

They lay back down, huddled together, still trembling.

In the early morning she said, "I can introduce you to Lili, a colleague of mine. You should hit it off. And Agnieszka if you want someone exotic. Don't ever forget that a whore is as mistrustful of you as you are of her, so find a way to gain their trust, because if there's a tiff, she's got the upper hand. If she asks you outright what you like, the way I did, it's to get rid of you as quickly as she can. If you want to spend the night with her, don't pay in advance because she'll wait for you to fall asleep and then she'll leave on the sly. If I teach you how to negotiate, after a few nights have gone by you won't be paying a premium anymore. And, if you don't take revenge on a whore for all your little woes, she won't take revenge on you for her hatred of men."

In a bistro on the Avenue de Friedland, at ten P.M. on the dot, Philippe Saint-Jean and Yves Lehaleur were commenting on the session that had just taken place, for the third time, in their little museum. The last speaker had embarked on a panegyric in praise of married men, leaving the audience speechless. He had separated adult males into two clans, *them,* the husbands, and *us,* everyone else, and he included, out of hand, those hundred attendees who had no say in the matter. *They* were the norm, the natural way of things; *we* were the anomaly. In an era rife with disenchantment, unbridled consumerism, the abdication of ideology, and individualism raised to the status of a dogma, most men, he said, still believed in the commitment that had been their fathers' lot and their fathers' fathers'. Millions and millions of men had taken a woman's hand in theirs and uttered holy vows in the church or at city hall, *to have and to hold, from this day forward, for better, for worse, for richer, for poorer, in sickness and health, until death do us part.* Any other life choice seemed dreary in comparison. Those who had made these vows included lunatics, wise men, torturers, victims, gangsters, believers, atheists, slave drivers, slaves, serial killers, misers, vagabonds. So why *them* and not *us?*

Philippe had to admit the fellow had a certain chutzpah; Yves envied him for his charisma, something he wished he had.

"What I appreciated about the way got his point across," added Philippe, "was that he set out the idea of commitment as a premise right from the start and not some sort of revelation that comes along when you actually meet someone. A touch of Pascal in his way of thinking. Faith first, happiness later."

Yves was incapable of venturing into Pascalian territory, but he said he was sorry the man's eloquent speech had not taken into account the evolution from one era to the next and the most recent threat to marital values, including the most dreadful threat of all: male strippers. For while the prostitute on her street corner had been a threat to marital cohesion from time immemorial, the go-go dancer was a very recent threat. The law, if not the biblical texts, needed a complete overhaul.

In a more serious tone, Philippe said he was concerned they hadn't seen Denis Benitez for the last three sessions.

"Maybe he found the answer he was looking for," suggested Yves.

The moment he got home from the clinic Denis fell ill; the illness had been faster than the ambulance. He left his bed only twice a day: first at around two and then again at nine in the evening, to make the only meal that didn't leave him feeling sick to his stomach, a slice of gruyere between two pieces of white bread, tasteless and odorless but substantial enough to stave off the upset stomach caused by every handful of tablets. The rest of the time he slept, but it did not seem to make anything better. Denis was at a stage where the causes of depression had been lost along the way, but that way stretched on ahead, through zones of insalubrity and endless tunnels, to end up in an empty lot where he would stagnate for days on end.

In the beginning his coworkers stopped by to visit, always in pairs to give each other moral support. *We're not the ones who miss you, it's the diners.* Denis thanked them silently, then turned off the volume on the television as soon as they left, to fall asleep with the images of a world as disenchanted as his own.

In the days that followed Denis made a few attempts to get back to normal. The scenario was always the same: he woke before noon, an insane thought running through his head: *And what if this ordeal were over?* A burst of energy would get him going, he tore off his pajamas as if they were dead skin, put on some pants, picked out a T-shirt, not the red one or the green one, above all not the blue one; maybe the beige. And then, discouraged by the dust, a reflection in a glass of water, a moped roaring in the distance, he went back to bed.

One evening, however, when his friends had deserted him for good, when his entire body had attained a state of utter inertia, when the power of his surrender had triumphed over any sort of hope, he heard the doorbell ring.

He had been asleep, and initially he thought this was a death knell from some terrible nightmare. He sat up against his pillows, waited for a moment, heard nothing more then burrowed down in the bed again to search for gentler dreams. The bell went again, for a long time, a threatening insistence: whoever it was, they were not about to leave. Denis imagined one or two hypotheses, glanced at the clock, which told him it was seven P.M., headed in the half-light toward the front door, and looked through the spyhole.

He did not recognize the person who went on ringing so insistently, filling him with exasperation: it was as if the entire human race were out there. He was going to have to tell this person that he did not belong anymore.

He trampled over the mail that had been shoved under his door, looked for the light switch, and his immediate reaction was to put on the door chain. The glaring landing light, on a timer, hurt his eyes. He brought his face into the doorframe, made gaunt with sleep and weight loss, covered with stubble.

A woman in a gray raincoat stood there, her arms crossed, a faint smile on her lips. They looked each other up and down for a moment then he emerged painfully from his speechlessness, while she remained motionless and silent. Denis felt obliged to call on the powers of speech sooner than he would have liked.

"Are you from the clinic?"

"The clinic?"

"They told me about some sort of psychological aid . . . Something like that . . . But I haven't seen anyone . . . "

Her only reply was to shake her head slowly, still smiling faintly.

"You're not a shrink? Or anyone like that?"

"No, I haven't been sent by the clinic."

"Then you must be the social security? Checking up? I'm on long-term disability. You should have gotten my papers."

"No, I'm not from the social security, either."

"What do you want?"

"I've come to see you."

"Me?"

"Yes."

"Do we know each other?"

"No. At least I don't think so."

"You're some sort of social worker? Caregiver?"

"No."

"Why don't you stop telling me what you are not and instead tell me what you're here for?"

"Do we have to stand here talking on the landing?"

"Listen . . . I'm not very well, I'm going back to bed. So either you tell me what you want or you leave me alone."

"Just let me come in, what difference does it make?"

"I don't know you!"

"What are you afraid of? Do I look dangerous?"

"Has someone sent you? Someone I know?"

"No, nobody. I don't think there's anyone we both know. So just let me in, why don't you?"

"You think I go letting strangers into my house?"

"We would look less ridiculous."

"Do I look ridiculous?"

"Frankly, with your head in the door chain, like an old lady . . . "

Denis was nonplussed. The woman waited.

"You're selling things door-to-door, is that it? Tell me outright, we'd waste less time."

"A door-to-door salesman, me?"

"If that isn't the case, then what's that in your suitcase?"

"My belongings."

Denis didn't know what to say.

"Come on, open the door, otherwise someone will come out of the elevator and what will they think?"

"This is all getting absurd, I will have to ask you to leave me alone, and above all, don't go ringing the bell again. Thank you."

He slammed the door, irritated for a thousand reasons: he'd been disturbed while he was peacefully feeling depressed;

she'd thrown herself on him like a bundle of dirty laundry; and, above all, she'd called him a little old lady—he had forgotten that human beings were such a dreadful species that one single specimen could be the source of several irritations at once, with boundless, stubborn determination. And, sure enough, the bell rang again right away.

After splashing his face with water, he drank a few sips of a flat drink, put on a bathrobe, then went back to open the door, careful to remove the door chain.

"I'm not well, I think you can tell that. So for the last time, either you tell me what you are doing outside my door, or I call the police."

"The police? You'd go that far? No kidding, you would call the police?"

"That's what you're supposed to do in situations like this."

Inwardly, he had to confess that situations like this tended to be rare.

"Go ahead, if it makes you feel better, but what do you think you'll say to them?"

"You're asking me that as if you intend to wait and find out."

"I'm curious to hear you call. 'There's this girl outside my door, I don't know what she wants but she's won't go away . . . '"

"Am I mistaken or are you taking the piss out of me?"

"They'll ask you to describe me, in case I'm some strung-out junkie, a delinquent, who knows. Above all, they'll try to figure out how urgent it is, because I expect they have other fish to fry. 'She's wearing a raincoat, officer . . . '"

But also a pair of old boots, half leather and half canvas, and a gray silk shawl all around her upper body.

"If I don't open, will you stay there all evening?"

"If need be."

What the—? thought Denis.

"Let me in. Oh, come on, it's no big deal."

"What have I done to you?"

"Nothing at all."

"So what's up? You don't know where to go? You want some money?"

"Not at all!" she said, shrugging her shoulders. "Who do you take me for?"

"Put yourself in my position."

"In your position, I would have already let me in. What do you have to lose?"

Of all the things she had said thus far, these were the words that gave Denis pause. His stiff carcass, curled up day and night at the bottom of a ravine, obliged to swallow blue, white and green things to chase away the pain of anxiety, his joyless self, the way he was these days, with neither energy nor illusions—did he have anything left to lose?

"Maybe I'm a little groggy but I can still tell when a situation is completely wacko. I am going to close this door, but first you are going to promise me that you won't ring the bell anymore."

She paused, then said half-heartedly, "I won't ring anymore."

"Thank you," he said, gently closing the door.

On his way to the bedroom he met a repulsive creature, and recoiled. That indescribable thing—hairy, bent over, rickety, slovenly, had suddenly appeared between a cupboard door and the entrance to the bathroom. Before going to lie down he forced himself to confront the monster in question and face the mirror.

So *this* is what he had become?

Ashamed to behold this shadow of himself, Denis shouted, *Would you look at yourself, for Christ's sake!* and lavished on his shadow enough scorn for all the scum on earth. He was tempted to shave, couldn't find the strength, and went back to bed, shoving aside any shreds of pride the way you shove aside a chore. What miracle had stopped this odd girl from being afraid of *that?*

He nestled into his blankets, glad to be left alone at last. Indignation, shame, anger, too many feelings all at once for a sick man who was still a long way from convalescence. Never mind if that weird girl left with her mystery intact; for certain phenomena here on earth there were no rational explanations, as Denis was paying dearly to find out.

He groped across his night table, grabbed a tube, and swallowed several tablets before the usual time. He'd been disturbed in his retreat, he was still all feverish, it would take him a while to forget. He had thrown in the towel: why was someone coming to bug him? He used to feel so good on the planet, he used to make sure there was plenty of room for fantasy, he had loved his life and dared to say as much—so why him? Now he had to thank God for making him mortal.

What did the girl look like again? Shoulder-length hair, light brown it seemed, and then? And then nothing, an ordinary face, a figure in a raincoat, an insignificant character of the kind you meet in droves whenever you're unwise enough to leave your bed.

Denis dozed off for a too-brief moment, then opened his eyes wide, filled with doubt. What if that insignificant person hadn't taken her mystery away with her?

He left his bed again, rushed to the door, looked through the spyhole: she was still silhouetted against the darkness on the landing.

"You're going to give me problems with the neighbors."

"What do you mean, I just talked to a very nice lady, on the right here, she didn't seem at all surprised to find me waiting. She said, 'He must be asleep, he takes a lot of medication.'"

Denis stared at her wordlessly.

"Having said that, I'd give anything to sit down for a sec and drink a big glass of water."

"Are you joking?"

"That's all I want."

"Who the fuck are you?"

"Marie-Jeanne Pereyres," she said, rummaging in her handbag.

She handed him her ID card. *Height: 5'6". Place of birth: Bois-le-Roi (Seine-et-Marne).* On the picture, her hair was slightly longer and she was wearing round glasses. Give or take a year or two, she was the same age as Denis.

If his antidepressants and anxiolytics had not inhibited his fear reflex, Denis would have wondered whether he was being smitten with a misfortune worse than his depression. This strange person might have come to tell him as much: he had to find out once and for all.

"So let's suppose I let you sit here for a minute, will you finally tell me what you want?"

"Yes."

At last she was allowed through the door, so she put her suitcase in the hallway and went on to discover a tiny, neglected space, furnished with an old sofa and a little console covered with various small boxes and containers.

"May I switch on the light?" she asked, while he ran a glass under the faucet.

Not waiting for his reply, she turned on the light, sat down at last, and gave a sigh of relief, massaging her ankles. She drank the water all in one go and thanked him with a smile. He cleared away the things that were scattered across the table and moved a few things into the hallway, restoring a semblance of tidiness.

"Don't bother for my sake," she said, unbuttoning her raincoat.

"Keep your coat on and tell me what it is you want so we can get this over with."

Avoiding his gaze, she hesitated for a moment. But as she had committed to a reply, she was trying to find the fairest, least threatening way to put it. In the end she chose the simplest.

"I want to stay."

"Pardon?"

"I want to stay."

"What do you mean by *stay*? Stay here? At my place?"

"Yes, here. I don't take up much room."

"You are telling me that you barged in here to move in? That this is some sort of nightmare I'm having here?"

"Don't get upset. That heavy medication you're taking is probably affecting your judgment."

Drained of his last remaining strength, Denis had to sit down next to her for a moment. The *heavy medication* was playing tricks on him. He must have made a mistake with the dosage, he must have confused the blue tablets with the white ones, must have taken too many green ones, he was already asleep and the nightmare would fade away as soon as he woke up. And yet the creature did seem to be made of flesh and blood.

"Before I throw you out of here on your ear, heavy medication or no heavy medication, I'll give you one last chance to tell me what you mean by 'stay.'"

"This living room is enough. I can sleep on the sofa. I won't make any noise, I read a lot. Once a day for the bathroom will be fine. I can eat out."

Suddenly Denis's affliction was mingled with sadness, and the sadness brought on so many other emotions, all contradictory, all too violent for a man who was so weary. He could not restrain a sudden onrush of tears, and he began to sob and weep, like a child who is overwhelmed by the injustice of the world.

After what seemed like an eternity he dried his tears on the handkerchief she held out to him. He let out a long sigh of exhaustion.

"I'm going back to bed," he said, almost gently. "I'm sick. I'm tired. I am going to sleep for a very long time. Tomorrow, when I get up, make sure you're gone."

She didn't say anything in reply, and watched as he vanished into his room. Denis collapsed onto his bed and fell into a deep sleep that lasted all night long, then all the next morning.

When he awoke, the woman's face emerged from his memory. He rushed into the living room and found her stretched out on the sofa, a book in her hand.

She had stayed.

5

Once he had turned forty, Philippe Saint-Jean no longer expected to know the joys of secrecy. He had never committed to a woman to the point of swearing he would remain faithful, other than with Juliette, whom he would not have betrayed for anything. So he had never known the delight of stealing moments from respectability, or the sudden intrusion of romance into the monotony of everyday life, or the inventiveness required to create an intimacy that no one else would know about. Mia was handing it all to him on a silver platter, with neither the guilt nor the pettiness of adultery. At a time when everyone was in search of his or her fifteen minutes of fame, these two were rediscovering the meaning of 'hidden,' like Romeo and Juliet in an era devoid of all romanticism. But the secret of their idyll would not last: already rumors were circulating about the special friendship between the beauty and the thinker; people who had seen them together had jumped to their inevitable conclusions, and all it would take now was for someone to do some cross-checking for their liaison to become official. Until then, they would meet when they could, in gilded hideouts that left their anonymity suffused with light.

Philippe, however, found it somewhat baroque, the decoration of this balcony overlooking a sparkling blue Eiffel Tower. A midnight snack had been set out on a little circular table covered with red roses and purple carnations, a glass candlestick, a little bust of a marquise, and two little bowls filled with Iranian caviar that Mia was sampling as if it were yoghurt.

"It's so nice to be able to eat outside," she said, "you can tell summer is coming."

"You've just come in from Vancouver and you're leaving for Sydney the day after tomorrow. How on earth can you even tell that summer is coming in Paris? I've been waiting for it for months, I've seen it getting closer day by day. In February I was surprised it was still light out at five o'clock, and it put me in a good mood all evening. Not even three weeks ago I hesitated to take a coat and I went out with just my jacket and I wasn't sorry. This summer is mine, I've been waiting for it, I deserve it."

"That's one reason I love to be in your company. All anyone has to say is 'the weather is fine' for you to get all worked up about it."

The moment they entered the suite at the Hôtel George V, Philippe started commenting on a host of details that Mia had ceased to notice since her agency had started putting her up in the most luxurious hotels on earth. The place was more spacious than his own apartment, and it aroused his class consciousness—a delightful sensation he rarely felt: astonishment at how the truly privileged really live, bathing in pink marble, slouching on their Louis XV chairs, and slaking their thirst with a *grand cru*. In addition to the life in first class she was inviting him to share, he particularly enjoyed the precious time she devoted to him during her brief stays in Paris—given the cost of one hour with Mia, just to appear in public, he could consider himself flattered. And when she left him for a catwalk halfway round the world, he was surprised to find himself switching on the television to look out for a commercial where she was shown running half naked through the Hall of Mirrors at Versailles.

"Tomorrow evening I have a meeting with some designers; it shouldn't take forever. Then I have to stop off at the inauguration of the Espace Guerlain. And I promised my agency I would have a drink with the head of a group who want me to be the face of their public image. But we could meet up after that?"

Just to make sure she understood that he too was a busy man, he answered, with a touch of mystery, "I'm never free before midnight on Thursdays."

"Good evening. My name is Laurent. I'm a swinger."

The man with the shaven skull who was introducing himself was dressed in a well-tailored blue suit and fine leather ankle boots, and he stood very straight, arms crossed, facing his audience. He had said it in a very natural way, *I'm a swinger,* and he clearly wasn't trying to surprise or shock.

"I'm fifty years old, I buy advertising space for a major food distributor, I'm married and have two daughters. For over twenty years, sex has been a central part of my life. A passion I share with my wife and my friends, one which fills all my free time, my evenings, weekends, and vacations."

In the little projection room with its black walls and rows of red seats, you could sense a sudden rise in the level of attention.

"The way other people devote their time to making model aircraft, or river rafting, or politics, or fixing up their country house, I make love. For what it's worth, let me point out that I am not a ladies' man or a Don Juan. I don't hunt, I don't conquer: I consume. My wife and I go regularly to swingers' clubs, but we also organize private evenings with various circles of friends, who have their own overlapping networks. In addition, we spend weekends with couples we find on the internet, and we go on vacation to specialized clubs where we find other like-minded people. No matter the context, my wife and I arrive together, and we leave together. Sometimes the evening might be planned so that it's especially pleasant for me, and other times I arrange a session with Carole's pleasure in mind."

The men in the audience respected the tradition of silence,

even though most of them would have liked to cry out, Give us examples, dammit!

"Yesterday evening we went to a club just outside Paris. Well acquainted with my taste, Carole quickly zeroed in on two women, and she was the one who approached them and served them to me. I spent the night with all three of them. Next Friday we are going to a private party where the ritual dictates that Carole will be at the center of a group of four or five men—I'm the one who picks them out and makes sure everything goes according to the rules—and in these cases, I'm just a spectator."

This man who defined himself as a swinger was driven by a desire that most men would never know. He was consumed by a rare fever that compelled him endlessly to seek out new bodies, new experiences, new combinations, in a never-ending quest for ecstasy, which made him a blissful slave to his senses.

Like the others, Yves Lehaleur was dying to know how far the man's escapades went, what limits he had set on what was taboo. But while he might admire the man's frenzy, under no circumstances did he share it. To be sure, it would have been unthinkable not to take his pleasure from a body he was paying for, but he was not about to even think of giving pleasure to a prostitute, or trying to obtain any favors she reserved for the man she loved. Yves's recently aroused need for variety was not in response to some voracious appetite: the more time he spent with these women, the more he realized that the real pleasure consisted in breaking through their tough outer shell, hardened by so many consensual rapes. More out of pride than out of the goodness of his heart, Yves tried to find the woman beneath the whore, and to relieve her, for a night, of the disgust her clients aroused in her. Yves Lehaleur thought he would be capable of finding the core of every woman he invited into his bed—her secret zone, somewhere between her head, her heart, and her sex, a place where the key to her entire being lay hidden.

"On the rare occasions when we have our experiences apart," continued Laurent, "it is always by mutual consent. For example, I sometimes play the 'sexual coach' with women who complain of erosion in their relationship before it has even fully blossomed. I offer to spend a few afternoons with them until they have experienced all the different orgasms a woman can have. I make their inhibitions and taboos disappear, so that their pleasure will reassure and guide them, and so that they can return to their husbands and share that pleasure with them, foster it and experience it again and again. As a rule, I never hear from them again. As for Carole, she sometimes spends the evening with one of our friends who suffers from a distinctive feature that is all too rare among men: he is oversexed. The size of his member is enough to frighten off any partners he might have, and Carole is probably the only one who doesn't run away."

Philippe Saint-Jean refrained from taking his notebook to write this down. In his life, he had encountered any number of boastful guys who could not shut up about their performance, real males who needed to shout it loud and clear in order to convince themselves of the fact. Laurent the swinger didn't belong to this category; his direct, prosaic way of speaking of his *passion* was not out to convince, and not for one moment did he give himself away by any ribald gestures or innuendos: just the opposite of a pervert. In Philippe's circles, few practiced swinging but many tongues wagged; there were quotations from Restif de la Bretonne and Georges Bataille; the misfortunes of virtue were set against the prosperity of vice; Japanese erotic cinema was discussed; sometimes dirty jokes were told, but always in a tongue-in-cheek manner that made them acceptable. Like the others, Philippe had spent time in the circles of hell in his library, and he'd never quite made the return journey. In his essay on the collective conscious, he had included an entire disquisition on the persistence of taboos, a brilliant combination of Freudian theory and the seven parts of the *Kama Sutra*. But so many views from the mental perspective rarely passed through the filter of experience. So much literature, for hardly a frisson!—that was what he was forced to conclude that evening, as he listened to Laurent the swinger. He suddenly took the measure of how conventional his own lifestyle was, for in bed he was neither bold, nor very creative, nor even sure of himself, no more than any other man, no more than women were. But what was the point of worrying about it, after all? No one could be Laurent and Carole the swingers, ceaselessly driven by their boundless quest for pleasure. And nothing, not even the fantasy of ultimate ecstasy, could match the fantasy and lightness of the nights he spent with Mia. Right at the start, she had had a fit of hysterical laughter as she watched him studying every part of her world-famous anatomy—as he caressed her legs, he had said, *I already know these legs, I saw them in L'Express magazine.* The high point was when he rhapsodized over the "three ochres" of her sex, confessing to her that making love with a *métisse* was something completely new for him. In one night, Mia's body had made him forget Juliette's.

"What I am about to say may seem like a paradox, but I think only swingers have attained true sexual equality. Neither one of us makes sacrifices, or looks for compromises, or simulates or dissimulates, or forces him or herself to do something to make their partner happy. I might add that, in spite of our multiple partners, the most intense pleasure we ever have is when we are just the two of us, alone, in our bed at home. The love I feel for Carole remains the most powerful aphrodisiac I know."

Up to now the audience had been captivated: they wondered why this swinger was in their midst. In spite of his crude explanations he had never been indecent, but he might prove so after all if he went on flaunting his marital happiness and his talents as a sexual conquistador. If he did not justify his presence there among the brotherhood very soon, his listeners would begin to view him as a despicable agitator, and that very evening they might well be provoked into their very first attempt at lynching.

From the very start, Denis Benitez hadn't listened to any of it, so he expected nothing from what was to follow. Still, after many long weeks, he was there, present. At the brasserie, they had greeted the rebirth of the prodigal child, not as cheerful as he used to be, but ready for an active convalescence—to serve up a plate of leeks vinaigrette with stuffed cabbage was, for Denis, tangible proof that he had returned to reality. At the rate of three hundred place settings a day, Denis was reconnecting with his fellow human beings. He agreed to do two services and even stayed late after closing; he had plenty of energy. Everyone saw this as a sign that he wanted to make up for lost time, but everyone was wrong: he was forced to flee his apartment, now that an intruder had moved in.

The very evening that creature had stepped across his threshold, Denis's final certainties had melted away. The four walls that had been protecting him from the outside world had now become a theater of the absurd, home to outrageous situations. His refuge was a danger zone, and the vast outside world had become a refuge. If only these men here tonight, this brotherhood, knew how much their stories, which they thought were exceptional, seemed insignificant in comparison to his ordeal! But while they had once listened to him and felt sorry for him, this time they would merely view him as a lost cause, driven into mental confusion by his celibacy.

After a brief silence, as if to announce an epilogue, Laurent said that he too was puzzled, why had he felt this need to share his private life with a group of strangers, who must have envied his healthy debauchery?

"I am one of those people who believe that all life on earth is subject to a certain logic, a certain equilibrium, that there is a price for happiness, and a flip side to every coin, even if we don't realize it until the time comes for the final reckoning. By making love with thousands of woman, perhaps I've violated some natural law and I ought to fear some sort of retribution. Perhaps I should be prepared to have to sacrifice something precious. So far, I don't know what that might be. But I promise you that if any such misfortune befalls me, you will be the first to know."

No sooner had they poured their beers than Denis, Philippe and Yves were drinking to the health of Laurent the swinger, paying tribute as if he were there with them.

"This evening I have learnt something yet again," said Yves. "Women keep you young!"

"Not exactly," said Philippe. "What keeps you young is knowing not to do your head in over them."

He had deliberately used one of Mia's expressions, which seemed to suit the occasion. In a literary gathering he would no doubt have turned the phrase differently, to convey the notion that only those rare male specimens who had been liberated from their emotions, their jealousy, and their predatory instincts could attain any sort of eternal carnal bliss.

Denis agreed with a smile. What he wouldn't give to feel even just a tiny bit casual around women. To be able to stop seeing them as creatures who could be magical or diabolical in turn, and view them rather as individuals whose mechanism might be intricate but certainly no more complex than his own.

Over their beers they continued to chat without any further reference to the session they had just left. They did not broach any subjects that were too personal, or display any curiosity about the others' future, yet god knows, since they had first met, each of them had experienced things that were far more disconcerting than anything anyone had come out with in public.

Philippe resisted the urge to tell them about his night with one of the most coveted women on the planet—most men would dream of making such a confession between two pints. Making his buddies jealous would be less important than his need to describe his extravagant affair for the very first time. Once the moment of astonishment was over, he would answer their eager questions less from a sense of boastfulness than to see his fair mistress through their eyes. Out of superstition, he would start off by saying, *We have nothing in common*, because he had learned at his own expense that those stories that start off *We are made for each other* come to an abrupt end. He would also like to affirm that he was not in love: *I tend to fall in love at first sight but in this case, no.* Neither Denis nor Yves would believe him, and to convince them he would have to tell them the story of his first love, at the age of eighteen. Two years of passionate love, followed by three months of living together in a maid's garret to get over it. Juliette came almost ten years later. Everything since then in Philippe's life had been nothing but the post-Juliette era, an afterwards. Even Mia was part of this ongoing period, but the most delightful, the most unhoped-for part of it. Then Denis and Yves would press him to describe her *the way she really is*, and Philippe would make a stab at this mandatory exercise, but how could you describe Mia other than to say she was a young lady who was capable of simplicity, with the naïveté of a young woman of her age, and the seasoned nature of a young woman of her time? Burdened by the image of herself that the world sent back to her, yet aware that all this hullabaloo would not last, that life already had episodes in store that would prove far more authentic. At the risk of disconcerting them, he would describe her as an aquatic creature, with an insular soul, who even in the heart of Paris lived as if she were by the sea. That was how he saw her, that Thursday night, but Philippe would not break their pact, he would keep their idyll a secret as long as was necessary.

Yves's secret, far less romantic, would be no easier to confess. If one woman had come into his life, he would not have
hesitated to share his happiness with witnesses—but ten?
Which name would he choose? Sibylle, Claire, Jessica, Samia?
How could he introduce Sibylle other than as a gray-eyed
brunette, fortysomething, with a body capable of bending
itself into positions so indecent they were outlawed? And what
about Lili, brainy Lili? More than just a pair of buttocks, she
was a shoulder where a lost man could find refuge—a guy like
Yves, obviously upset about something, but instead of trying to
find women to hit on he paid a prostitute for the night. But the
questions Lili asked him revealed more about her, and while
Yves had stood fast and never mentioned Pauline's name, Lili
had cracked and gone on to describe the way her ex-husband
had snubbed her. Claire was more reserved, almost shy,
ashamed no doubt at being a sex worker, as she confessed her
lack of experience to Yves, who had so little himself. She had
gone through the gestures she thought a pro would make, all
of them clumsy. He had clearly had been one of her first
clients, and surely one of the last. Then he had met Jessica,
through Sibylle; Samia had been sent to him by Jessica, but
Yves already liked Agnieszka best of all. He did not know her
yet, but Kris had lavished praise on her charms.

Nor would the name Marie-Jeanne Pereyres be spoken that
night, any more than Mia or Kris. Denis had kept quiet about
the reasons for his illness, and he would have been incapable of
coming up with any reasons for his sudden recovery either. By
moving into his place the intruder had dispossessed him of his
right to complain. His long bout of despair had yielded to an
indignation that awoke his faculties of resistance; the superb
thing about trying to come up with explanations for the presence of this intruder in his house was that it had unblocked the
gears in his mind and restored his fighting spirit.

By ordering a third round, they were extending their post-session ritual. The three of them enjoyed each other's company, but they didn't realize it. Philippe Saint-Jean, in his everyday life, rarely came across people like Yves Lehaleur or Denis Benitez. No matter how he lauded the reigning eclecticism and dreaded the degeneracy of milieus that were blood relations, he rarely took the time to get to know the man in the street, unless there was some immediate benefit to be had—his wine-seller, his computer consultant, or his ear, nose, and throat specialist—they could boast that they knew him. Unburdened at last of his role as a thinker, of his defects as a dialectician, he could savor the sweet futility of their confabulations at the bistro. Denis Benitez appreciated the way in which the *intellectual* refrained from being judgmental, but remained attentive, ready to learn—and even if it was all a pose, their exchange seemed sincere. And Denis also appreciated the outspokenness of a man like Lehaleur, his independent spirit, the fact that he did not seem in the least inclined to make this into a pissing contest. In fact, Yves knew how to avoid the usual guy talk or any topic that might lead to discussing their hopeless fascination with performance. He was thankful to Philippe and Denis for sparing him the usual clichés, and the tiresome complicity of men among men.

Everything seemed to indicate that Marie-Jeanne Pereyres had finagled her way into Denis's house to seek revenge: was there any other explanation for this kind of meddling? He must be paying for some major sin committed long ago. When he was around twenty, Denis and a buddy had embarked on a tour of all the nightclubs in France, getting themselves hired as waiter and bartender respectively. Three months in Marseille, two in Antibes, the same in Montélimar, ten days in Bordeaux—but what a ten days it had been!—and short stays everywhere they were wanted, and even where they were not wanted. They had filled their pockets, and fornicated like devils, clearing out at dawn; they had sown their wild oats to the point of exhaustion. How many Marie-Jeanne Pereyres had they met and charmed and intoxicated and betrayed with complete impunity? Was it not obvious that sooner or later, even twenty years later, one of them would call them to account? Someone had caught up with Denis at last for his juvenile misconduct: it made sense. The intruder was clearly of the opinionated sort, not to be deterred from her goal, and when that goal was revenge, she would mete out her punishment, ineluctably, ever harsher as time went by. Perhaps women were more spiteful than men when it came to things like this, and there were a good number of such crimes that knew no statute of limitations.

The intruder lay sprawled on the couch, her nightgown up to her knees, white socks up to her calves. With her glasses on her nose, she was reading a book that looked like a guidebook to some faraway country.

"You're back early," she said, without budging from her languid position.

"You seem annoyed."

"Not at all, I'm just surprised. Usually you don't finish your service until after midnight."

"Usually? What usually? What do you know about my life and what I usually do or don't do? Do you even have any idea what I was doing this evening?"

"No idea."

"Well, I spent the evening digging through my memory and I couldn't find you. Maybe we've already met somewhere, but for the life of me I don't know where or when, and do you know why?"

"No."

"Because you don't look like anything. And I'm not even saying that to hurt you."

Denis had studied her from head to toe, spied on her as she slept, clothed her in a host of different outfits: no memory of Marie-Jeanne Pereyres.

"Not like anything at all?"

"Everyone has some distinguishing feature. You don't. Your shape is the kind people meet all their lives, in the street, in a corridor, but which leaves no impression on the retina or the memory. Everyone knows that people like you exist somewhere, but they don't really want to know where. For me you represent, all on your own, exactly what goes to make *other people*. You're a kind of vague, indistinct entity—at best, you could be characterized as a woman, but your specificity goes no further. And on that very point, you may not believe me, but as a rule I have a sort of gift for decrypting women, I know where they come from and where they're going, I can sense instinctively what is missing in their lives, what they desire more than anything. With you I can't see a thing, nothing at all, no matter how much I watch you sleep or move around, you don't give off any particular truth, nothing in your physical being gives me the slightest clue, you are indescribable. For example, the impression you give is that you have brown hair, let's say a light chestnut, as indefinable a color as it gets, like gray walls and off-white raincoats. But in artificial light you look blonde, a kind of half-hearted blonde, not forthright, not the blondness of a blonde. Likewise, it is impossible to say what color your eyes are, and yet eyes are supposed to light up a face, to release a kind of inner light—well, in your case, nothing. Apparently you're of medium height, and when someone sees you coming from a distance they might say, 'Look at that little woman over there,' but when I see you curled up on the sofa here, I get the impression you don't know where to put your legs. Your features could correspond to absolutely any professional profile; you don't look right for the job, you look right for every job. You could be a dental assistant as easily as a senior executive, the kind who's always in a hurry, who lives intensely, or you could be the head of a team of hostesses at a convention or a car show."

"My eyes are green."

"Oh, no, you may like to think so, but you're wrong. Your green is more like sludge, it gives you the kind of expression that belongs to people who are forgotten. You're not even ugly. If your looks were the kind where people say, 'God, that girl's ugly,' at least you'd leave an impression, you'd be identifiable—but not even. So, if I've already met you in another life, you left my memory the moment you left the picture."

As she watched him leave the picture in turn to go and hide in his bedroom, a stunned Marie-Jeanne said to the empty room: "If we had met in the past, I wouldn't have forgotten you . . . "

"You'll see, she makes love without subtitles, and she knows how to drink. Don't ask her to marry you, she's likely to say yes, but not just to please you."

Yves could not resist Kris's description of Agnieszka. He made an appointment with her for Saturday afternoon with the prospect, if they hit if off, of a weekend behind closed doors. He opened his door to the loveliest surprise of all these last weeks: eyes like dark pearls against fair coloring, high cheekbones, coral lips. The beautiful Polish girl took off her raincoat, uncovered her shoulders, revealed her neckline, smoothed her satin dress over her hips, then sat down in an armchair, waiting for her host to take charge. Yves launched into a long greeting, the only word of which she understood was *tea,* which she accepted, in English, with a simple *yes.*

"How long have you been in France?"

Silence.

He tried English. "In France? Long ago?"

"*Wan ear,*" she said, raising a thumb.

"I've always heard people who live in Eastern Europe are good at languages."

Again, a questioning silence.

"I speak as much English as you do French. Just a little English."

She nodded, registered the word *little*. They smiled, sipped the scorching jasmine tea in a silence impossible to fill. To erase any further doubt, he asked, "Is it really possible to be a prostitute without speaking one intelligible word?"

She stared at him wordlessly.

"Or are you taking me for a fool?"

Nothing.

"Maybe you speak French better than you claim to, in order to have an unfair advantage that might turn out to be important somewhere down the line."

Agnieszka was afraid she might have found herself one of those clients who need to tell their life story, to unburden everything they cannot tell their wives, chattering away to hide how nervous they are—the weekend was shaping up to be one terrible misunderstanding. She knew how to give her body to perfect strangers without having to say a thing to them.

"Czy pan chce, żebym została na cały weekend?" she said, pointing to the wall clock.

" . . . I thought it had all been agreed with Kris. You know who I mean, Kris?"

"Tak, tak, Kris, jest tak jak się umawialiśmy. All weekend? To jest ciągle aktualne?"

"Until Monday morning, is okay for you?"

"Yes, Monday morning, okay."

Without counting them, she put the banknotes he handed her into her bag. Then there was one last smile and a new silence, as each one waited for the other to relieve them of a cloak of gravity. The lovely mute woman seemed unable to decide to head for the alcove on her own initiative—the only gesture which, in Yves's opinion, she could have made without saying a thing, and which all the other women had made for him—Kris had settled into his bed as if she had been his mistress forever; Marie-Ange had taken off her shoes the moment she arrived; Samia had said, *I'm wearing something special, want to see?* And the frenetic Céline had placed her hand straight off beneath his shirt to caress his torso. Agnieszka was happy just to wait, accustomed to allowing the language barrier to free her from any initiative. Yves was almost annoyed, for he felt he was paying enough as it was not to have to go through a maneuver that reminded him of his youthful procrastination, something which may well have deprived him of a career as a Casanova—could one ever know how many men chose to marry just to relieve themselves of the burden of having to make the first move? That first move toward intimacy, signaling all the others to follow, where the male was duty bound to be daring, at the risk of being snubbed, rejected, and scorned. An impulse which, since it was in fact premeditated and constantly brushed aside, was never really an impulse. A man who paid women should no longer have to go through it, for Christ's sake, and yet this evening Yves had to force himself to say a few words she would not understand but whose tone could leave no doubt.

She let her dress slip to the floor, then her stockings, then she lay down in her matching black silk bodice and boxer shorts. Afraid he would be misunderstood, Yves refrained from saying, *Take me in your mouth, now, right away,* so he put his hand on the back of Agnieszka's neck and guided her toward his cock, which she took whole into her mouth. He let himself go for a while, then caressed his partner's back through the fabric, slipped his hand into her shorts, which she removed without pausing in what she was doing. He pulled her rump toward him and rubbed his face against a hot, streaming sex, already open, and this gesture seemed far more natural to him than so many others.

"Mia? Why don't you come and spend the weekend at a place that would be the height of exoticism for you."

"You know, as far as trying to blow me away with anything exotic . . . "

"A place filled with History, which in its way is a synthesis of all human culture. Full of an enlightened disorder, but conducive to introspection. One of the very rare places on earth that is still safe from the chaos of technology, where you can hear yourself think, where the stripped down décor stimulates inner peace."

"Where's that?"

"My house."

His three-room apartment in the Latin Quarter had, despite the passage of time, preserved a pseudo-Bohemian air. The parquet floor creaked, the walls were covered with books and files, there was a smell of newspaper and incense, the kitchen was that of a confirmed old bachelor, the bedroom that of a student. For Philippe, this was a test: was Mia ready to do without her usual VIP comfort and immerse herself in a world so diametrically opposed to her own? Was she, quite simply, curious about him?

She arrived on Saturday at the end of the afternoon, sat down in an ageless armchair and did not budge from it, as if she were the prisoner of a citadel of knowledge.

"Did you know that every worthy thinker in France has sat in that chair? Card-carrying editorialists, persevering researchers, disenchanted essayists, hundred-year-old ethnologists, ruthless biographers, suffering academics, gloom-mongering bon vivants, crypto-Nietzscheans, post-existentialists, disillusioned visionaries, still-green academicians, and even one or two ministers who'd lost their bearings. You are without doubt the first supermodel."

Mia, fascinated by so much austerity, slightly dazed by the crushing quantity of books all around her, asked the most predictable question: "Have you really read all these books?"

"Almost all of them. And I plan to read the others."

"Even *The Economy of Primitive Societies*?" she asked, picking up a book at random.

"Fascinating!"

She asked another, more sensitive, question about the gaps in her own knowledge, her absolute lack of references, having excluded herself from the spheres of thought—after all this time spent with a renowned philosopher, she had eventually begun to have a complex. When she had tried to read his essay on the mirror of memory, she got the impression that a hundred more essays were missing from her general culture if she were even to begin to understand. Between the references to Plato and an Oceanic tribe, and quotations from Spinoza, she had gotten lost among the various concepts, which had all been dealt with already in the dozens of books listed in the bibliography. Whenever she thought she had discovered an essential truth in life, that truth was contradicted an hour later by another current of thought. It was fairly common to see the philosopher contradicted by the psychoanalyst, the psychoanalyst by the chemist, the chemist by the sociologist, and the sociologist by the philosopher.

"So what are we supposed to do, *the rest of us*, other than throw in the towel?"

Out of his comfort zone, Philippe would have given an easy answer, since the point Mia was raising—is there any meaning to meaning?—was about to smash him in the face like a cream pie. That evening, the bookshelves around him enfolding him like a nice old coat, he wanted to encourage his companion's first halting steps along the path—well-worn for him, but still untrodden for so many others. He had to banish from her mind the idea that the intellectual life was an infinite puzzle from which, for her, a piece would always be missing. Rid her of the idea of *understanding,* to give herself a chance to *feel.* To learn to listen to herself and not the contradictory injunctions of leading opinion makers, both those who were sincere and the impostors. Prove to her that those who confess to having neither the instruments nor the substance have already so many convictions and intuitions, so much experience, that all it would take would be a simple triggering event in order to combine all those experiences and reach an *epiphany*, one of those illuminating moments that strike so powerfully that they light the rest of the way forever.

After which, they made love, without wondering whether there was any meaning to it.

Agnieszka and Yves embraced until late at night, making little sighs that were intelligible in any language. She seemed to find pleasure in her work, and even if that were not the case, Yves was grateful to her for having shown such fervor. At two o'clock in the morning, he set out on the coffee table a selection of zakuski he had bought that very morning at a Polish delicatessen, then he took from the freezer a bottle of red vodka and two tiny iced glasses.

"A kiedy przyjmujesz Szwedkę, to podajesz akwawitę?"

He thought he caught a hint of irony in her intonation.

"I made a detour to the tenth arrondissement to find this stuff. Tell me what you think."

She drank her shot of pepper vodka down in one, and tapped her chest with the palm of her hand to get rid of the burning sensation.

"Pieprzówka . . . Nie wiedziałeś o tym, ale trafiłeś akurat na taką jaką lubię."

Agnieszka too had given up trying to communicate, at least through words, and like Yves she enjoyed chatting away without worrying about being understood—after all, what did they have to say to each other that was that important? Savoring a second pierogi, she waved her glass, already empty. The feeling of calm the vodka gave her was yielding to another: in these two days she would earn enough to be able to go away for some thalassotherapy, to make up for thousands of late nights; she'd be able to abandon her body to other hands, expert hands, with no evil intentions.

At the brasserie, the Saturday night service ended at roughly two o'clock and was often followed by a drink at the bar, the time it took for the brigade to coordinate the next schedule before the Sunday break. Denis knocked back a good strong Calvados, then went home to slip into bed without waking his intruder—that was the term that suited her best, like some permanent reminder of danger. He slept late, but not long enough to recover from the fatigue he'd accumulated from his self-imposed schedule. He felt the urge for a cup of tea, got up, and walked through the living room without having any unpleasant encounters, but a vision of horror awaited him in the kitchen: Marie-Jeanne, a sponge in her hand, was tidying up and cleaning the countertops.

"Who said you could touch anything?"

She didn't answer.

"In case you didn't know, I work in the restaurant business. I know what a kitchen is and how to keep it."

"All I did was move a few utensils that were on the counter, but I won't do it again."

"If we let things get messy during our service, we're fucked, but what you saw on the counter was not mess."

"Sorry . . . "

"What were you thinking? Since I'm here, might as well make myself useful? Or something like, 'Oh, men, the minute you let them loose in a kitchen . . . '"

"Nothing like that."

"Don't try to make yourself useful, you'll never be useful in this house. You are the opposite of useful, you're in the way. Maybe if I lived in a huge villa with corridors as far as the eye can see and one room after the other that I never went into, maybe then, one day, by chance, I could open the door of a storage room and find you there, in which case I would close it again at once and leave you there and take special care to forget you. But here! You're in the living room! The main room! I open the door and there you are!"

"Do you think I take up a lot of room? And yet I'm trying not to leave anything lying around."

The intruder's entire life seemed to fit in a black wheeled suitcase, always closed, put away between the closet and the armrest of the sofa. No obvious accessories—hairbrush, handbag, cell phone, various lotions—nothing, only two or three books, a few magazines, and a pair of reading glasses, all neatly kept in a pile behind the other armrest.

"So you don't work? You don't need to earn a living?"

"Not at the moment."

"Are you rich? Live off your income?"

"No, but I change jobs regularly. Just now I'm between jobs."

"Between what jobs? How long does it last, your between jobs?"

"I can give you the details, but it's really not very interesting."

"Between what sort of jobs, dammit?"

"For a long time I ran a toy store, then I was the administrator in a little local crafts museum, and then I got fed up with that so I opened a travel agency with a friend, and that went pretty well, but then I got fed up with that, too, so I sold her my share, and since then I've been hesitating to go and join my sister who lives with her family in Nouméa. I've already been offered a job coordinating the tour operators from mainland France."

Denis sat down on the edge of a chair and stayed there for a moment, unmoving, hesitating between retreat and an assault that he didn't feel up to. With an air of detachment she alone was capable of, Marie-Jeanne Pereyres had just summed up the last twenty years of her life for him, wondering all the while about the next twenty to come—with her, overseas had better watch out. In response to a question he had not asked she added, "It would be a big leap into the unknown."

She seemed sincere, oblivious to any irony, forgetting for a moment that she had invaded the territory of a man she claimed to know nothing about. And as for Denis Benitez, there was nothing where he was concerned even remotely resembling a *big leap into the unknown*, he was not intimidating, he inspired no sort of caution, there was nothing mysterious about him, you could even set up your bivouac in his place without ever wondering whether there was a law against it. To be sure, he had never known any other life besides that of a waiter, the life of a waiter who, in any case, had never thought of going into business for himself, the life of an eternal waiter who would have liked by the time he was middle-aged to settle down with a companion, someone straightforward and not proud, his type of girl, someone just the opposite of Marie-Jeanne Pereyres. So why was this independent, determined woman, perfectly capable of breaking down barriers, still hesitating between a tropical destination and a rotten sofa, in the middle of a room in an apartment with no natural light, shrouded in Parisian gloom?

He decided against the tea and went back to his room, exhausted, ready for the next twenty-four hour ritual. As he was drifting off he saw himself as the poorest man in the world for having lost the only thing left to those who have already lost everything. *Oh, my solitude, sister of silence and mother of contemplation, I have been duly punished for having doubted you.*

Philippe Saint-Jean did not treat Sundays any differently from any other day; as a matter of habit he would go down for the mail and come back up empty-handed, then make up his list of the day's little pleasures and sacrifices: the Vietnamese café was closed, there would be the humorous column in *Le Journal du Dimanche*, he would go wine-tasting at the wine merchant's, the streets would be deserted and the parks crowded, there was always a film on television at midnight on Sundays. But this Sunday, however, had been planned out long in advance in order to keep Mia as long as possible on his planet. He saw there was a rare Japanese film at the Champollion cinema, a funny, baroque sort of film, that he'd like her to discover. Then they would linger in the Jardin du Luxembourg to read in the sun, drink a tea at the *buvette* and have a laugh at the expense of the joggers going by. Late in the day he would invite her to the Closerie des Lilas to surprise her with a dry Martini prepared especially for her by his friend the head bartender, in order to show Mia that he too had his hide-out, his ritual, and his cocktail. But to start with, Philippe would serve her a breakfast tray luxurious enough to compete with the fancy hotels', and filling enough to keep them going until evening.

"You're an angel, but take those croissants from my sight, I have a show in eight days and two pounds to lose."

Philippe had not even had time to share his program with her before Mia suggested they have lunch with her parents.

"Are they in Paris at the moment?"

"No, they've invited us to their place in Provence."

Philippe looked at her questioningly.

"I'll call the agency and she'll take care of everything. We'll be back in Paris before midnight."

"How long have you had this up your sleeve?"

Mia cuddled up to him, far too cuddlesome to be honest, already prepared to defend her whim tooth and nail. *I want them to meet you because you mean a lot to me.*

What wouldn't he have given, a few years earlier, to hear Mia's proposal coming from Juliette's lips? He had been the one to insist on meeting her parents at last, the old-fashioned way, like some future son-in-law who wants to be in his father-in-law's good books. For Juliette, he would even have made a solemn declaration, his knee on the floor. He would have said *I do* in a church and run an announcement in *Le Monde.* And in all likelihood, his wedding gift would have been a short, fervent text written to celebrate the day when he had laid eyes on her for the very first time.

Yves had been awake since dawn, and for a moment he watched Agnieszka sleeping before he quietly left the bed. He put on a jacket and went for a good hour's run in a nearby park, then came back to find his guest sitting watching a Polish channel on cable.

"Mamy taki sam internet. To jest program 451."

Yves recognized the world "internet" and then she added, pointing to the full coffee pot:

"Pozwoliłam sobie zrobić kawę."

Utterly surprised by the way she had taken over the place, he tasted the coffee and found it was very different from the one he made. Then he took a long shower before joining her in the bed, nestling against her side, breathing in her warm odor, and he sat by her side watching the weather forecast.

"I understood *celsiusa* and *hectopascali,*" he said.

"Jest jeszcze chłodno, u mnie. 14° w Lublinie."

She in turn took a shower, came back out of the bathroom in her peignoir and pointed to her clothes folded on a chair.

"Mam się ubrać, czy tak zostać?"

"Get dressed? Yes, go ahead. Tak!"

Yves reached under the cupboard for another scooter helmet.

"Would you like to go and have it off outside?"

She stared at him.

"Outside."

"Outside?"

She gave him a somewhat dubious look, fearful of some dicey plan. She'd been through too much not to dread the perverse imagination of her clients.

"Where, outside? Ja nie mogę sobie pozwolić na chryje z policjantami!"

He guessed she saw something depraved about him, and reassured her with a word he thought must be universal.

"Picnic."

Denis slept for a long time, a daytime sleep, more guilty than it was pleasurable. He was assailed by a dense, disturbing dream, where his face was reflected to infinity, covering posters, on the front page of all the papers: people recognized him in the street and pointed at him.

When he woke up he tried to find the key to this jumble of images, and he pursued a new hypothesis for the intruder's presence—a Machiavellian one, to be sure, but only too plausible in these morbid times where the spectacle of mediocrity fascinated the crowds. Marie-Jeanne Pereyres had chosen him as the subject of a reportage for a news magazine, or worse, as a guinea pig for one of those reality TV shows which transformed human drama into a prime-time program. Interference in other people's lives was already on offer in any number of forms, but in the overall effort to constantly push back the boundaries of voyeurism, there were always new things to try. Cameras were hidden in the rooms of troubled adolescents, or of couples going through a crisis, or of families being wrenched apart, all of whom were seeking some sort of catharsis, all of whom were ready to sell their privacy at a discount, to put their daily life on stage in exchange for a brief moment of media glory. The true identity of Marie-Jeanne Pereyres? A special correspondent, a champion of the ratings, a reporter without scruples. She'd have a field day! Exaggerate the caricature, turn Denis into some sort of fairground monster, an empty creature in a life that was every bit as empty. *Denis Benitez: neither husband nor father nor lover: is he still a man?* She would shape the prototype of the contemporary male, an obsolete entity, incapable of making himself useful, creating far more problems than he resolved, doomed therefore to disappear before long.

"It's all becoming clear: prime time! You've got hidden cameras in the home of a single man who's in a rut, and you're on the trail of his bad old bachelor habits. To go and look for misery wherever it hides, that's kind of *trendy*, no? You've got hilarious jokes and emotional sequences planned for the *Benitez Show*, right? With a *best of* at the end of the week?"

"If there were such a program I wouldn't miss it."

"Instead of interfering and acting all mysterious, why don't you put your cards on the table? Why don't you just ask for an interview and stop hiding what you're really on about? I'm prepared to testify, if you promise you'll work in broad daylight and if it's really the only way to see you get the hell out of here."

"I'm not a journalist and I'm not planning to do any such thing. Besides, if I were going to do a portrait of you, it would be that of a man who can get along quite well without a woman. A man for whom household chores are not a problem, who doesn't see women merely as some pleasant complement to his virility, and who could even, if he had to, bring up a child on his own. Exactly—what if you, Denis, were the man of the future?"

"Over there, in the clearing, at the foot of that tree?"

"Moim zdaniem tam jest za płasko."

Agnieszka added to her hesitant pout an arm movement which seemed to indicate a more rolling landscape. Yves turned the ignition on the scooter and they headed north. In the end she was the one, five minutes later, as they were going through the forest of Saint-Cloud, who pointed to a forested hillside, totally isolated, irresistible. They found a spot at the summit, shared their sandwiches, each one chatting in his or her native tongue—perhaps they were sharing secrets which the other would never be able to give away. At the end of the afternoon he pulled her over to him, lifted up her skirt and entered her, their bodies open to the sun and the springtime breeze.

Taking her there, Yves experienced a moment of supreme harmony, something he had never known, a sort of fulfillment where forces of earth and sun fused within him. He was at the center of everything—of her, of nature, of the universe, and if the earth was still spinning, they were its pivot.

Vibrant with desire, pressing into the moist earth, protected by a tree and calmed by the sun and the breeze, the whore and her client re-created around them the lost paradise of virgins and innocents.

At 11:45 a taxi came to fetch them at the exit to the Avignon airstrip, and left them off thirty kilometers from there in the little village of Baux-de-Provence. In the shade of an old farmhouse, a family was impatiently awaiting the arrival of Mia's new boyfriend. Philippe had been through far too many exams in his life to let himself be intimidated by this one. During lunch, he amused himself by playing the perfect son-in-law on Mia's arm; she was far more nervous than he was. He was surprised to see how she reverted to being a little girl with her *Mamina*, how she allowed herself be teased by her older brother, and how she asked about everyone in the village, neighbors and shopkeepers, coming up with a childhood memory for each of them. She cast off her usual jargon, which was a mixture of cosmopolitan expressions, shortcuts from the fashion industry, and an untold quantity of useless Anglicisms. Surrounded by her own people, she lapsed back into the local accent, a language filled with Provençal turns of phrase and other purely idiomatic expressions that were part of her family heritage. They sat Philippe next to Roland, her father, who was eager to subject *the philosopher* to a carefully prepared interview.

"Did you know Papa has read one of your books?"

On learning that his daughter was seeing a renowned intellectual, Roland had gotten hold of what the local bookseller said was the most accessible of Philippe's works. With patience and concentration he sat down to *Prayer of Expectancy*, an essay on the passing of time, how modern man is wasting time because his desire to conquer it is too great. Roland praised Philippe for his theories—most of which he thought he had gotten the gist of—and Philippe accepted the tribute paid him by this unassuming man, who'd stuck with determination to his reading, even if what he retained was only the first pressing. To pay tribute to him in turn, Philippe began a light, courteous game of dialectics, letting the father dare to draw a parallel between *Prayer of Expectancy* and his own experience of the passing of time. Philippe, who knew how to place himself on the level of less agile interlocutors—he was constantly called on to do just that with TV presenters—emphasized the most important points and asked questions, and Roland, emboldened by the rosé, prided himself on being able to answer. In short, the other diners at the table witnessed an amiable verbal sparring match, where the man of books and the man of the earth exchanged essential truths about an eternal theme.

A short while later, while she was showing him the garden, Mia's eyes misted over, and she threw her arms around her lover, to thank him for the most wonderful gift she could ever have dreamt of: Philippe had made a philosopher of her father, for the rest of his days.

6

E veryone knows that the devil's first ruse is to wear the rags of modesty, candor, and abnegation. When Manon came into my office for a job interview, her resumé was that of an orphan in distress. But so willing, so much promise!"

For the last few weeks Denis Benitez, Yves Lehaleur and Philippe Saint-Jean had been sitting side by side, and they did not refrain from a nudge of complicity or a muttered comment during the confessions.

"As the months went by, she gained more self-assurance, and turned into an ally no one could resist, not even me. Add to the formula my shaky marriage and a mid-life crisis, and I fell into a trap as old as free enterprise, the boss who sleeps with his secretary."

As he was neither boss nor secretary, Denis Benitez gave the cliché the benefit of the doubt, then allowed his attention to wander. Since he did not have the courage to stand up and reveal the presence of the intruder, he was hoping for an impossible miracle from these Thursday meetings: to come across a situation similar to his own. But how could he possibly believe for even a moment that his strange story might have a precedent? Who might possibly have suffered as he had from an unexplained presence between his walls? At first he had thought she was a ghost from the past come to make him pay for his sins, but the more time he spent with her—and she was both terribly present and terribly discreet—the more he leaned toward a theory that was the exact opposite. For what other reason would a woman move in with a man if not to see him, hear him, feel his presence, and be part of his life no matter what?

Was the intruder one of those secretive lovers who sighs in the shadow of the man she adores? By knocking on his door, had she taken a step that no other woman would dare to take? Was it so impossible for a man like him to arouse immoderate, unshakable feelings? Why not picture Marie-Jeanne Pereyres as a passionate woman who had thrown herself on him, the living proof of her passion?

"Not long afterwards, I fell ill. I was in bed for several weeks, unable to react, drained of all my strength, incapable of saying a word. The doctors didn't make a diagnosis, other than some sort of aphasia that was not the same thing as depression, and I was the only one who could know where it had come from. Deep down I knew that Manon's presence in my life was going to drive out everything else, and it was this certainty that had made me ill. I am sure that many of you have gone to pieces over a woman, otherwise this brotherhood of yours would not exist."

The rule in the audience was not to react, even if some of those present, including Philippe Saint-Jean, felt it concerned them. There had been a time when Juliette aroused feelings so intense that, like the witness, he had collapsed on the floor. A doctor had prescribed a series of tests, all of them useless, because to recover from such a seismic event in his life all Philippe needed was to feel Juliette's hand in his—only the woman who had been the cause of the illness had the power to cure him. Two weeks later, when he had regained his speech and the use of his legs, Juliette moved into his place for good. Their first year together they were so intensely close that they dreaded being apart for even one hour, and went to their respective appointments together, until no one would even schedule an appointment with either of them. Philippe would never forget one morning when Juliette went out to do the shopping, on her own, and came back with a black eye because she had slipped on the tiled floor in a shop. He had drawn some very Freudian conclusions: Juliette had punished herself for this first separation, as she had punished the man of her life for having let her go off without him, and the guilt the incident inspired bore a disturbing resemblance to the shiner an abusive man can deliver. They knew too that other people could not stand to be around them—they were little cooing lovebirds, but they could not behave in any other way: they would only go back into the world once they'd had their fill of each other.

"Passion is a serious illness, a hard drug. After the first exultant moments comes the labor of obsession, then dependency. Manon the moment I opened my eyes, Manon when I laughed, Manon when I cried, Manon in my dreams. There was only one answer to all the questions, all the doubts: Manon. *What time is it?* Manon. *Would you like something for dessert?* Manon. *It looks like it's going to storm.* Manon."

Fortunately, Yves Lehaleur had rid himself of those devastating, exhausting emotions, which could leave a human being feeling neglected. He thanked the heavens for leaving him with peace of mind and a wandering cock. Furtively, he consulted his cell phone to see whether Kris had left him a message. He'd been trying to make an appointment since morning, not so much to sleep with her but to tell her in detail, with irony, about a calamitous evening he'd spent with a certain Brigitte. *She wore me out, your colleague, and not the way I would have liked. Call me back.* Before she'd even removed her coat, Brigitte had taken a call on her cell, excusing herself in advance: *I never pick up, but in this case I have to.* To be discreet, Yves shut himself in the kitchen, but could not help but overhear bits of her conversation. *Did the doctor come? . . . Her insurance card is in the dresser drawer, where else did you think it would be? . . . There are some fish sticks left for the little one, and you can make her some macaroni.* Yves came back in, his head full of scenarios that were anything but erotic: Brigitte working by day and prostituting herself by night because an unemployed husband can't help her make ends meet. A husband who feels cramped wearing the costume of the passive pimp, but times are hard. And the little girl asking as she stares at her macaroni: *Why is Mommy never here at night?* No sooner had Brigitte put her phone away than she broached the financial question: *€200 for two hours, then I have to get going.* Of all the women he'd had at his place, she more than anyone gave him the impression that she was at work, convinced she had a power that she did not have, the power to excite the senses of a man who is paying her—and that was surely the most exasperating thing of all, her presumptuousness in calling herself a prostitute, as if all it took was for her to spread her legs. In spite of this, he reckoned that if they chatted for the first hour he would desire her enough to be able to give her a tumble during the second, but with every word they exchanged they sank further into reality, of the most pragmatic sort, that of time racing by as quickly as credit. Trying to act like a professional, she was dead offhand with him: *What d'you feel like, then?* For the first time Yves realized just how vulgar those simple words could sound. Tired of resisting, he offered her a deal: he would let her leave again without even having to get undressed, provided she came out and told him her story in depth. *What story? What are you talking about? You want to know why I'm working as a whore?* Yves had to rephrase his request: what circumstances could be so terrible that they prevented Brigitte from staying home with her sick child at that moment? Because only a heroine out of Zola could have such a tragic fate that she has to sell herself to buy medicine for her kid. Yves was annoyed because of his €200, and he expected to hear something grandiose—an ancestral curse, a childhood destroyed by secrets, a passionate love for a monster, a betrayal straight out of Dante. Brigitte merely mentioned child support that never arrived, a new boyfriend who was crippled with debts, and stubborn bailiffs. Then she left, a few banknotes richer, but unburdened of a pallid reality that no one had ever cared to worm out of her before.

"After that everything started happening at once. I left my family to go and live in a furnished apartment. Manon was there with me in the beginning. We dreamt of a radiant future together, full of passion and power. I ruined myself to give her everything she wanted, went into debt to build the house of our dreams, of which she would be the sole owner—I remember insisting, *If anything were to happen to me, I want to be sure you're taken care of.* At the office, she volunteered to take over the more routine accounts, then she lured me into a subtle chess game within the company. One day she handed me a file containing the equivalent of my death warrant, and I signed it without even reading it. Then she agreed to a promotion and began her incredible climb through the ranks. She ate out with colleagues most of the time, and then the bosses. *You have to forge alliances,* she said. She started coming home later and later, and when I complained, she found ways to silence me in bed. She kept coming up with various pretexts for postponing the marriage, and she assured me she'd stopped taking the pill. One morning I saw her sitting among us at the board meeting. The next day she left me."

Yves didn't believe these stereotypical stories where a man is ensnared by a venomous creature. The guy had to be making it up, for what would be the point of demonizing his mistress if it were not so that he could free himself of his original mistake? Why bother trying to convince his audience if not to rehabilitate himself in his own eyes?

Having burned with that same fire, Philippe did not doubt the man's sincerity. He too would have signed any document on earth Juliette placed before him; he too would have laid everything he owned at her feet.

As for Denis, all he retained of the story being told were the elements that supported his thesis. How far can you go for love? If a man could ruin himself, abandon his family, and make himself sick, then couldn't a woman force her way into the home of her chosen man? And, sooner or later, force her way past that other door, the one he never opened, the door to his entire being? Without a doubt, Marie-Jeanne Pereyres was laying siege, and he himself was the stronghold.

"And now I'm still living in that furnished apartment, alone. All the redundancy payments I get go to pay alimony and child support. My ex-wife hates me, my sons don't want to see me. The few friends who'd absolved me for leaving my wife and kids have gotten sick of hearing me go on and on about Manon, and they've dropped me, too. I screwed up and it's all my fault, and, although it may not look like it, I didn't come here to complain, but to make an offer, if there are any among you who will help me obtain my revenge . . . "

Everyone in the audience who'd been expecting a solemn conclusion or contemplative silence suddenly pricked up their ears at his last words.

"I suppose some of you have seen Robert Bresson's film *Les Dames du Bois de Boulogne.* If you haven't, well it's the story of a woman who is jilted by a man she is passionately in love with. She decides to get her revenge by placing an irresistible young woman in his path. His turn now to know the suffering of passion and abandonment."

Denis, Philippe, and Yves looked at each other, intrigued by the strange turn this testimony was taking. Philippe had seen a connection between the guy's story and some pre-war melodramas, but not with Bresson's film, which he loved as he loved all Bresson's films, and which seemed to him way off the subject. Denis had not seen it, but it was enough to hear *She decides to take revenge by placing in his path an irresistible young woman* for a new theory to come out of nowhere: the presence of the intruder as the instrument of another woman's revenge. But in spite of his paranoia, this hypothesis did not stand up to even one minute of cold analysis: to make sure he fell into the trap, whoever it was would have surely chosen choose a femme fatale, and not such a . . . well, not this Marie-Jeanne in any case. Besides, the thought that anyone could manipulate Marie-Jeanne was simply inconceivable.

Yves didn't remember the film at all, but the guy's summary made him want to see it; this girl being shoved into the arms of the protagonist: was she a prostitute or not? What other woman would go along with such a ploy? What sort of talent would it take to make it work? Which of the girls he was seeing might have that sort of temptress's power?

"I will offer a considerable sum of money to whoever will agree to seduce Manon, drive her crazy, and ruin her life the way she ruined mine. Together we'll come up with an infallible conspiracy. I know all her addresses, her habits, her faults, her weaknesses, her deepest desires, I know the words to get through to her and the gestures to flatter her. In less than three months, she'll be eating out of your hand. If one of you is interested, please come and meet me afterwards on the way out so we can discuss it in detail."

From the day it was founded, the members of the brotherhood had seen all sorts of witnesses come and go, and while sometimes their stories overlapped, each one of them remained unique, complex, and worth listening to. But as far as anyone could recall, in all that time there had never been a single individual ready to recruit another in order to exact his revenge. The oldest members, furious that anyone might think they could stoop to such sinister manipulation, broke the law of silence to inform the interloper that he'd come to the wrong address and, while they were at it, they showed him the door.

Philippe Saint-Jean took a hasty leave of his companions at the intersection at the Avenue de Friedland, jumped in a taxi, pulled a bow tie from his pocket, and knotted it over his wing collar, thus adding the final touch to his brand new tuxedo, which no one had noticed during the session. In their usual bistro, no sooner had Yves sat down than Kris called him at last and accepted his invitation to dine after one last appointment—Yves imagined her trying to get her client to climax as quickly as possible so she'd be on time at the restaurant. Before long Denis was alone with his drink, and as he did not feel like going home, he ordered another one, at the risk of exacerbating the waitress's bad mood—he himself knew how to cast black looks at customers who delayed closing time by twenty minutes with their last orders. Denis noticed from her quick, precise gestures that she was a professional, not one of those dilettantes who condescended to wait tables while waiting for their exceptional destinies. If he indeed had a talent for decrypting women, then this woman—thanks to their shared profession—seemed far more legible than any other.

After she's set the table, tidied up the sidewalk seating area, done the register and mopped the floor, she'll go back to her studio, where no one is waiting. She'll take a shower to wash off the smell of burnt fat, and she'll stretch out, her legs heavy, in front of the television, which has place of prominence at the foot of her bed. All her emotions transit through that box. It makes her laugh and dream, sometimes cry, it gives rhythm to her life, wakes her up but above all puts her to sleep, otherwise she's good for a bout of insomnia, and that would be tragic, because sleep is her second passion. She says so herself: my bed is my life raft. *Occasionally on a Sunday she'll let herself drift on it all day, eyes on the screen, ready to doze off between two series. Sometimes she tells herself that there isn't room for two on her raft, that no man would cast himself adrift with her. Sometimes she's glad, too, that she has no children, all she has to do is watch the news to find ten good reasons for not conceiving. Her choices came naturally, as a matter of course. And they haven't been such bad choices, have they?*

Denis's daydreaming was interrupted by a sudden revelation: how could he ever have imagined that Marie-Jeanne Pereyres might be driven by noble sentiments? Only her dread of living alone, getting old, and ending up alone could explain her determination. Plagued by an identical despair, he'd merely sunk into depression, with dignity, without harming a soul! Marie-Jeanne Pereyres had preferred to get ahead of her sad destiny and abandon a raft that was taking on water, to end up on someone else's; and now, she was clinging to that raft like a survivor.

Kris called Yves "the hauler," as if it were his profession. She knew nothing about him, other than that he was not a hauler, or a boatman, but that he installed windows and he enjoyed it. If a few days went by and she heard nothing from him, she began to think of him as a co-conspirator with whom you're dying to share the latest gossip. For someone as confident as she was when it came to dividing men—unpredictable little creatures that they were—into two or three categories, with the hauler she had lost her bearings. And God knows how many sick minds she'd come across since she started in the business, and not just sexual perverts, but also men whose hidden motives revealed the meanderings of a tortured spirit, all the more so if they prided themselves on their feelings. Her experience, acquired in pain, had taught her to flee from those who, sooner or later, would reproach her for the desire she elicited in them. She knew how to spot the ones who, for all their gentlemanly air, were on the lookout through their association with prostitutes for psychological degradation. She was also wary of the gallant knight ready to go on a crusade to *get her out of there.* Just as she dreaded the ones who insisted on kissing her on the mouth for the very reason that she wouldn't allow it. Lehaleur did not seem to have any personal shame, or scorn for his temptresses; nor did he have a virgin's romantic side; he asked for nothing extravagant but obtained more than the others did. He had a unique way of sussing out women, of observing them to know what made them tick, of complimenting them on an asset they were proud of, or taking them in his arms without it seeming out of place—this guy knew instinctively where the border between tenderness and intimacy lay. It was almost annoying, how gifted he was at drawing the map of emotions so precisely, as if it were the map of an empire carved up between ruling powers, each of which was seeking to preserve its own borders. She found him dominating, affectionate, curious about her, always elusive. Kris knew the power her sex had over men, who were feverish and prepared to accept anything to find relief, but that power didn't work on Yves. His ability to go from one woman to the next and his perpetual need for diversity kept her from being unique in the eyes of the only man to whom she would have truly liked to be unique. She could, however, boast of having been the first, his original whore, the one who had given him a taste for all the others.

"This one's on me, to make up for sending you the wrong girl," she said. "Brigitte must have been having an off day, don't hold it against her."

"If I pay for girls it's also for their mystery."

Surprised by his firmness, Kris took it as fair warning. To calm things down, he added, "But as long as you go on sending girls like Agnieszka, I'll do my best to forget about the ones like Brigitte."

Reduced to her role as a pimp, Kris realized that henceforth she would have to hold her own in this procession of women. And she would not give up her position in that procession for anything on earth. Because now that she had slept in the arms of the hauler, she felt ready to take on all the brusqueness, resentment, depravity, malaise, and misogyny of a man in his prime.

Philippe was aware of his good fortune, being able to adapt his speech according to circumstance. The philosopher of the modern era had the resources to cloak himself in legitimacy for any occasion, a knowing combination of intellectual agility and bad faith, hard-won through his experiences with the media and their tendency to resemble a lions' den. In some extreme cases, Philippe could hesitate between two perfectly contradictory arguments and decide on one or the other on a whim. One day, in an almost empty auditorium where he was supposed to be giving a lecture on the democratization of knowledge, annoyed at having attracted such a thin crowd, he launched into a celebration of intellectual elites. Conversely, on a radio program together with a young singer who had gone to the trouble to read his work, Philippe had shown enthusiasm for the lyrics of his song, even though they were singularly inept. In a major newspaper, he had praised an essay on language published by a friend, when only the night before he had described it to Juliette as an *extinguisher of semantics*.

This evening, with his dashing bow tie, as he stepped onto the red carpet, photographers clicking madly away, he would need all his rhetorical skills to regain some of his legitimacy as a thinker. Mia and Philippe had decided to go public. In less than an hour, their idyll would no longer be mere rumor. For their first official appearance together, they had to choose an event that had nothing to do with their careers, in order to show that neither one was the consort of the other. Philippe had seized on the premiere of a blockbuster movie about the cultural explosion of Paris in the 1920s; they wouldn't attend the screening itself, but would meet up at the luxurious reception given at the Hôtel Crillon. When Mia asked him why *that* event rather than another, Philippe gave several reasons. But he kept silent on the real reason.

Once he was past the entrance, he was directed to a salon sparkling with white silk and pink champagne, where designer gowns of the sort only someone like Mia would truly have done justice to mingled with tuxedos that looked far more attractive on others than on Philippe. Under no circumstances, this time, could he allow himself to stand back as an observer or play at the sneering ethnologist: he was one of them. Feeling cramped in his worldly uniform, he was losing the right to decode the signs, interpret the gestures, decrypt the behavior; he had forfeited his grain of salt. This was the price to be paid for yielding to the glitter of the privileged classes. Seeking to strike a pose as he hunted for his girlfriend, he grabbed a glass of champagne in passing, then went to drink it out on the terrace, and enjoy one of the finest views there is: the Place de la Concorde, all lit up, and the entrance to the Tuileries with its Ferris wheel. No matter how marvelous it was, he still felt awkward and, until his little pest arrived, had to resist the urge to flee. This from a man who, years before, had visited an old people's home in Bombay, wandering easily among the beds, witnessing the extreme poverty and watching people die, exchanging smiles and words with the patients; he had seen those dying people preparing for the great departure, and never had he felt more like a *philosopher* than that afternoon. This evening, to the contrary, he found it impossible to mingle with people he suspected of being intolerably futile. What was worse, he was ashamed of himself for recognizing so many faces—actors, presenters, demi-princesses, jet-set celebs—how on earth had all these existences managed to make themselves known to his cortex and mobilize so many precious neurons? He hardly ever watched television, and at the barber's he read his own books rather than let himself be tempted, incognito, by the celebrity press. The question eluded the gauntlet of his fine analysis: how had this fringe element with their para-cultural activities managed to impregnate his mind and niche themselves among his pantheon of Greek philosophers, his catalogue of literary giants, and his cartography of so-called primitive people? How had he become the receiver of so many insignificant messages? As a sociologist, he could have made himself an ideal subject of study: to what degree could an individual bent on preserving his or her concentration as much as possible, creating an impregnable barrier to the ambient noise, still be invaded by a subtle capillary action? Philippe could not even claim to belong to that group of researchers who scrutinize the media, seeing it as a laboratory for decomposing ideas, so he had no excuse for knowing the name of that nineteen-year-old starlet who had just started a career as a singer, and was now stuffing herself on *bocconcini*.

As he walked into another salon he finally espied his fair lady, surrounded exclusively by men on the young side who all seemed perfectly at home in their bespoke tailoring, luxury leather and Swiss watches. Philippe stood to one side for a moment to enjoy the spectacle of the fuss they made over her and observe the posturing of a handful of predators. Among them was a mega-rich captain of industry, a good-looking playboy by vocation, all of which made him the likeliest pretender to a woman like Mia. Far from viewing him as a serious rival, Philippe, as a good entomologist of human behavior, identified him as an insect of the arthropod variety, which includes spiders but also crabs, creatures that move tangentially, qualified as *pests* for the environment. Philippe had always been fascinated by the spectacle of arrogance in action, for he found therein an absolute lack of self-doubt that summed up the contemporary era. He could just imagine the witticisms spouting from the man's mouth, pathetic outbursts which, once they'd been stripped of the cynicism stolen from thoroughgoing sniggerers and insolent mediagenic posers, were proof of a rare vulgarity. Of a refined vulgarity, of the educated sort, knowing how far was too far, capable at any moment of brandishing the grain-of-salt card when an interlocutor verged on complacency. If Philippe Saint-Jean had ever been out looking for his perfect symmetrical counterpart, the obscene version of his *ego*, as of tonight he knew what he looked like.

Mia spotted him at last and motioned to him to join her. With one furtive kiss on the lips, she decreed who was chosen and who was damned. Arrogance had changed sides. As he savored this rare moment, Philippe knew he had just avenged the little boy he once was, for the time when the prettiest girl in school only had eyes for the bad boys—and it was partly her fault if the shy boy he had once been turned into a contemplative soul. The dashing CEO found it difficult to hide his shock upon hearing the word *philosopher*, which delighted Mia. Thus, this creature with her divine measurements was sleeping with a thinking entity? Was this how the supermodel got her rocks off? With this egghead, this pinched intellectual? A guy who was neither loaded, nor dead handsome, nor world famous, but who had dreamt up a few ideas and published books that changed hands at the Sorbonne? Who would have believed it? Ordinarily, sirens like her swallowed the bait on the shiniest hooks and were easily reeled in from the side of a yacht. Not to lose his haughty stance altogether, the deposed admirer displayed a knowing scorn for all things written and thought. He was practically boasting about confusing Schopenhauer with a Formula 1 driver; he was lousy at spelling, but his two assistants, with their postgraduate degrees, could take care of that; he had not read Sartre's *Being and Nothingness* but he would rent the DVD. When faced with ignorance that was flaunted as a banner of social standing, Philippe never hesitated to brandish his fists—he had wiped out bankers, speculators, self-proclaimed artists and *sons of* who were only too happy to follow in Daddy's footsteps. This pinched intellectual boxed in a category that could knock out any arrogant jerk who even tried do battle by the word. His challenger, beaten before he'd begun, knew when it was time to throw in the towel.

A few photographers had been allowed into the salons, and when Mia spotted them starting to head their way, she led Philippe out onto the balcony, asked him to put her glass somewhere, adjusted the top of her gown and took his hand as she turned to face the cameras, with the Ferris wheel of the Tuileries in the background. The photograph would be perfect, and the moment was, too: a high point, no doubt, of the kind that leaves one, already, nostalgic.

At the Montparnasse stop all, of a sudden the carriage emptied out and then filled again just as quickly; Denis Benitez could not help but envy all those people who were about to go home for dinner and would be able to sleep peacefully, their minds at rest. The closer he got to his home, the more the image of Marie-Jeanne Pereyres in her nightgown took over, the woman more ensconced than ever, silent but ready to face a new onslaught of questions. What really got to him was the way she reversed the roles, acting patient, even kindly toward her host while she got in his way, to the point of seeming surprised by his mood or his eagerness for things to return to normal. And there was no way he could go to the police or file a complaint for forcible entry, he could just imagine the duty officer's look, and his reaction as he wrote down the complaint: *This is really a very ordinary case you're bringing us, Monsieur Benitez, me too I wake up every morning with a perfect stranger in my bed, the same one for the last twenty-five years, impossible to get rid of her, and I still don't know what she wants from me.*

A woman in her fifties came and sat down on the seat opposite Denis, glanced at him briefly, then opened her magazine.

She wears her hat as if it were a crown, and her gaze says, "I may be taking the métro but I have a life elsewhere."

What use was this power of his to decrypt if the only woman he needed desperately to decode remained opaque? There must be a meaning to this mysterious irony, but what was it?

He saw a young teenage girl a short distance away, leaning against the door.

She's pregnant but not flaunting it, her features are relaxed, she's not sorry to be swapping her role as a girl for that of a mother.

Sometimes Denis wondered why none of the women he had known had seen him as a potential father. No doubt he didn't inspire the trust and solidity that create that desire for fusion. Not one of them had been reckless enough to say, *Let's make a human being we can be proud of.* Not one of them had wanted to embark on that adventure with him, even the ones who had loved him.

But what could one say about the intruder?

About her stubbornness of tempered steel? Her formidable talent for interfering? The way she could strut about on a dingy sofa? How stupid could he get, not to have thought of it earlier! It was as old as the dawn of time! It went round and round, like a biological clock. Why waste his time on the romantic hypothesis that Marie-Jeanne Pereyres was some passionate heroine, or even the more pragmatic theory that she was an old maid looking for an end no matter what? There was only one hypothesis that made more sense than all the others now: Marie-Jeanne had tried everything to get pregnant.

As lovers filed by one after the other, she had persevered until she had her fortieth birthday in her sights: if she couldn't find a father, she'd make do with a genitor. A guy just passing by, a guy she'd recruit for the occasion, a married man, already a father, in good health, and who would never find out he'd been used. But as each of her appointments with her ovular destiny failed, she turned to science and test tubes. Alas, the lady at the Center for the Study and Preservation of Human Eggs and Sperm had pronounced her far too single to aspire to insemination, and Marie-Jeanne had gone away with a heavy heart and an empty gut. The most preposterous ideas had crossed her mind: ask a friend, present the scheme to him as a joke, a proof of friendship. She'd take care of the diapers, all he had to do was come over one night with a bottle of vodka for Dutch courage and then he could disappear. The lad wasn't too sure about it all, but he was flattered, then he vanished without a trace. In spite of everything, Marie-Jeanne Pereyres had not yet reached the limits of her imagination or of her patience. There must be a solution, however extravagant. Any woman who had ever burned with the desire to have a child would absolve her. What better way to get pregnant than to take a man hostage?

Kris was clearly the one who was more ill at ease, as she wondered what the true purpose of this impromptu off-duty meeting was.

"Would you like a little limoncello, Kris?"

"What I would like would be for you to call me by my real name, Christelle."

This sounded like a far more intimate request than some new variation on the lotus position. For a whole hour she had talked about herself, how she'd interrupted her studies too soon, her wild youth, her future dreams. He had listened to her the way he did between two bouts of lovemaking, because he listened to all the women, and each one imagined she was the only one entitled to such special attention. Kris allowed herself a brief incursion of insane ideas, Edenic images. Having a never-ending affair with her special client. As for Yves, he was merely spending a pleasant moment with one of his bed partners.

"You've always told me that prostitutes play a role, and that their pseudonym is a part of it, just like their look and the way they speak. You are prepared to abandon that persona, just because we've shared a plate of *spaghetti al nero di seppia*?"

And here she'd thought she wasn't the least bit vulnerable, not even to insults: it was as if she'd been slapped.

"With you I can't be Kris anymore."

Yves suddenly found himself in the position of an ingénue who thinks she's with a confidant when he's really only another suitor in her wake. He was flattered, but he was afraid he'd made a gaffe inviting her to dinner like this, since now it looked suspiciously like a romantic tête-à-tête. In her features he suddenly saw Pauline as she had been during their first times alone together—the modestly lowered eyes, the flushed cheeks, the impish smile. It was precisely the sort of face that he no longer wanted to see, that face of disarmed sincerity, pure intentions, and infinite tenderness to come. Ever since women of easy virtue had begun parading through his house, so many other emotions had become indispensable to him. In addition to the fever a stranger's body could provoke, with that frenzy of immediate nudity and the bliss of hitherto unknown caresses, there was also the terrible pride of seeing the women leave his bed less mistrustful than upon arrival. This was essential: he had to get her to let her guard down, this woman who saw him either as an embarrassed fool, a cash register, or an enemy. Yves was not especially gifted as a lover, and had a perfectly ordinary body, but he knew now how to tame the wildest among them, and after a night or two he had them eating out of his hand. And so what if he never became a one-woman man ever again, if he never knew the joys coupledom: let his peers take care of that, they had the skills and the patience. For every Asia, Jessica, or Victoire who ardently impaled herself upon him, there was a Pauline he could thank for having betrayed him, for having released him from the duty of constancy.

"You don't think it suits me?"

"What?"

"Christelle."

"It does. Makes me imagine the little girl you used to be."

That little girl was coming to the surface now, impressed by an adult, a man she wanted to charm with candor and frankness, the opposite of her usual weapons. Not taking his eyes from her, Yves tugged discreetly on his sleeve to look at the time, then asked the waiter for the check.

"Are you going home?" she asked.

"I can give you a lift, I have two helmets."

Resolved to confide further in him, to confess what she felt for him, Kris decided that this night would be her treat. And a luxury for herself at the same time.

"I'll come with you. On me this time."

Not to ruffle her feelings, Yves tried to think of a way out, and could already hear himself lying about how tired he was, how he'd woken up at the crack of dawn. But what was the point justifying himself to Kris: didn't he pay her in order to see her appear and disappear without having to owe her any explanations? He had almost reacted like a husband, or even a single guy bogged down in a relationship. As he was neither, he laid his hand on Kris's and told her, as he generally did, the truth.

"Tonight I have an appointment with Kim, a Vietnamese girl who Jessica recommended. She wasn't free until one in the morning. I can't cancel. You don't like it either, when a customer does that to you."

She didn't know what to say.

"I've never made love with an Asian woman, I've been looking forward to it for weeks. I've often told you as much but you don't know anyone."

What Kris heard above all was that he had trusted someone else for that sort of recommendation.

"You won't hold it against me?"

"Me, hold something against you? The only clients I hold anything against are the ones who beat me up."

Once again she was the whore, he was the john, everything was back in place. Kris might feel hurt, but he had broken no rules, he had never come to her wearing a mask, he had never reneged on a promise. He was simply, calmly pursuing his quest to the end.

Before leaving the table, she could not help but give him a warning.

"You can forget what I'm about to tell you, but I'll say it all the same. Be careful. Be careful with your freedom, the ease of what you've chosen. I know where it leads. Today you can pick up the phone and have all the women you want, and this can go on as long as there are men with money in their pockets and women ready to relieve them of it. But ask yourself what you're sacrificing by giving up the hunt, by not playing the charm game. Sooner or later your senses will become dulled, you won't know how to recognize the signals anymore, you'll no longer take the risk that a woman might read into you, and you'll lose your fine casual attitude. Promise me you'll think about it."

He promised her, although he didn't really think he would. Once they were outside he kissed her on both cheeks and left her, saying, "Bye, Kris."

Philippe Saint-Jean was now the partner of one of the most beautiful women in the world, and the world had just found out about it. Thus, their few months of clandestine existence had come to an end, an existence that had given them the illusion of overcoming certain hurdles, of creating their relationship *in opposition to*, of deserving their future. By becoming Mia's official companion, Philippe was in danger of finding himself in the public eye far more than he ever had been as a philosopher; no doubt that was the price you paid, but why turn down such an adventure? Even if he refused to see his companion as a trophy, her exceptional fame had played a huge role. He had always known the importance of another person's gaze on the object of one's desire and, in the case of someone like Mia, that gaze was multiplied by a global coefficient; a simple exponential calculation allowed him to conclude that you don't get tired of a girl like her: he had the odds on his side. And anyway, he felt he deserved Mia, she was his just reward for so many years spent defending just causes, separating truth from falsehood, advocating Beauty and Good, preserving his faith in humankind. Philippe may not have believed in fate, but fate, not one to hold grudges, had seen the wisdom, not once but twice, of placing Mia in his path.

He did, however, have one last reason to be seen on Mia's arm that night. And that reason wore a pearl gray dress whose neckline proudly revealed, above her breast, a swashbuckler's scar that Philippe could not get enough of. Mia could sense her boyfriend was troubled.

"Do you know her?"

He only ever ran into Juliette by chance, now; he refused to convert into mere friendship a love affair that had been so intense. They sometimes came across each other at lunchtime in a restaurant on the Rue de Bièvre where they used to dine together, back in the days, or in the corridors of a shared publishing house. As a rule, he acted indifferent and gratified her with a compliment taking them back to their lost intimacy. In those furtive moments he had to restrain himself from lifting his hand to stroke those curls he had smoothed so often with his fingers.

However, this sudden encounter in the gilt of the Hôtel Crillon owed nothing to chance. Because she had written a significant work on turn-of-the-century artistic movements, Juliette had been a consultant on the film being honored that night. Philippe had always known this.

"Go say hello to her," said Mia.

He did not need her permission, but he thanked her with his eyes.

"Still six foot one and a hundred and thirty-nine pounds?"

"What are you doing here? In a tux no less?"

Somewhat too evasively, they both tried to find out whether the other was seeing someone. Not wanting to face the answers, Philippe refrained from asking her the questions that were burning his lips. He would rather preserve his image of a Juliette finding it hard to get over their separation, incapable of falling in love from that moment on, feeling somehow soiled if she spent the night with another man. On the other hand, he managed to slip the words *my partner* into the conversation fairly quickly, pointing her out a short way away, where she was surrounded by admirers.

"She's famous, that girl, what's her name already?"

"Mia."

"She's magnificent."

"And not just on the outside."

"I remember, you met her at a dinner one night. You thought she was ordinary and full of herself."

"I gave her a second chance."

Philippe was about to add, *I was so afraid I'd see you on another man's arm that I grabbed the arm of one of the most desirable women on the planet. Take that as a tribute.*

Marie-Jeanne, languid, put her reading aside for a moment to sit up on the sofa and greet her host with a smile. He ignored her the way he generally did, and went into the kitchen in a tomb-like silence to fix himself a sandwich. Exhausted by all his speculation about the intruder's presence, he preferred to avoid any new hostility and headed straight back to his bedroom. She was too quick for him.

"I have a request for you this evening, but promise me you won't take it badly."

"Too late."

"I know this will seem somewhat awkward to you, and I will understand if you refuse."

"The more you try to take precautions around me, the more exasperated you'll make me."

"I would like to sleep with you tonight."

He stared at her inquisitively.

"Don't go imagining anything sexual. In short, let's say that this promiscuity between us is beginning to have undesirable effects."

" . . . Have what?"

"Seeing you shut yourself in your bedroom like that, day after day, because you're afraid I'll attack you has made me see you as an impregnable fortress. Obviously this has been making me think."

"A madwoman has moved into my house—"

"In other words, I don't want to go away from here with the memory of your terrible mistrust. Sleeping together just for a night is probably the only way to lay down our arms."

"This woman is out of her mind."

"Let me tell you a childhood memory: when my parents first took me to the Louvre, I came upon a canvas by Toulouse-Lautrec entitled *The Bed*, which shows two people sleeping side by side. I must have been five or six years old, and I was incredibly moved by the impression of peace and abandonment coming from the painting. I thought it must take a tremendous amount of trust to dare to sleep next to someone."

Denis looked at her questioningly.

"Moreover, I haven't spent the night in a man's bed for a long time and, oddly enough, what I miss more than anything is not the usual acrobatics but the sleeping in the same bed. So you have nothing to fear, I'm not even going to touch you. All you have to do is lie down on your own and go to sleep, and I'll slip under the comforter and you won't even notice, and tomorrow morning, before you wake up, I'll move back to the sofa. And I promise never to ask you for anything again."

Denis didn't know what to say.

"Go on, it won't cost you anything . . . "

"You're sick in the head, you need medical attention."

"It's not like I'm asking for something extraordinary. You'll be silent and calm, close by, breathing deeply, your weight on the mattress, moving about while you're dreaming."

"I haven't had a single dream since you moved into this place. My life is nothing but one long nightmare, and if I'm lucky I can escape from it at night when I'm dead tired, for a few short hours before the alarm goes. And now you want to take that away from me?"

"A woman who wants to sleep by your side for one night, is that the end of the world? What can be so awful about that?"

"I know exactly what you want, trying to get into my bed. You have some plan."

"A plan, me?"

"You got hooked on me already a long time ago. I don't know where you saw me, maybe you were having dinner at the brasserie where I work, I must have served you a dish and something was triggered, I became your obsession. A woman consumed by passion can quickly turn into a stalker, there's no lack of news items to prove it."

"You've asked me a hundred times if we've already met. And a hundred times I have told you the same thing. You are suspecting me of feelings that are just too strong. I'm not made of that sort of stuff. And, with all due respect, neither are you."

"If you're not crazy about me, then that's all the more deplorable, you're being purely calculating. Your true motive for butting your way in here is your fear of ending up alone. You want to hook up with someone, that's normal for a woman your age. You spotted me long ago, maybe you live nearby, or some mutual friend told you that I'd be easy prey in my psychologically diminished state, and that's when you decided to strike."

"The fear of ending up alone . . . That's the best one yet! Have you taken a good look at me?"

"What is it, then? Are you looking for a donor?"

"I beg your pardon?"

"A genitor, a guy stupid enough to let a woman have a kid behind his back? We spend one night together, and then another, and you continue your siege until you fall pregnant. So you figure no one can resist Marie-Jeanne Pereyres? You actually believe your little ploy might work?"

"What sort of nonsense is this?"

"Why me, damn it? Do I look like someone whose genes are in good condition?"

"What makes you think I don't already have children?"

"Do you?"

"No. I'm sterile, I found out very early on. At first it felt like a punishment, but over time I've come to terms with it. I have a whole tribe of nephews and nieces who adore me. And who knows, maybe some day I'll adopt. There'd be no risk in taking me in your bed. Do you really think I'm after your body?"

"And why not? I've attracted other women, you know."

"You can be sure of one thing: the night you stop coming home alone, I will disappear on tiptoes."

Which she did now, turning around, her head down, to go to her sofa. Hurt, like any rejected woman who thinks that only men are meant to be rejected.

Denis now knew how to get rid of her.

7

After six weeks spent in the museum's projection room—an ideal venue given its size, comfort, acoustics, and décor—the members would henceforth be meeting at the Rue de la Convention, in the fifteenth arrondissement, in the basement of a little apartment complex. It was a long, vaulted cellar, clean and heated, equipped with benches and recycled chairs, and had been set aside for the co-owners' meetings, but was also used for parties and various rehearsals.

Very different from the usual solemnity of the Thursday gatherings, a silence reigned like a voiceless accusation against one of the attendees. As the brotherhood had neither spokesman nor chairman, no one was prepared to express their indignation, and yet everyone was looking stealthily at one of their number. For the first time Philippe Saint-Jean felt he was not welcome, and he prayed the session would begin at last so they would stop staring at him.

Three days earlier, his publisher, stunned, called to tell him that a photograph had appeared in the press showing Philippe arm-in-arm with a famous supermodel. Philippe's family were the next to call, then a few friends who conceded they, too, had seen the magazine. After the fifth phone call, Philippe decided to go down to his usual kiosk, where his vendor was waiting for him, full of admiration. Back in his old threadbare chesterfield, Philippe was at last able to see the famous photograph for himself. He studied his image for a long time and found he was not as ridiculous as he had feared—almost handsome, in fact. He had even managed to look surprised, as if he were trying to overcome his natural discretion and was embarrassed at having to pose, thus preserving a certain dignity. Lesser-known acquaintances got in touch at the end of the afternoon, the same people who liked to remind him of their existence whenever he happened to be on television. All this solicitude ended up annoying him: if he happened to put his name to an article, whether it was about Freud's Spinozism, the manifestations of the sexual revolution, or the impermeability of the middle classes, absolutely no one gave a sign of life.

Later that night, Mia called him from Montreal *between two shoots* to tell him how pleased her agency was about their relationship—far more efficient, as far as publicity was concerned, than an ordinary scandal. The next morning, he was woken by a press attaché who was delighted to relay the requests for interviews emanating from the various media who had just learned of his existence. The high point came when the proprietor of his regular dive treated him to an aperitif for the first time in ten years—a kir that Philippe bought dearly with his person by posing for the guest book. After gallantry, then annoyance, came bitterness: never had he been as popular as when he was the opposite of his true self.

In fact, the vast majority of the men gathered there that Thursday had seen the photograph or spread the word. Once they had recognized Philippe in the picture, they went on to find out that he was a sociologist, curious about human nature, but with few kind things to say about his own era. How could they help but see this mute witness as a threat to their occult community? In the philosopher's eyes, would this handful of individuals not represent a subject worthy of study, a societal oddity? Should they not be afraid he was preparing a work on the bankruptcy of the male of the species? Was this brotherhood, founded on trust and sharing, not harboring a traitor?

While most of them found it hard to hide their concern, the more fatalistic among them admitted that sooner or later their cenacle was bound to lose its anonymity; it was even a miracle that it had been kept safe over the decades from journalists and other assorted sneaks. How could they have imagined, in this so-called era of communication, which encouraged self-promotion and keeping a close watch on others, had no regard for privacy, and violated what ought to be sacrosanct, that their little secret meetings every week would continue to prosper behind closed doors? It would be so easy to portray their existence in a cynical light! While there might be a hundred ways to revile the brotherhood, there was only one way to present it in all its simplicity, and it was to be feared that Philippe Saint-Jean might have chosen precisely that way.

And even if he had no evil intentions, how dare he sit among these men who were often distraught, frustrated, or disappointed—he who seemed so fulfilled in his professional life; he who, if one were to go by the photographs, moved in posh circles and, above all—and herein lay the ignominy—was going out with one of the most adulated women in the world? This could be seen as the height of provocation, and the unhappier members had the right to feel offended.

Philippe could discern the true message of this stubborn silence; he was being targeted, to be sure, but they were giving him a chance to explain himself, to reassure his peers. All he had to do was find the courage to abandon his insidious wait-and-see attitude and confess the true reasons for his presence there.

Philippe looked to Denis and Yves for encouragement; they were both already looking forward to giving him the third degree over a beer. They didn't hold it against him for keeping Mia's name from them, and they couldn't care less about the brotherhood's anonymity: this was their buddy sleeping with the girl who was showing herself all over town in her underwear. Not even encouraged by his companions, Philippe stood up to go and face an audience that was vastly different from that of his seminars, lecture halls and television studios. This time he had not prepared a thing, and he did not feel protected by any sort of argument or technique; he would do as all his predecessors had done and let one sentence lead to the next, even if it meant getting lost in digressions, repetitions, and contradictions.

"My name is Philippe, I'm a researcher in social sciences. Only a few months ago, I was still trying to recover from a broken heart. I'd thought I was cleverer than other people, I thought I'd be able to avoid the pain of missing someone by making it a subject for reflection. I reasoned that if I put it into perspective often enough I would be able to empty it of its melodrama, and see just how trivial and foolish it was, so I'd soon be rid of the pain. It didn't take long before I had the proof that I was no better armed than the next man to fight against that pain. I began to despise the classics; they provided no answers. I hated language, I cursed reason, loathed dialectics. The essence of my conscious thoughts could be summed up in four words: *Juliette has gone away.*"

Philippe spared them those details which failed to portray him in a flattering light: the sleepless nights next to the telephone, the photographs he'd torn up, the spiteful insinuations he had made to mutual friends. But his spite was no more successful at putting her behind him than his great literature had been.

"That was when I found out about this . . . this circle—I may have baptized a few concepts in my life and given names to the most abstract forms, but I still don't know what to call our assembly this evening. I remember very well my state of mind when I came to my first session: the analytical machine was plugged in and I was expecting the worst. How pretentious could I get, wanting to decipher the meaning of these meetings, when I myself didn't know why I was attending? Since then I've listened as dozens of guys have told their stories, then disappeared. You can't tell how a story will end when it's being told by the main protagonist. Over the weeks I've been drawn by the intensity of these spoken words; it's manna from heaven for a guy like me, so eager to define what constitutes a Human Being that he forgets the individual and the charge of reality each of us carries within. Oh, reality . . . irreplaceable reality, the way it defies the imagination and sometimes even understanding. It's been a joy to witness the complexity of all the men who've trooped through here. There are those who dread truth far more than lies, those who prefer great sorrows to petty compromises, those who prefer to make a petty compromise rather than risk great sorrow, those who go from Greek tragedy to Italian commedia, those who sacrifice flesh and blood creatures to their mental creations, those who invent brand new feelings, those whose dick shows them which way is north, those who prefer hatred to indifference. In the long run, I forgot that the people speaking were actually men, they could just as easily have been women or extraterrestrials. The only thing that mattered was to be in contact with another way of seeing, however disturbing it might be. As I found myself actually enjoying listening to other people again, I began to take a second look at all my convictions about the principle of otherness, and I had to concede that my hostile feelings toward the woman I had once loved were exceedingly vain."

His words would never be recorded anywhere. He was very pleased with the thought.

"Without a doubt, I owe my surprising recovery to these Thursday sessions, but I have since noticed a pernicious effect which means I will have to stop coming: an excess of empathy has dulled my critical faculty. Every testimony is admissible, every wild imagining is good to hear. In other words, I always agree with the last gentleman to have spoken, which is never a good thing for a philosopher . . . "

Philippe succeeded in making a few listeners smile.

"I won't come back next week, or in the weeks to follow, but I swear to you that in my work I shall never use a single word I've heard here, and I will never reveal anything about these meetings, except to someone who might need to attend."

Contrary to tradition, the men applauded him, with the sense of relief only trust regained can bring.

"Will the two of you stop beginning all your sentences with 'Is it true that'?"

"Is it true that she has a pet ferret that goes with her everywhere on a leash?"

"Is it true that she eats nothing but green seaweed available only in Japan?"

"Is it true that she gets $25,000 for one hour of posing?"

"Is it true that she has a ring in her clit, like in *The Story of O?*"

"Where on earth did you hear all this rubbish?"

Denis remembered a television commercial where you could see Mia through a translucent screen rubbing cream all over her body; he had told himself then that perfection did exist in this world but that he would never see the shape of it elsewhere than on a screen. As for Yves, he still hadn't gotten over the cover of *Elle,* where Mia's insolent eyes seemed to be saying to him, "Lehaleur, I want you!"

"Is it true that some financial bigwig offered her a Ferrari just to have dinner with him?"

"Is it true that she's had floating ribs removed to make her waist smaller?"

"Guys, look, this isn't the jealous boyfriend talking, it's the sociologist: where on earth did you dig up such exaggerated information? I'm serious, I want to know. In my essay on the memory-mirror, I examined the endemic impact of rumors. I wish I'd known you at the time!"

What did this intellectual have that they didn't, that entitled him take a living myth into his arms? Just because they served *oeufs mayonnaise* or installed windows, did that mean they were not worthy of pleading their case with someone like Mia? He must have reeled her in with his fancy phrases! He must have come up with a whole slew of woolly theories to get her into his bed!

"What's she like in real life?"

"I don't know. With her, life is never real."

As he refused to be judgmental where his friends were concerned, Philippe decided to sidestep the issue gracefully. If he was not always lucid with people he liked, it didn't weigh on his conscience. And yet, he could not help but interpret the signals Mia sent out, and that endeavor left him nostalgic for the amorous blindness he had once known, that sweet distraction, that total lack of distance which compels one to paint another person's faults as virtues. Did it mean he was not really in love if he could see through Mia so well?

He had noticed that she was very demonstrative in public, yet far less so once they were alone. At her parents' place she fondled him to the verge of indecency. In the street she walked in step with him like some Siamese twin. Around photographers she clung to him as if to a life buoy. But behind closed doors Mia immediately asserted her need for personal space, and she even went so far as to make fun of self-sufficient little couples with their sappy kissing. He had observed the way she held back, giving only the absolute minimum, in order to keep her partner in a state of dependency—something Philippe referred to as *emotional Malthusianism*. He preferred to see this not as emotional self-restraint but as naïve calculation, in order to keep him with her as long as possible. A third clue, even more worrying, was Mia's refusal to envision her future, the day when her approval ratings in the glamour world began to decline. Philippe had asked her, *Have you thought about afterwards?* Initially she had dodged the subject, convinced as she was that nothing could be as good as the life she was leading at the moment, and then she replied, *Have children, and then, we'll see, maybe become an actress.*

"'With her, life is never real' . . . Do you think we'll be satisfied with that?"

"Do you want proof? This time next Thursday, I'll be in a luxury hotel in Bali, with one of the most beautiful creatures in the world. I'll be sipping on a dry Martini by the pool, looking out over the ocean, while you will be surrounded by a hundred sniveling guys in a concrete basement. Console yourselves with the thought that all this good male bonding will make you better people."

A six-day photo shoot for Vanity Fair, that was how Mia had presented it to him. Six photos for an American monthly. The ordinary paradise of fashion magazines, the lazy imagery of a dreamlike otherworld. Philippe wondered how, in the third millennium, that cliché could still sell. *I managed to slip you into my contract, my agency will take care of everything.* Philippe Saint-Jean, no less, who had attended lectures with Michel Foucault at the Collège de France, had been *slipped into a contract.* Travel first class, stay in a luxury suite at the finest hotel in Southeast Asia. *All you have to do is say yes.* Philippe had nothing against the idea of saying yes, but yes to what? To the change of scene? To the luxury? To the colors of a postcard? *In case you're feeling guilty, tell yourself that you'll get a lot more work done there than in your dried up little study.* Phrased differently, that was the only argument that seemed admissible. Philippe never left Paris other than to attend a seminar or a book fair. Back in the days when Juliette agreed to go along with him, that could mean an escapade in a boutique hotel, with some local sightseeing and time for tasting

THE THURSDAY NIGHT MEN · 153

regional specialties: quite an adventure for a guy like him. He felt no need to disrupt a work routine that allowed him to travel much farther than any tour operator could. To him, the word vacation had a nuance of vulgarity, unless he lopped off the suffix and was left with the verb and its emphasis on desertion. And now the intrepid Mia was disrupting his everyday routine, pointing to a certain ossification: what if, because it had never been questioned, his beloved routine had turned him into a sluggard? A puny intellectual crushed by his sedentary lifestyle, drained by inertia, worn out before his time? The trip she was suggesting would be the perfect opportunity to take a good look at his working methods. For that reason alone he agreed to follow her to the antipodes, and he planned to take no computer and no books, only his little notebook, just in case he felt inspired as he sat beneath a palm tree.

Certain that this would be his last glass in the company of Yves and Denis, Philippe took his time. He knew how partitioned the world could be, how life could dismiss the people met in exceptional circumstances, how much memory disposed of those who had witnessed your moments of weakness. And the further behind he left the Thursday sessions, the greater the risk he'd have nothing to say to these two, and his search for that lost complicity would be in vain. Moreover, neither Yves nor Denis suggested meeting again, elsewhere, later on, as they might have done had they felt the bonds of true friendship. They weren't kidding themselves, so all that was left was to say goodbye, with a touch of irony.

"If we haven't swapped phone numbers up to now," said Yves, "we're not about to do so this evening."

"You never know," said Philippe, "I may need some new windows. Now that you've introduced me to the charms of galvanized metal windowframes, I've gone back over some of my preconceived ideas. What does a philosopher do, other than look at the world through his window? He is duty bound to keep up with the latest technology in the domain—good soundproofing so he won't be distracted by the racket of civilization, and reflective film to be able to see without being seen, like some kindly observer keeping an eye on everything. Yves Lehaleur, you can make me into that superior being."

"I'm going to miss not having any intellectuals among my acquaintances. It's some consolation to think that at last I'll be able to read one of your books. As long as we were buddies, I kept putting it off, I was afraid I wouldn't understand a thing and I said to myself, 'Can you go on drinking beer with a guy when you can't make head or tail of his theories?'"

"Read *On Being Casual.* I don't really know what you mean by theory, but there isn't any in that book."

"And I'd like to invite you to come and dine at the brasserie," said Denis, "but only if you come with Mia. I don't need to tell you how many brownie points I'd get with the boss if you did."

"If you cook up that green seaweed you can only find in Japan—you're on."

Philippe got up, shook hands, and headed home, already nostalgic for the mysterious postures of those who, once upon a time, were members of a secret society.

Ever since one woman had scorned the regular nice guy he had been trying so hard to become, a hundred others were now contributing to reveal the new Lehaleur, a guy he'd never have imagined even in his wildest dreams. This man used to be married? Had to be an impostor. In the long run, he wouldn't have known how to keep up the act: he'd have languished, would have allowed bitterness to eat away at his relationship and he'd have ended up blaming his wife for all the women he'd never known. And what a sacrilege that would have been, never to have known Beatrice, who had told him about Albane, who'd introduced him to Mariya, who'd recommended

Éléonore. Yves quickly forgot the bad experiences and kept only the magical moments, without trying to retain or reproduce them.

Kim, his first Asian, had scrubbed and massaged his entire body. A treatment fit for a warrior. In the morning he had felt strong enough to raise an army of samurai, but he'd done nothing more than go and install windows. Mona, between two depraved adventures, had asked to be spanked; Yves had managed to assert enough authority to spice up the game and act the dominator. In the grip of an irrepressible strength he discovered how much female docility could excite him, as part of a tacit, sealed pact. This was confirmed to him several nights later when Camille suggested bringing her friend Rachel along. *She's a she-devil . . .* A dream was about to become reality, and he hadn't even had to wish for it. The two of them had given him an infinite number of enchanting experiences, all of which he'd been eager to try. When they saw how presumptuous he was about his abilities they made fun of him, but respected his stage directions. In the morning he awoke with Camille lying curled against his side, and Rachel curled against Camille: clearly the most delightful of all their postures. With Éla, the redhead from the Middle East, he had dared far worse by reversing the roles; during the entire session he had treated her like a client who is paying for a gigolo: *What would make you happy?* A question that is eminently more delectable for the one asking than for the one who hears it.

However, the delightful frisson he had felt whenever he opened his door to a stranger eventually began to wear off. His frenetic search for novelty was exhausting him physically, and the two or three sessions required to wear down a newcomer's mistrust were taking more and more out of him. Yves preferred to devote his time to the girls he explored a bit more with each visit, of whom there were four, not counting Kris.

Agnieszka, his Polish girl with her angelic face. Instead of driving them further apart, the language barrier had brought them closer. If she could talk about herself without a care whether she was understood, Yves felt no need to try and convince her. Their squeals, laughter, caresses, and the way they raised their glasses to each other were far more eloquent than any articulated sentence might have been. Between each bout of lovemaking they rambled, got carried away, made fun of each other.

"Jak będę kurwić się dalej to nie ma mowy o yało żeniu rodziny."

"Who do you sleep with without getting paid?"

"Nie bądź za dumny z tego twojego kutasa."

"Yesterday I installed electric shutters at an insane asylum."

"Tęsknię za rodzicami i za siostrą też."

Between two naps, they opened their hearts, moaned, consoled each other. Their intonation was often enough to indicate when they were being ironic, or naughty, or serious. Their silence spoke of sadness, calm, or trust. Thanks to Agnieszka, Yves had regained an acute ability to listen, something he had lost after a few years of marriage. He no longer blamed his ex-wife for it, he alone was at fault; over time he could not hear anything in Pauline's silences anymore, not even distress, boredom, or disappointment. Laziness had prevailed over male courtesy, criticism over praise. With Agnieszka he need not fear the erosion of the lovers' dialogue. Yves indulged in the pleasures of another conversation, bringing his lips to her sex, to her own fine lips, mute until he kissed them.

With Sylvie, time went by just as sweetly, but on a very different register. She belonged to a sort of daytime variety that bloomed in natural light. Whenever he managed to have a free afternoon, Yves would entertain her until the fading light drove her away. Sylvie was a greedy, voluptuous creature, a subversive sort. Buttocks, hips, breasts of total impunity: her curves were outrageous for the era but she assumed them, arrogantly. She

summed up in her person so many of the lost battles of her sex.
She couldn't care less about independence, and was fully prepared to live off the largesse of men. The word effort was not
in her vocabulary, but excessive hedonism was; even as an adolescent she had not tried to fight her tendency to put on
weight, but had made it her own style, her way of life. She liked
to be naked, she liked sitting around doing nothing, she liked
posing for imaginary painters, she liked surrendering completely to her indolence. She was mad about pears, no matter
the season, and she ate pastries straight from the box. If a
stranger in the street called her fat she just laughed, and if
someone tried to reduce her to the rank of an object, she gladly
pictured herself as a monumental sculpture, replete with sym-
bolism. She purred when Yves caressed her from head to toe,
on a tactile journey that frequently explored unexpected
detours. She called her clients *my men*, and she respected them
all, for they all sent back to her the reflection of an earth goddess. Two of them, however, had a special status.

Like so many of her co-practitioners, Sylvie was saddled
with a meal ticket man, an indulgent boyfriend who was a borderline small-time pimp, acting mister tough guy at home, then
going for a stroll when madam had company. Yves could not
understand how such a likeable, tactful person as Sylvie could
be infatuated with such an odious partner, a nervous, cowardly,
authoritarian little guy, whose sole empire here on earth was
the one she let him have. *He's mean and nasty, I know, but he
has no one but me.*

Fortunately, the other man in her life, a certain Grégoire,
who'd been her client right from the start, had confessed his
feelings to her one day. And this man's story, absurd and whim-
sical, would have been perfect material for the Thursday
evening crowd. Grégoire was rich, good-looking, and single as
well, but he was incapable of assuming his passion for Sylvie in
public. Not because she was a sex worker, but because he was

the most sought-after dietician in the capital. *His problem is that he can't get it up with anorexic girls . . .* Grégoire venerated Sylvie's body the way a powerful man venerates his dominatrix. Sometimes they met in his office, where she would play the part of a patient obsessed with her weight, and he would fall at her feet, overcome by an irresistible desire to throw his arms around her waist and press his head against her belly in a sweet, regressive pose. When he invited her to his house, he had to take a thousand precautions so that no one met her in the stairs, but once they were behind closed doors he allowed his untold fantasies of opulence to run wild, along with his raging desire to lose himself in the folds of her flesh.

"It took him years to create his range of products, meal replacements, draining teas, things like that. He's opening stores all over. He's friends with movie stars. Got his picture in *Paris-Match.* It's not that he'd mind having a whore on his arm, on the contrary, it would be *the* trendy thing. But a fat one, well . . . "

Yves listened sympathetically, but cautiously refrained from reacting and left Sylvie torn between her pathetic pimp and her shame-riddled client.

Then there was Céline, the hot-blooded beast. Yves had found his female mate in her. Arch, claw, grunt, gnash, devour. Their desire was of the rutting kind, their moans were growls. When they had an appointment to meet that evening, Yves would spend the day in a feverish state until she arrived, at which point she would show off her ever-changing lingerie before throwing herself on her client. Céline did not have one ounce of modesty, nor the slightest complex; she went along with everything, and never stood on ceremony. Back in the days when he was married Yves had always been careful, as had Pauline, to respect a certain limit, which had never been set: the limit where something intimate could lapse into something *dirty.* All it had taken was a few gestures of avoidance on either one's part for them both to identify and proscribe that dark territory where only the depraved made love. Did you have to be tormented by vile instincts to strive never to yield to them? Céline was so carnal that what came across was her innocence; nothing was dirty or perverse, it was all divinely natural. Yves saw it as nothing more, or less, than the expression of a licentious tenderness.

I love sex, but that's not why I'm a whore. Céline had another professional ideal which seemed far less accessible to her than prostitution.

"I was trained as a ceramist."

Yves gave her a questioning look.

"I was trained in Sèvres, I have a diploma in applied arts, and I did my internship with the best potter there. I know how to produce and paint plates and vases, I even designed a few models that are still on sale. There's one of my coffee cups in the shop at the Musée d'Art moderne."

"So what are you doing here with me, stark naked, instead of standing by your kiln?"

"I still don't know if I'm a whore with a certain talent for ceramics, or a ceramist who'll be a whore until the day she can live from her art."

While Yves loved these three women for who they were, he loved Maud for who she was not. Right from the start she had made it clear to him that she was not a prostitute but an *escort,* and she claimed that she herself chose the men to whom she dispensed her favors, never the contrary. She thought of herself as high-class, a thoroughbred, a geisha, the noble fringe of whoredom. To hear her, you'd think she spent her days in luxury hotels, surrounded by the great and good who paid dearly for her company. Did she herself believe it, or was it enough for her to convince others of it? Maud was a counterfeiter. What a joy it was to see her arrive in her Chanel uniform, with her Dior glasses and a Jack Russell under her arm—the poor beast was used to waiting patiently on a rug in a corner while his mistress purveyed her services. Maud wore just enough makeup to look her best, and relied on a year-round suntan that was hardly the result of sun in the Seychelles, but rather that of exorbitantly expensive sessions on a sun-bed. She would sit sideways on the sofa, legs crossed, sipping a cup of Darjeeling with a spot of milk, always poured afterwards, not before, then she would tell him some story about a *mission* overseas that was virtually a state secret. Yves found her lack of self-knowledge touching: did it require the candor of an adolescent to see oneself as a courtesan in the new millennium? What was Maud's backstory, to have reached this point? Perhaps it was nothing more than a summer spent on a yacht, with a millionaire persuading her to satisfy his whims; a summer that had lasted long enough for her to be introduced to other millionaires determined to have a taste of her youth. At the end of that summer, obviously unable to maintain the lifestyle, she had adopted Maud's persona, never to leave it again.

Whatever you do, don't get undressed! ordered Yves before taking her standing up, in her suit and lace stockings. Oh, how talented Maud was at appearing respectable. Mannerisms of a dowager, a *demi-mondaine*'s erudition, the learned phrasing of a Lady Bountiful. Through her, Yves was fucking the schoolteacher, the lady of the manor, the wife of the mayor or the banker, not to mention all his inaccessible window clients in posh neighborhoods. How many Mauds had he visited dressed in his overalls, burdened with fanlights and soundproofing material? Almost all of them had offered him a beer and called him a *technician* to avoid using the word *worker*. He was amused by the way they would say *This is for you* as they slipped a bill into the hand of the laboring man. Wrapped in silks, with a whiff of Guerlain, rarely haughty but just a bit too affable. Maud incarnated them all. Enough to cure him most delightfully of his class complex.

Unable to find a rational explanation for the intruder's presence, Denis was forced to reconsider his own mental health. After all, as he had never so much as touched or even grazed Marie-Jeanne Pereyres accidentally, he had no proof of her physical existence. She had appeared when he was in the depths of his depression: perhaps she was some emanation of his unconscious, sapped as it had been by five years of frustration? Plagued by a syndrome of delirium, his troubled mind had fabricated the obsessive image of a desire: Marie-Jeanne Pereyres did not exist. Had he been given more effective medication, she would never have materialized.

A grave symptom like this must have an entry in the big book of psychiatry, but there was still one reason to doubt the entire hypothesis of a hallucination. If Marie-Jeanne Pereyres was no more than a pathological projection, why had he subjected himself to such a lackluster fantasy? Why the stringy hair, the faint twist to her mouth, the boy-scout knee-high socks? Why not a figment of his dreams, a mirage of a woman, born of a thousand unfulfilled desires? He had been hoping for so long, he had sought her in his bed on waking, so many times he thought he had seen her in a crowd, had dressed and undressed her endlessly: that being the case, why had he shown so little imagination in his mental fabrication? If his projection had been one of dreamlike perfection, Denis would not even have tried to cure himself of it. On the contrary, in his madness he would have set up house with her and closed the door on the doctors and their pathetic therapies, to live in endless happiness, in love with an illusion—but then, weren't all men in love with an illusion?

No, nothing seemed to confirm the hypothesis of a projection. Unless there were a way to unearth an even deeper and more troubling truth in that projection. And what if, instead of representing the woman for whom he had waited for so long, Marie-Jeanne Pereyres was the shadow side of Denis Benitez, his obscure double? The reflection of his ego, more accomplished or more hideous, the side one does not dare to confront but which, one day, will prevail, either to hear our grievances, or announce a tragic fate. Denis could see his painful dialectic with the intruder as a permanent debate with himself, the perfect utterance of his desires to a hypothetical *Other*. But even there, why did he chose someone like Marie-Jeanne Pereyres to be a mirror to his soul? How could he imagine *her* as his malevolent twin? It was enough to dissuade you from the temptation of an alter ego! Why wear himself out trying to express his hidden truth to this vision in a nightgown, sprawled lopsidedly on a threadbare sofa? Even the most uninspired psychotic could do better.

He might as well face the facts: nothing confirmed to Denis the certainty of his own mental dysfunctioning. Besides, the moment he put on his waiter's apron, he forgot the intruder's very existence, and he lost himself in the deadening, incessant hum of the restaurant, the demands of a hundred patrons, all in a hurry, fussy, lonely, authoritarian or stingy: how could you stay on course in such an ocean of nervous commotion without seeing it as irrefutable proof of sound mental health? When a hundred times a day you had to reply to the question *Can I have green beans instead of rice?* and never tell anyone to go fuck themselves: was this not the sign of supremely solid nerves?

But for all that, Marie-Jeanne Pereyres remained one of those inexplicable phenomena that drive the most rational individual to venture into the tenebrous zones of the paranormal. Ever since she had made her appearance, Denis had revised downwards all his pragmatic certainties. No one liked to see strange manifestations appear suddenly in their life, yet one could not help but imagine the intruder as some sort of supernatural presence entering the physical world in the form of an ectoplasm, or even a phantom come to inhabit the mortal coil of a certain Marie-Jeanne Pereyres in order to carry out some obscure design. Several new hypotheses arose: if the intruder had moved into his house with no intention of leaving, could it be that the place of habitation was much more important than the tenant? Perhaps she was a wandering soul who had come to haunt the space where she had once experienced some dramatic event. If this were the case, it was pointless to hope he could get rid of her unless he set fire to the furniture, or waited until the ghost found her own deliverance. Unless the intruder was one of those phantoms animated by kindly intentions, whose mission was to bring a message from the beyond to a human in distress. A plausible premise, but then, for Christ's sake, what was the message?

According to popular wisdom, *the best moment with a prostitute is when you're walking up the stairs together.* Kris liked to turn the assertion the other way around: nothing could rival that short minute she spent climbing the two floors up to Lehaleur's place. An appointment at her *big-hearted client's* meant she was in for a calm, sincere moment, all simplicity, no haggling or struggling. When she arrived at his place she could make herself at home as if she were an old friend, she could sprawl on the sofa, drink from the glass he handed to her, and take off her shoes—*I spend my days in a taxi and yet my feet ache like some old streetwalker's.* Then they would have dinner together like an old married couple, and according to their ritual Yves would tell her his latest experiences with her colleagues. She would listen, occasionally allowing herself to comment, but she wouldn't let her anger show: *I cannot stand the way you talk to me about them, I'm discovering an unfamiliar feeling that frightens me, a whore doesn't have the right to be jealous, it's absurd.* After a tender night in his arms, Kris's anger would flare again in the morning when she saw the money tucked on a corner of the table.

"I make so many others pay. Why should I make you?"

"You have to earn a living."

"Don't I have the right to make a gesture? To use my free will? Will I only ever be a whore for you?"

Yves preferred not to see the signs of her attachment, her questions that were too direct, her confessions—*You can kiss me on the mouth if you want, but if you do, then you mustn't kiss anyone else.* While he had a great deal of respect for her, he did not love her enough not to pay her. Why take the risk of changing the slightest component of their equation, of endangering the fragile balance obtained through a transaction? The pecuniary aspect, far from seeming sordid to him, guaranteed both pleasure and detachment. Yves paid a prostitute with the same fervor that a prostitute put into being a prostitute. And it could have gone on like that for a long time had Kris not fallen into a trap that he had, involuntarily, set for her. From the moment they met, she had fought against any sort of feeling, seeking to repress him no matter what, to file him away, along with the others, in the clan of the weak or the wily. In spite of her best efforts, it was impossible to knock him out, to make him cry or beg; impossible to reduce him to a vice or a plea or a feeling of inferiority; impossible to despise him for his brutality, familiarity, or meanness; impossible to scorn him for his male arrogance; impossible to ridicule him for his childish whining; impossible to lead him around by his dick. Kris had been undefeated up until now, but this was one battle she had lost. Henceforth, whenever she felt those hands all over her body, whenever she had to tolerate male members in her every orifice, when evening came around it wasn't an urgent need to take her body back for herself that she felt, but rather rush headlong into Lehaleur's arms. You could have fooled her: the bastard looked like the companion of a lifetime.

The more he saw her taking unexpected liberties, priding herself on a legitimacy she'd acquired who knows how, or claiming her status as initiator, the more Yves wondered whether their relationship ought to continue. He had been waiting for that evening to talk to her about it; he was concerned, wanted to understand what was upsetting her, and perhaps hoped they'd be able to go back to their good old routine. He did not have time to broach the subject. She did it for him.

Lehaleur, I have to talk to you.

She felt tired and vulnerable, lost in a way she'd never been since she'd started in this profession.

I have to try and make some sense of all this. I've been thinking about it for weeks already . . . It's gotten too difficult . . .

Yves was sorry he hadn't spoken up first.

I'm not independent enough to go on by myself . . .

Her speech was already disjointed, when she began to describe in detail her house in Ville-d'Avray, at the edge of the forest. Well-maintained, quiet.

But it's been way too big for me since my parents moved to the South.

What came next was unbearable.

No one has ever taken care of me the way you do here . . . We could make a good team, you and I . . . I earn a lot, you know . . . You wouldn't have to work so hard anymore . . .

And suddenly, silence.

Yves was wearing the smile of the idiot who refuses to understand. Everything he had just heard reminded him of the failure of his previous life: talk about a roof, money, a couple, but coming from Kris, those words suggested another word.

"I must not be hearing right. You're asking me to play the pimp?"

"Why do you go and use a word like that? I need a man to think about when I leave for work, I need to know he'll be there in the evening, that he'll heal my wounds, the ones you can see and all the others too."

What sin had he committed to find himself confronted with

such a loathsome offer? Even to suggest such a corrupted image of happiness showed she had failed, totally, to grasp who he was. Something was pursuing him, choking him, making him feel completely nauseous, and he had to tear whatever it was to pieces.

"I have a question for you, Kris. Is there something shameful about going with prostitutes?"

"What do you mean?"

"I mean, sooner or later, you come up against the question of whether it is moral to pay for as many girls as I have. Do I even have the right to resort to women like you? A lot of people would say I'm a stupid jerk. They might see it as the ancestral domination of a man over a woman's body, the centuries-old need to turn her into a piece of merchandise. There are other times when I don't feel guilty at all: these women who sell me their bodies—or at least the ones I want to see again—don't seem to be throwing away one ounce of their dignity. I treat them with a respect that they give me in return, and I don't judge them for choosing to put a price on their charms. But no matter what, I will never be at peace with my conscience, and there will never be an answer to these moral issues, they're as old as the world."

"What are you driving at?"

"I can try and understand what's going on in the mind of a gangster or a murderer or a mercenary. Maybe I could get interested in the case of a psychopath or someone who's mentally ill. I can try and go beyond my own taboos to understand another person's way of thinking, even if it's hideous. But if you put me next to a pimp or a rapist or a man who beats his wife, it makes me ashamed to belong to the male tribe. Guys who exploit or mistreat a woman's body have forfeited any right to call themselves men: they're beasts. The hatred I feel toward men like that is so strong it could turn me into the worst kind of torturer. And you are prepared to offer me such an abject arrangement?"

Kris stared at him, speechless.

"I have just understood why they sometimes call a brothel a house of tolerance: whores will tolerate anything."

She still said nothing.

"You have wounded me in my dignity as a man this evening. And I'm afraid I will never forgive you."

"I hope you don't mind, the concierge slid the mail under the door so I put it on the little console."

Marie-Jeanne fell silent, fearful she had already said or done too much. Denis was looking at her piercingly, ready to fight, praying he could be ruthless. This evening he felt strong enough to have the ghost's hide.

"Have you already lived here?"

"Pardon?"

"Don't make me repeat myself: were you already acquainted with this apartment before I made the disastrous decision to let you come in?"

"No, never. I barely even knew your neighborhood."

"Did you suffer here, in another life? I'm ready to believe anything I hear."

"Suffered? In another life? Now what have you gotten into your head?"

"Answer!"

"Never in this life, nor in any other. Although, in this life, you're not exactly easy all the time."

"Do you know what a poltergeist is?"

"No."

"And a perispirit?"

"A what?"

"It's the second body which the soul of a dead person inhabits."

"I have the sneaking suspicion you've been reading the dictionary."

"Do you like your mortal coil? Do you feel good in it?"

Marie-Jeanne looked down from her torso to her feet, put her hands around her waist, and lifted up her nightgown to inspect her calves, no longer hidden because her socks had fallen down around her ankles.

"Yeah, it's okay."

"You don't leave a single trace anywhere in this house—not a crumb, not a shred of tissue, not a hair in the tub, it isn't human, especially for a woman."

"Sometimes I envy you, Denis. You live in this magical world where the most ludicrous details become fascinating."

"Do you eat? Do you wash? Do you even belong to the material world?"

"Make up your mind. As a rule, you reproach me for being too present and too heavy, and you reproach me for having a body."

"As a matter of fact, I'm going to tell you: you don't exist. You are a projection of my sick mind."

"A projection? God, what wouldn't I give to be some man's projection! A fantastical creature, an ideal, with just that little bit of *fatale* to hint at perfection . . . Especially as whatever your projection is, it must be really hot."

"Unless you're just some ordinary ghost, the kind you find in legends, rumors, old houses and country inns. I prefer the second hypothesis by far. You correspond totally to the way I imagine an ectoplasm. An invasive presence that has no reality; you're just haunting me."

Marie-Jeanne suddenly felt powerless in the presence of so much fantasizing.

"Alas, I am not pure spirit, but a creature made of flesh who needs her two thousand calories a day and often goes well over that. I like to take hot foot baths at the end of the day, I add coarse salt to the tub and I don't really know what good it does, but my mother used to do it so I do it too, otherwise I wouldn't enjoy it as much. I sleep in a white cotton nightgown that has almost the same consistency as linen; I can't do without it, ever since that morning when I went to get the mail the minute I got out of bed and a neighbor said to me, 'It looks nice on you, that little summer dress.' I've got cellulite, not too much for my age, but I also have a bit of a spare tire on my stomach that seems to have settled there, sometimes I think about having liposuction but never in earnest. I do my laundry on Thursdays so that I can iron on Friday, but when the weather's really humid I do the laundry on Wednesday so it has time to dry. I've had heartburn forever, I always have a blister pack of Maalox on me, and if I drink champagne I take two ahead of time. Apparently I snore when I've been drinking but I refuse to believe it. Another detail for when I've been drinking: I don't have the strength to brush my teeth, and I go straight to bed and collapse. I hate cutting my toenails, I have to get into this ridiculous position, and all too often I wait for my tights to start running at my big toe, it's not very feminine but that's just the way it is. I remember going for a three-day hike once where I didn't wash, and I have this nice memory of my sour smell. When I dye my hair with henna, I lock myself in the bathroom with a plastic bag on my head to wait for it to take. I wax my legs. I have a pin in my left knee. My stomach rumbles at noon sharp, especially if I'm on the bus. I know how to make spring rolls like a real little Vietnamese woman. It may not look like much but it's not that easy, you have to get all the soybeans going in the same direction, then you sprinkle them with chopped mint, grated carrot, and angel hair, and you put the shrimp in an S, but the hardest thing is to roll it all tight with the corners tucked in so that the roll stays sealed. To get the knack, you need a lot of experience of the real world, of everyday life, of the physical realities that govern our little lives here on earth, you can't live in some parallel world full of fairies and ghosts."

A creature made of flesh, she had said.

Denis had doubted her, and doubted her still, and an irrepressible impulse compelled him to find out once and for all.

Marie-Jeanne was sitting on the arm of the sofa, her hands tucked between her legs, waiting defiantly for whatever came next.

He wondered if this was the only way he could find out.

She would not help him: he would have to find the proof his faith required.

But wasn't that proof going to cost him more than his doubts did? Did he have the nerve to risk seeing Marie-Jeanne Pereyres as anything but a dream, an essence, a specter—to see her, quite simply, as a woman, here and now?

She would not help him. Perhaps he still saw her as a strange body.

Denis had forgotten that silence.

She smiled at him, like a friend. She found him touching, the way she found all men touching when they were prisoners of themselves.

He held out his hand to her.

8

The Anatra suite in the Watu Hotel, on the Nusa Dua peninsula in Indonesia, had a 360° panoramic view of the ocean. The suite was actually a villa, set apart from the others on the top of a hill, made of little ochre walls and glass partitions that flooded the three thousand square feet with light. The infinity edge swimming pool skimmed the southern façade, extending into an enclave designed to cool the bedroom, where an immense bed, right on the floor, was level with the water. Spare furnishings in black wood created an illusion of separate rooms—living room, study, open-air dining room. Tall exotic plants stood out against the empty space, the indoor ornamental pond, and the terrace. On the northern façade, beyond the flower garden, a cubic construction of openwork wooden slats did not seem to have any particular purpose; it could be a play area for children, or a canopy battered by sun and rain, or even a purely decorative modern sculpture. A narrow path of teak planks led down a gentle slope to the main building of the hotel and the everyday bustle of tourists and servants. From there, one had access to a white sand beach covered in deck chairs, parasols, changing cabins, and bars. The waves seemed gentle as they came to die at swimmers' feet, but in the distance a violent, continuous surf broke against the coral reef. The temperature for the month of June, still tolerable for a Western tourist, was 86 degrees, and the humidity 77%, and this would vary little until sunset, at five in the afternoon.

Philippe Saint-Jean left the villa as little as possible and used the phone to order his meals, which he took most often on the terrace, facing the endless blueness. Ever since his arrival in paradise, he had been trying to feel at home—mostly in vain, for he was convinced he had become part of the furniture, not very useful, not even matching. The worst ordeal, by far, had been learning to dress lightly. To free himself of the weight of cloth. To let go of his *petit Parisien* get-up in order to survive in the tropics. Into the wardrobe went the tweed, velvet, and plaid. Philippe had to uncover himself, and uncovering oneself always entailed surprises, as the philosopher in him was well positioned to know. How far back did he have to go to find his last confrontation with his own nudity, other than in the semi-darkness of the bed or the narrow confines of a bathroom? Since he viewed aging merely from the perspective of the mind, and he viewed his mind as his primary asset in the charm department, for fifteen whole years he had forgotten his body. Now, he was thousands of miles from home, there for all to see in the harsh light of the sun, and the naked truth was glaringly obvious: folds, sagging, gray skin, liver spots, flabby muscles, spare tires.

How could he have so ignored his own body? Why had he treated his old bones as little more than a vehicle? He had celebrated *the living* with so much eloquence, and now he was obliged to remind himself at last that he was made of flesh and bones. So what if he had always admired those wrinkled faces that had been through so much, with their slow, bent, infinitely touching bodies: his own reflection now showed him nothing but negligence. So what if he had always tolerated other people's physical disparities and imperfections: now he pinched his skin the way one inspects an overripe fruit.

When she was unable to find anything in Philippe's wardrobe suitable for minimal coverage in ninety degrees in the shade, Mia raided the trendy boutiques: short-sleeved shirts in

Egyptian cotton, brand-name Bermuda shorts, leather sandals, boxer short swimming trunks, and a light linen jacket for the evening. No sooner had they arrived than she was already caught up in work, so she said, *Enjoy your time, darling.* He replied, *That's the worst thing you could ask of me.* Enjoy? It was a verb he despised, as he despised any injunction to pursue pleasure. And yet, he had harnessed himself to the task under cover of an entirely new experience: he would seek out the subtle sensations linked solely to the pleasure of existing. His living organism, back in its original bath, the sea. Once again he would be a naked aquatic creature, his skin wearing nothing but a faint tan; he would swim among his fellow fish. He would disregard his desires, fears, and questionings, to attain the age-old dream of the ancient Greeks: that point of equilibrium and harmony. He would find humility among the elements once again, he would be satisfied with the horizon without seeking beyond it, he would venerate the sun as the atheist's only god.

But to attain that old dream, he would have needed the courage to confront the infinitesimality of his being, to consider himself as a simple organic entity, infinitely fragile, emptied of thought, gregarious. He would have had to go against his nature, cease to invest himself, and accept the feeling it induced; he would have to restrain his mental machine until he found it ridiculous and vain. Leave aside the fear that nothing had any meaning. Forget everything and nothing, to have the physical experience of everything and nothing. Accept that the supreme stage of consciousness consisted in denying one's consciousness.

But how could he stop being Philippe Saint-Jean, even for one hour? Where could he find the necessary detachment to become relative to his own self? From the moment he became stuck in Bali, the good old Cartesian *I think therefore I am* had been taking on an entirely new meaning. In the early morning, once Mia had left to join her team, he began to wonder how he would spend his day and, feeling guilty that he had no idea, he clung to one principle: *I think therefore I do not "enjoy" and I am content merely to resist.* At the end of the morning, after a quick perusal of the international press, he dipped up to mid-thigh in the blue water in hope of stimulating his entire body and finding an entirely new energy to draw on. As a rule, one lap around the pool was enough: *I think therefore I paddle joy-lessly around a private swimming pool.* At the end of the after-noon, and there was no glory in it, he would compile the list of the day's activities prior to Mia's return, for she would be pro-viding him with the detailed narration of an infinity of minor events. And then he would feel just that tiny bit more excluded: *I think therefore I exist as a thinker in a world which often discourages such individuals.* Late at night, when she went off to sleep, he would at last, on the terrace, have a taste of sus-pended time and of the spindrift carried by the winds. *I think therefore the life of ideas is my only rampart against insignifi-cance.*

He found himself stuck at present in a picture postcard décor, and that was just too much for someone who, whenever he received a postcard, never looked at the picture but only read the text; an unconscious mechanism which spoke vol-umes about both his need for self-expression and his lack of interest in places and landscapes, even at the other end of the world.

And so it was there, on a deck chair in the antipodes, in his Bermuda shorts, that he could see as clearly as a furrow drawn in the sand what the rest of his life would be like. He would grow old in Paris to the rhythm of the seasons, increasingly out of his depth in the speed and ferociousness of his beloved city. And that is where he would die, because that was his only nat-ural element. Climbing the three flights of stairs to his apart-ment would become more and more trying, but he would not move house for fear of losing the waves, the vibrations, the fluids, the phantoms that had been accumulating there from the very first day. And as long as possible he would continue to orbit around a concept, until he had the illusion he had been all the way around it. When he went out on his walks, wherever he happened to end up, he would always linger in a bistro at the bar, sipping his espresso, jotting something down in his notebook, and eyeing a passing skirt. Sooner or later he would be awarded a chair among his peers in some academy. With his little following of exegetes, who would be quick to deep-freeze his memory before he had even died, he would indulge in a few whims, a few outbursts. And one fine morning, with a peaceful expression on his face, he would be placed in a coffin in a good old tweed jacket, ready for that final journey whose destination he had questioned so often.

On opening the red lacquered drawers of an old Chinese chest, Yves Lehaleur had a bizarre intuition: a stranger's hand had been rummaging among the old things collected there. This was confirmed when he discovered the absence of a whisky flask that had been stamped with the initials of his paternal grandfather, an old rascal who had lit up his childhood. The magnificent Horace had given him that flask the way others give a fob watch, explaining to his grandson that there were times when a flask filled with strong liquor could save a life, but a watch, rarely. In general, this was followed by his anecdote about the time in the winter of 1954, when he got lost in a forest in the Vercors and the temperature was only ten degrees. *Without my flask of gin, I'd be there still, damn it!* Yves was more attached to that object than to any other, not so much for its clever design—curved to fit against the chest muscles, with a screw top held by a thin bar—nor for its noble craftsmanship—repoussé silver and peccary leather well-burnished by the old gent's heavy paw—but because it symbolized the eccentricity of the Lehaleur clan. Even if he had no children to pass it on to, the disappearance of that object cut Yves off from his lineage, dispossessed him of his role as a transmitter of family memory. From another drawer, a brand new Dupont pen had disappeared. Yves had restored a friend's shutters, and unsure how to pay him, the friend had thanked him with this diamond nib pen, which gave him the handwriting of a monarch for someone who wrote so little. Yves hadn't known what to do with it, so he had put it aside for the day when he would have to write a love letter, or a letter of farewell—yet now, he had freed himself from love, and no longer ran the risk of a breaking up with anyone. He hunted around for his pocket movie camera and, as he expected, failed to find it. No matter how Yves tried to resist any kind of nostalgia, that camera was the only present from Pauline that he had kept. He had destroyed all his pictures of her, even the ones from the wedding, but in that camera—although he never looked at them—were a few short films that bore witness to his lost happiness; only moving pictures had that power. He had filmed Pauline while she was driving along a mountain road, they were headed for the chalet some friends had lent them for Christmas. Radiant, her cheeks rosy with the cold air, she was already describing the child they would conceive that very evening by the fireside; Yves had reflected that the day they showed it to their first-born child, that film would take on all its potency. Filled with a dread foreboding, he rushed over to a closet, opened a large metal box that, until then, had contained a leather document holder with a score by Erik Satie, annotated in the composer's own hand. Yves's mother had given it to him, and she had inherited it from her aunt Alice, a pianist who had met her master in 1920 at his house in Honfleur. Yves, who was utterly incapable of distinguishing the key of A from the key of D, used to feel a curious sensation when he looked at that handwriting, with its instructions for certain musical phrases: "Unostentatiously" or "With vigorous sadness." A bitter smile on his lips, Yves wondered whether the thief—and she had to have been a woman—had stolen the score for what it represented, or merely for the value of its document holder, Cordoba leather inlaid with gold leaf.

Which one? he wondered.

Which one of his fair ladies of the night had committed this pathetic petty crime?

There had been one incident three months earlier, but it had finished happily: he had caught Annette red-handed in the middle of the night pilfering a few British pounds he'd left lying around. She'd been ravaged by guilt, and Yves had consoled her, but not before lecturing her at length about trust betrayed. At the end of the night, she had obtained her pardon with the supple movement of her hips. So now the only possible culprits were Sylvie, Céline, Agnieszka and Maud, but Yves could not bring himself to suspect any of them. Sylvie even less than the others. Sylvie, the indolent quasi-ingénue, who one morning had returned a surplus banknote to him which in fact he had slipped into her previous remuneration. Céline? Céline insisted on paying her way at the restaurant, and there were times she left Yves's bed forgetting to ask him for what she was owed. And Agnieszka? She was greedy, to be sure, but would be terrified by the thought of aggravating prostitution with a run-in with the police. Suddenly a memory came to him, so obvious it was wrenching, and yet it had been so pleasant at the time: Yves, relaxing in the bathtub, while Maud used the time to run an errand: he told her where the spare keys were, she went out for a moment, then came back to join him in the foamy bath. The next morning, all she had to do was slip the keys into her bag before leaving, then come back to the apartment once she had seen Yves ride off on his scooter to reap her villainous little harvest, before putting the keys back on the nail in the fuse box.

Maud. The phony great lady. She'd worked so hard at seeing herself as elegance incarnate in the guise of a whore that she'd become vulgar. Far too inclined to lecture others to be innocent. After selling her body, she was reduced to selling her pride at a discount. Yves paid a great deal for her class fantasy, as he called it. Since that night, she no longer incarnated respectability but degradation; the vilest little street thief had more ethics and panache. Just as Yves thought he had been delivered from his past, now he felt dispossessed of the only key moments in his entire history.

The prospect of confronting the villain was repulsive. Yves could already imagine the scene: first she would deny it, then she would try in vain to hide her shame with forced indignation. She would not learn her lesson from this mediocre end to their relationship, and he could never put aside his resentment. He wanted to leave her a chance to recover a bit of self-esteem.

"Hello, Maud?"

"Yves?"

"It's never been so hard to get hold of you."

"I've taken on too many appointments, you know what it's like."

"We'll go on acting as if you hadn't robbed me."

"I beg your pardon?"

"We'll just say that you had to write something down in your diary and you inadvertently dropped my pen into your bag. We'll say you needed a movie camera so you borrowed mine. We'll say that to learn to play the piano you decided to start with Erik Satie."

"What on earth are you talking about?"

"You're such a sensitive woman, how could you be so lacking in dignity?"

She didn't answer.

"You can keep it all, except the flask, it's been in my family forever and you won't get anything for it."

"Am I to understand that you suspect me of having done such a thing?"

"I can just see you in the act, trying to figure out if this or that item had any market value, how much you could get for it, and where to offload them. You might get a thousand euros at an auction house for the musical score. Let me know when the day comes."

"How dare you accuse me like this—it's absolutely hateful. Why don't you ask some of those low-level whores who parade through your place instead."

"Return the flask and we won't mention it again."

"And even if I were guilty, what would you do? File a complaint?"

"I wouldn't stop there."

He did not know Maud's last name, or even her real first name, so finding her would not be easy, but Yves had time to lose and patience to spare. To obtain redress was not so important. He felt he was entitled to a genuine farewell.

Whether God existed or not, an angel had fallen from the heavens into Denis's bed.

Whether God existed or not, the visitation of Marie-Jeanne Pereyres was the irrefutable sign of a celestial decision.

Whether God existed or not, Denis had suffered the torture of martyrs. He had been deprived of the earthly love to which all men are entitled, then thrown into an abyss of asthenia, until a herald angel had rung at his door.

Whether God existed or not, Denis was being inducted into paradise, after five long years of purgatory. In a single night, Marie-Jeanne Pereyres had erased his rancor and his loneliness, had brought a long-overdue gratification to his senses. Denis had dozed off, his hands clutching her buttocks, his face buried in her thighs, finding his oxygen in her scent and nowhere else, her hips his only mooring.

Whether God existed or not, a superior being had the power to combine all women into a single one, to give her the perfect curves of a creature Denis could curl up to, as if she were the missing part.

Only unbelievers need proof. His proof was breathing, alive, in his bed. Whether God existed or not, Denis would never doubt her again.

Mia was dropped off at the hotel at nightfall, then she walked up to the villa where Philippe was waiting, irritable with boredom, ready to light the fuse to an arsenal of complaints. So he had to force himself to ask her how her work day had been, already dreading that she would utter a certain word.

"We were at this sort of artificial inlet on the western tip of the island. This morning I was wearing a pareo and a straw hat. This afternoon I was wearing a one-piece flesh-colored Érès bathing suit. The second shoot lasted three hours and forty minutes."

Philippe didn't mind people coining words, making up idiomatic expressions, if they enriched the language. But this use in French of the English word *shoot* carried with it too many despicable connotations and in itself alone summed up the ridiculous urgency of representing a world that did not have the slightest material reality. For Philippe, that single word conveyed all the pugnacity of advertisers, the hysteria of fashion designers, and the machine-gunning frenzy of the photographer with his unconscious desire to *shoot* at a living target.

If Philippe went out of his way to criticize the clichés of the fashion industry, neither did he spare any other aspect of the art of photography which, in his opinion, no longer served any purpose. After a century overloaded with images—in newspapers and advertisements, exciting or subversive, incriminating or decorative, full of lies or blaring the truth, all of them esthetically perfect—there was not a single photograph that still had the power to charm, inform, shock, or even inspire a daydream in the man on the street—who, with a cheap camera, could very well create his own iconography. The sole vocation of so-called professional photography in this day and age was to wrap up the merchandise or rob other people of their privacy. In either case, Mia was indeed a target, both as a provider, and as a victim, and Philippe took it on himself to remind her of the fact, just to reduce her value close to zero.

"Fill me in: does this word *shoot* mean anything other than someone *filming* you with a camera? A simple *photo session*? If so, why do you call it *shoot* when all you mean is a photo session?"

"Not even two days ago, you explained to me that the term *Dasein* referred to a philosophical concept which could translate to *being-in-the-world.*"

Philippe looked at her.

"So why do you use the word *Dasein* if all you mean is *being-in-the-world*?"

Over time Philippe no longer got annoyed with this sort of argument. He was so nimble in his use of words, so quick to develop an idea; yet with Mia, he had given up on verbal sparring, went no further than the hypocritical barbs of someone who has quarreled long enough and, worn down by the other person's arguments, is weary of trying to defend his own. Worse still, this man whose vocation was to express the world had now refined the art of saying nothing to a level of applied dialectics. Thus, he refrained from replying, *I could explain it to you, but I am afraid you might fry your precious neurons,* and chose simply to say, "Tomorrow I'll try to imagine a fusion between the *Dasein* and the *Shoot*, it will keep me busy."

Mia was feeling the same erosion, and protected herself in the same way. Used to sending everyone packing, she was making an unprecedented effort to silence all the things she wanted to throw in Philippe's face.

"*(Why are you so hostile the minute I get back after working ten hours in the blazing sun?)* And how was your day?"

"Same as yesterday, nothing special."

"Why don't you go for a tour of the island? You might find some locals to communicate with. *(And you could go into raptures about how rich their culture is, the ancestral rites that they've managed to preserve amidst all this Western decadence—of which, in your opinion, I am an icon.)*"

"I'm afraid, my dear, that the locals, as you call them, might all be trilingual and very well-informed as to the exchange rates. *(Which would fit better with your vision of the world: a playing field, inhabited by individuals of every race, all born to serve you.)*"

"Try at least not to go back to Paris as white as when you got here. I've completely burned up my sun capital but you should take advantage of it."

"*('Sun capital' rhymes with 'dumb commercial.')* I'm glad to know I'm in charge of so much capital, my dear."

After the customary pleasantries, they dressed for dinner at the hotel restaurant, where they were the center of attention when they came in. Mia signed autographs, responded to greetings, and above all got a dose of her companion's irritation with each consecutive interruption. Then there was a call from her agency, who had to make the most of the time slot between work and sleep to keep her up to date on her pending assignments. Philippe listened to every word, stunned by how unyielding she was the moment the subject was money.

"What festival? Haven't a clue. For less than €150,000 I won't move an eyelash."

For such an amount, how could she be so hardened, when she didn't even know what a euro note looked like, when she never paid a single bill or fee or restaurant check, and let her assistant to take care of the tip? Mia went around the world without a penny in her pocket, and all she had to do was point at whatever she wanted to have it served up on the spot and on a platter. Her astronomical earnings piled up and the debit column never varied. How could a young woman gauge so precisely what her appearances were worth when she didn't even know what money was worth? Philippe, with his renowned, scathing pen, was forever struggling with the spiny issue of fees and royalties, and he accepted the basic rate without daring to negotiate. More often than not, people waited for him to complain before they paid him, and sometimes they were surprised when he did complain.

"If it's cocktail *and* dinner, it'll be €25,000 extra, nonnegociable."

On the way back to the villa, he indulged in a cruel calculation: in order to earn the equivalent of what his girlfriend was paid to show her pretty face at some run-of-the-mill opening, Philippe would have had to write five hundred pages of something like *Metaphysics of the Unthought,* and it would take him several years of his life.

As soon as they were back in the villa, Mia immersed herself in the *New Yorker* that had arrived that very morning. Philippe was surprised by her sudden interest in a magazine which he knew to be intellectually rigorous, rather than one of those rags where she might come across a defamatory article requiring an immediate lawsuit. Perhaps he was being a bit too rigid, always wanting to file her in the bottom drawer without giving her a chance to surprise him. Perhaps she had begun to question choices she herself found frivolous. Ever since that famous picture taken on the terrace at the Crillon where she was holding his arm, Mia's image in the media and in her entourage had been changing. Not a single interview or gossip column did not mention her relationship with the thinker-writer-philosopher. Nowadays, she was questioned more often about her reading habits than her measurements, invited to cultural events, and asked to model for designers who qualified as postmodern. The height of recognition: a few of her colleagues were actually jealous, unable as they were to shake off the usual athletes or rock stars. To see Mia concentrated like that on the pages of a magazine that had virtually no illustrations might suggest that her new status as *a beautiful girl who also has something in her head* meant she really had attained a certain awareness, and that it was not just some sort of perfectly conceived marketing strategy.

"In your opinion, Philippe, if men were a handicap, which would it be? Deaf, blind, or mute?"

He looked at her questioningly.

"I can't decide between deaf and mute."

"What are you reading exactly?"

"The *New Yorker.* My subscription follows me wherever I go. I don't understand a thing in the articles but there's the test by Matthew Sharp."

"The what?"

"The guy's a genius. He designs these tests you take blind. You never know what you're being tested on, so that keeps you from trying to skew your answers."

Philippe didn't get it.

"So, spontaneously, do you associate 'cliff' with a) vertigo, b) rappelling, c) murder? You have to wait until the following week to find out the results of the test and what you were being tested on. It could be something like 'Are you a new reactionary?' or even 'Client or prostitute?'"

Philippe was silent.

"Don't tell me Philippe Saint-Jean has never heard of Matthew Sharp's tests!"

"I have."

"So try it: if men were a handicap?"

"How are you supposed to react to such a terrible question? *(You frightened me, honey, for a moment there I thought you were interested in something besides a citrus-fruit diet.)*"

"You don't want to answer because: a) you're a man, b) you think the question is ridiculous, c) you haven't a clue."

"The question in and of itself obliges whoever answers to flounder in generalities. In addition to which, I don't believe in characteristics being specific to one gender or another, it's nothing but a cesspool of clichés that serve to fuel ordinary misogyny and foster hostility in couples. But if I had to play along, I would say that men are accused above all of being mute, because men do not know how, or do not want, to express their feelings. Either because they're repressing them, or because they're afraid of seeming less virile. But it is also common knowledge that men are deaf to women's grievances. Either because they're too self-absorbed, or in order to avoid assuming responsibilities. Which leads to another cliché: God, what cowards men are. But let's not forget blindness for all that. Men don't see a thing, it's a well-known fact. A woman will immediately spot the trace of another woman on her husband. A man, never. A woman knows at first glance whether a guy is depressed or in love, whether another woman is pregnant or jealous; a man, no. She'll often say, 'You never notice a thing . . . ' So, to sum up, if men were a handicap, they'd be all three at once. Fortunately, women are there to restore the balance. Women listen to others, sometimes to a point of complacency. Women observe, sometimes to the verge of indiscretion. Women express themselves, sometimes to the limit of chattering. Have you had your fill of received ideas or do you want some more?"

Disappointed by Maud's betrayal, Yves Lehaleur was annoyed with himself for having believed they were ever close, just as he was annoyed with her for causing him to suspect the other girls as well. But in all likelihood, he was being naïve to imagine that trust was included in the price of a trick, and vain even to have assumed he'd created a special bond with any of the girls. Tormented by a sleepless night, of the kind he had not known since he broke up with Pauline, at 5:05 in the morning he was trying one last time to fall asleep when the doorbell rang.

What he saw through the spyhole caused him to recoil, a nightmarish vision. In the semi-darkness of the landing he saw a mask of swollen skin, disheveled hair, bloodshot eyes, a shivering body.

" . . . Agnieszka?"

Her only answer was to rush into his arms and burst into tears. He led her over to the sofa, where she collapsed, her hand in the small of her back to stave off the pain. Through the torn stocking on her right leg bluish bruises appeared; the belt had been ripped from her dress, and drops of blood fell from her nose onto her cashmere cardigan.

" . . . I'll call an ambulance."

"Co?"

"Hospital . . . " he said, in English.

"No! No hospital! No doctor! Przyżeknij mi, że nie sprowadzisz lekarza! Oni robią zeznania na policji!"

"You can't stay like this."

"Boli mnie! Masz jakieś środki przeciwbólowe? *Painkillers?*"

"It hurts?" Yves was not sure he understood the word in English.

"Byle co, co tam masz . . . daj nawet wódkę jak nie masz nic innego . . . "

Yves thought he heard the word vodka without being sure, then in his medicine cabinet he found a handful of capsules that she swallowed all in one go. With his fingertips, he lightly touched the injuries on her face, her back, her thighs. Others would probably surface.

"You need to have X-rays."

"Próbował mnie zgwałcić i jako, że nie dawał rady, to pobił mnie po twarzy."

Yves picked up the phone and dialed the number of the doctor on call, but Agnieszka found the strength to tug the phone from his hands: *Nie lekarza, mówię ci, nikogo! Będzie dobrze, odpocznę trochę a jutro zmywam się.* When it was obvious he would not get his way, Yves tried to administer first aid himself, and before acting the nurse he was the one who needed a big swallow of vodka. While he was wiping her injuries with disinfectant, he listened as she murmured the story of her attack, as if to chase it from her memory. *Facet o dobrych manierach, starannie ubrany . . . Wyjął z walizeczki jakieś przybory . . .* Since he did not understand, Yves had to imagine a scene straight from a secret drawer in his unconscious, where some perverse script was still lying around and which basically was something of a collective fantasy. He imagined a sadistic monster avenging his own failings on the pretty blonde whore. It was not enough to subjugate a body with money, he had to kick her and make her bow down. *Nie przyełam pieniędzy na robienie jego świństw . . .* Insulting her, mistreating her had not calmed him down, either; he had to distort her fine features with his fist, abolish her smile forever, break her lovely figure, mark her with fear. *Ugryzłam go w rękę aż do krwi.* He had wanted to get his own back, on all women, all at once, from the very first one on.

She looked at him, begging him for a spot on the bed. Yves put his arms around her and kept watch over her, with a hand on her brow, until she fell asleep. Agnieszka's ravaged face was the true face of prostitution, the one he had preferred never to see head on, whenever he brought home a woman who was selling herself: the makeup hiding the wounds. He had tried in vain to keep his door closed against the sordid side of things, but it lay crouching in the dark, fully determined to sneak in, and tonight it had. Once the sun rose, Agnieszka would recover from her ordeal, ready to head back to the front like a good little soldier. Once again, Yves was astonished by the endurance of these girls, their ability to overcome the most barbarian reality.

Until that time, it was not the disquieting Agnieszka he would hold in his arms but a lost, abused little girl, and that image would no doubt prevent him from ever seeing her again.

Had Denis ever truly loved before?

The simple fact of having to scrounge in his memories gave him the answer.

When he was a little boy, there had been that curious feeling he discovered when a little pigtailed thing came up to him; only the day before he'd been tormenting her. His lifelong enemy had triumphed, and made a gallant knight of her defeated opponent. That was love.

No, that wasn't love, since love was Béatrice Rosati, in middle school. Her and no one else. How do you prove it? You hold her hand in public, you want the wider world to know. All weekend long, life keeps them apart. Sunday afternoon is torture, Monday morning a deliverance. That was love.

In fact, he would fall in love for good in the bed of that beautiful stranger whose name he had forgotten, at the campsite in Royan, the summer of his final exams. All in one night, an intense, Biblical bonding, that was love.

Or was it? No, love would come a few years later, when he moved in with Véro. Ikea, joint accounts, talk of marriage. Sharing, future, that was love.

Three years later, free again. Denis had decided to favor women over love. If love really did exist, if it was as powerful as everyone claimed, let it prevail.

Now that he was well past forty, love finally had prevailed, so violently, so late, that Denis found himself foundering, engulfed by passion. He decreed that everything was sublime; he swooned over the most trivial things; he celebrated his partner relentlessly. And in spite of Marie-Jeanne's wish to remain among the rank and file of ordinary humans, to him she was a fairy, an angel, a goddess. When from time to time he managed enough distance to accept the part played by the divine in every love story, his own still remained exceptional, and he had the proof: a stranger had knocked on his door to save him from misfortune. How many people could say as much?

"Denis, I have something to tell you."

"You can tell me everything."

"I'm going to be leaving soon."

For several days now, the storm had been brewing, and that evening Philippe could do nothing to stop the deluge. In the realm of domestic spats, he still had everything to learn, as his former companion had always spared him in that respect. Juliette had a talent for never falling into the trap of moodiness, for never doubting what really mattered, just because of some gaffe or misplaced word, nor did she try to assert herself no matter the cost or the situation. She accepted that she was fallible, and preferred to learn a lesson rather than content herself with being right. Philippe translated all these virtues into one word: Juliette was an *adult*. For him, this was the supreme homage: he knew so few real adults, even among his eminent colleagues. Young Mia had a good heart, in many lovely ways, but was she not still tilting at windmills? How many more revolutions did she have to fight? Philippe would not wait.

"Tell me the truth. Do you think I am: a) superficial, b) a spoiled brat, c) a complete idiot?"

"None of the above. Let us say that the god glamour is your only religion."

"You see me as a *fashion victim,* because you think you can give me more than all those guys who are only interested in my looks. And do you think I don't realize because all I care about is my looks?"

"At the moment you are doing what is called secondary rationalization."

"*(You love playing professor.)* What is that?"

"It's when you reformulate an event, or an irrefutable fact, to make it acceptable in your eyes or in someone else's eyes. *(You are the Monsieur Jourdain of secondary rationalization, you do it all the time without even realizing.)*"

"In sum: I'm an empty shell, and that means I'm incapable of saying what I think."

"You are completely entitled to say what you think, but from time to time, try to think things through before you think."

Mia could not possibly win at this game. She had to strike a blow now, so hard it hurt, below the waist if need be.

"To claim that I'm interested in nothing but appearances, that's a bit rich coming from Monsieur Philippe Grosjean."

For a moment he acted surprised. But he was not a good actor.

"That's your name, isn't it?"

He looked at her, speechless.

"Don't waste your time, I found out when we were going through customs and you asked me to get your passport out from the bottom of your bag. Philippe Grosjean *aka* Philippe Saint-Jean, plain for all to see."

He did not know what to say.

"Grosjean doesn't sound much like a philosopher, now, does it? Grosjean doesn't sell as well as Saint-Jean? Doesn't get your little sociology students fantasizing over their professor as they write their dissertations about you?"

From the day the administration had allowed him to change his name, his secret had been kept for seventeen years. Grosjean *aka* Saint-Jean. His parents had absolved him, although not without a certain bitterness. But how could anyone have taken him seriously—a dissertation on collective memory by an author with a name like Philippe Grosjean? Ever since, he had had to live with the remorse of having forsaken his real name, of having rid himself of a name with provincial echoes, and of having adopted pseudo-aristocratic airs, all as if he were ashamed of his humble origins. What wouldn't he have done, now, to put that youthful error right?

Unable to justify himself, he left the room without looking at Mia and sought refuge under the mysterious canopy, the use of which he might have just discovered: a space where he could be left the hell alone.

As a rule, Philippe knew how to stave off reminiscences of his former life, but this evening he'd been driven to the brink by a birdbrain who reproached him for having betrayed his own self, and he could not help but remember the little Grosjean he once was, in a public school in the outskirts of Paris; how he questioned everything. Nothing back then set him apart from any of the other boys, other than the unvoiced intuition that throughout his life it would be as hard for him to obey orders as it would be to give them. And that, already, his spiritual imaginings would provide a far better refuge than any tree house could.

In the beginning there was Madame Lagirarde. The good Madame Lagirarde, who assigned analysis that was far too difficult for her eight-year-old pupils. She liked nothing better than to ask questions which children of that age were quite incapable of answering, as if to console herself for being forty. *Can one of you tell me why the child in the poem is listening to the rain from deep within the cellar?* Answers came thick and fast, each one more banal than the next. Little Grosjean sat cogitating like a devil: *rain + cellar = . . . ?* There was surely an explanation to justify the entire poem, otherwise what would be the point of so much languor, cold, fear? *Rain + cellar = war!* The stunned, almost annoyed look on Madame Lagirarde's face was worth far more than any good grade.

Back then, they still played cowboys and Indians in the schoolyard during recess. But little Grosjean did not give himself a choice: he would be an Indian, even if it meant dying from a paleface's bullets.

And then there was Nathalie Brisefert and her budding breasts, which he glimpsed by chance one day on opening the wrong door during a medical examination. The temptation to boast about it to his pals had been great, but, after a night's careful reflection little Grosjean preferred to bind himself to Nathalie through the secret. *What one says belongs to others. What one keeps silent is for eternity.*

And how could he ever live down the shame of not being able to climb up the tightrope? Hanging there, halfway up, petrified, his arms drained, his bladder bursting. That's all it took to be excluded from the gang of tough kids and find himself relegated to the clan of weaklings. From then on, all he could think was that one day he would get to the top, and leave those who thought they were so strong far below.

Even more marginal than little Grosjean: Michel Guilan, known as the Fool. He was frequently absent, because he had leukemia. *We need a volunteer to take him his homework. Shall I choose someone at random?* An even greater misfortune had befallen the Fool: he had no television! The Fool didn't care: he had all sixteen volumes of the *Tout l'Univers* encyclopedia. Little Grosjean lost his bearings: was the Fool really such a fool?

And then there was the unforgettable day, two years later, when Madame Dourçat fainted. They could see her underpants. Since there were no girls in the class, none of the boys wanted to go for help: let the show go on. Little Grosjean pulled her skirt down over her thighs and went to notify one of the cleaners. *My hand brushed against Madame Dourçat's stockings and I saved her life. I am a man.*

On Wednesday evenings, Monsieur and Madame Grosjean watched the circus program on television. Little Philippe hated the circus: the clowns were trying too hard to make him laugh, the trapeze artists who were so good at climbing up the tightrope left him indifferent, and the spectacle of the elephants in tutus appalled him. He used the time to read the newspaper; he didn't understand a great deal, other than that he couldn't grow up fast enough.

And one fine morning, a revelation: everyone dies someday. *Finally a logical explanation for the fact that man created God in his image.*

Filled with nostalgia, Philippe wondered whether he had become Saint-Jean thanks to one of these tiny revelations, or whether, come what may, he would have followed his natural inclination to deconstruct the workings of the mind, in order to put them back together again, according to his mood.

To erase Maud's loathsome betrayal and forget Agnieszka's distress, Yves sought out Céline's passion. On the telephone she displayed the same impatience as her client, which he took as the promise of a night without end. All day long, Yves compiled his little inventory of Céline's bodily delights, her fantasy, and her furor as well, the most intense he had ever known. He was already looking forward to the games they would play, innocently perverse but genuinely rough. While with Maud he satisfied his class fantasies, with Céline he had very different fantasies that enabled him to live out his desire to dominate. Céline could go from the female in heat to the shameless bitch who needs a scolding, then she'd shift to the ancillary script of the naughty chambermaid, ever attentive to her master's bidding. Tonight he would be the satyr, and she his captive.

When he opened the door Yves saw in her expression a hitherto unknown gravity. Dressed in a dull skirt and a threadbare jacket, she sat on the arm of the chair and declined the drink Yves offered her.

"I'm late."

He raised his eyebrows.

"With my period."

"I see, but what does that have to do with me?"

She didn't answer at once.

"We've only ever had safe sex."

"Except once."

He looked at her, surprised.

"On the first of May. Remember, you said, *Do you work when it's a public holiday celebrating laboring men and women?*"

"I don't recall."

"You should, though, it was the night of the *pussy shots.*"

How could he forget their binge? With the right glass and a few contortions, he'd perfected a very particular way of knocking back shots of vodka from between Céline's thighs.

"You were so drunk that you put the condom on any old way, and when I woke up it slid out from between my legs."

Suddenly drained of all strength, Yves clutched at blurred images—him on his knees with Céline's open sex streaming with alcohol, then the two of them bumping into the furniture on their way to the bed, then nothing, total blackout.

"I'm still only just late," she said, seeing how defeated he looked.

"Have you done the test?"

"I was waiting to talk to you about it before going to the pharmacy."

"I wasn't referring to that test."

Quicker than any other feeling, than any logic or caution: fear. The abyss opening at the feet of a terrified man. All of a sudden, Céline was no longer a wicked partner arousing his senses. She had not even had time to revert to being a woman like any other, possibly expecting a happy event. She was nothing but a whore who serviced countless men after they'd been sticking their dick god knows where. The poisoned mistress. High risk in person. But what good would it do to look for the culprit, when for months he was the one who'd been playing with fire, the fire all those women had lit in him. How many hundreds of times had he escaped death? Would his punishment not come sooner or later, practically heralded, ineluctable? Yves abruptly left the present day to enter the world of nightmares. His living room stank of death. Céline's voice a bitter rattle. His whisky tasted of gall. Before the floor fell away beneath his feet he tried in vain to cling to some scientific hope. *Maybe you haven't been contaminated. People don't die of it anymore. How many weeks since the first of May?*

How luminous life had seemed, only two minutes earlier.

"I haven't passed on any diseases, if that's what you're afraid of. I have regular checkups, the last one only ten days ago and we haven't seen each other since."

He could not help but give a silly smile, reassured by Céline's sudden indignation. The relief he felt made his ordinary little misfortunes seem relative. How could he forget so often that he was happy, privileged, and still young? The future could start all over.

"I know it's absurd, but I don't want to be alone when I read the result of the pregnancy test."

What was she talking about, already? Oh, yes, about life. Yves had just stared death in the face and there she was talking to him about some hypothetical life to come. And her tone, so ridiculous, so solemn! So much drama in her pathetic *I'm late.* Yves had to keep from saying, *Those are the risks of the job*, merely replying, "Aren't you on the pill?"

"I use a condom one hundred percent of the time. The risk was infinitesimal."

"So what do you plan to do?"

"Take the test, first, and then . . . "

"And then what?"

"And then I'll see."

"What will you see, shit, make yourself clear."

"It might be the opportunity I've been waiting for for so long."

"Are you telling me you won't necessarily have an abortion?"

"A kid might be the answer."

"The answer to what, for Christ's sake?"

Yves was treated to a tirade with one convoluted, contradictory argument leading to another. While she never said outright that she wanted a child, Céline was wondering whether this would not be her chance to *stop being a whore* and *change her life.* The prospect of bringing a little creature into the world and raising it had not been taken into account; only her own revolution mattered, her new projects. Before the birth she would have time to take the plunge, to do what only yesterday she had dreaded, to set up a ceramics studio with an associate, get back in touch with former contacts, work with clay again, invent new shapes, design a range, her own line. At the end of her exalted, long-winded speech, the issue was no longer a test, or the responsibilities of pregnancy, but the design she would use to conquer the world. Yves understood the extent to which this late arrival of her period was a pretext, how Céline was suffering from having made such a mistake with her career—what was she thinking, to sell her body when all she wanted was to make teacups?—but was that any reason, when he'd only narrowly escaped certain death, to get him involved in a destiny that was not his own?

"Just tell me how much you want me to be involved, in case you insist on keeping it."

"If I'd gotten pregnant because of any other man's doings, I'd get rid of it, for sure. You are the only one of my clients I respect, because you're the only one who listens to me and encourages me. It's no coincidence that we get along so well in bed. I want to be able to tell my kid that his dad is a nice guy. I'm not asking you to recognize him or take care of him. I want you to know that if this child exists, every time he says the word 'daddy' he'll be talking about you. If the child exists you will know that someone, somewhere has your genes. That he'll be sure to ask for you. That he'll be waiting for you."

"What do you mean by *going away*?"

"I'm out of here. Isn't that what you wanted more than anything?"

"Why leave, now that . . . "

Denis hesitated, for fear of giving his whole self away in one sentence. Of opening a door too wide, too quickly, when it was still only ajar. But because he wanted to avoid a declaration at all cost, he yielded to the irony they were comfortably sharing after several weeks of querulously close company.

"Now that you've left the sofa for my bed."

"I have other ambitions in life, Denis Benitez."

"What is stopping you being ambitious by my side? I'm not the kind of guy who's afraid his woman might cast a shadow over him."

"Would you have the heart to deprive me of all the adventures waiting for me all around the world?"

"And wouldn't a life together be an adventure?"

It was her turn to hesitate, and she gave him a look that said she preferred to refrain from a long confession—painful, no doubt, but with a wealth of wisdom and lessons. Not to prolong an awkward moment, she kissed Denis's cheek with infinite tenderness. In that moment he understood that Marie-Jeanne Pereyres was about to leave his life the way she had entered it, without a word of explanation, and when *she* decided to.

Mia awoke in the middle of the night from a too-brief sleep. She looked for Philippe in the bed, and then in the rest of the villa, and finally found him under the canopy where he spent all his time. The night before, he had decreed that this space that served no particular purpose would henceforth be a sort of study for thinking, a means of extricating himself from spatiotemporality in order to regain his mental privacy at last. He had settled there with his notebook and a jug of water, and was reinventing himself as a modern Diogenes. Mia was not allowed within the confines of his space. Philippe liked signaling to her in this way that while the entire island might belong to her, these forty square feet would remain out of bounds.

She found him asleep, woke him with a kiss, and led him back to bed, eager to efface their resentment and give their dying idyll one last chance. The method had already proven effective in the past. But this need of theirs to embrace in order to banish their bitterness quickly faded in favor of a dreary routine. Philippe lingered over foreplay, which gave him time to feel comfortable with her again, but he made Mia ill at ease with his excessive tenderness. She knew when to arch her back in an obscene position that Philippe could not possibly resist, as she offered up her entire intimate self to his gaze in a single curve. He in turn brandished his sex in Mia's face; she grabbed it to make it stiffen even more. Then he came inside her, moving in and out, regularly, unvaryingly, depriving Mia of any divine slowness or firm acceleration. She eventually disrupted the rhythm by abruptly turning around, which left Philippe less range. She sat astride him, rode him with a fervor he did not share but which did have the advantage—the only one—of restraining his excitement. Just then he recalled the way Juliette, when adopting the same position, would press her knees against her chest, forming a block of flesh that rested entirely upon her lover's erect member—this gave Philippe the irresistible sensation of being a pivot for another body. Mia preferred to express herself through speech but, oddly enough, in English, which gave Philippe the awkward impression he had been replaced, in turn, by an imaginary partner—

an Irish bass player, an American actor, or even worse. Sooner or later he ejaculated and, as was the case each time, the word "reductive" went through his mind, like some Pavlovian reflex. And it had been like this ever since that memorable evening when Mia, surprised that Philippe had ejaculated inside her and not on her, had said, "Ronnie, my ex, always withdrew before and splattered my belly."

So what, said Philippe's expression.

"He said that ejaculating inside a girl was *reductive*. That was the term he used."

"Reductive?"

"He wasn't the only one. Corrado, the one before Ronnie, used to do it, too. But you're fairly old school in that respect."

"Did you all learn how to fuck in front of the Saturday night porn flick?"

Philippe could quite easily conceive what might be *reductive* about the philosophical message of a Schopenhauer or a Heidegger, but what on earth could an English pop music bass player mean by the same word when referring to his orgasm? Philippe had been in for other surprises too as the months went by, which caused him to question many of his certainties regarding his sexual practices, and left him feeling moralistic at times and completely square at others. The day Mia declared she had no objection to sodomy he had almost been disappointed. What for him might be a gift of supreme intimacy was for Mia nothing more than a jolly variation on everyday coitus.

Instead of bringing them closer, this return to the alcove merely widened the gap between them. They would not get any more sleep than on the previous nights.

"I thought I was open-minded enough to respect your values, but I just can't. You are young, you are beautiful, you are living a dream life, but you represent a certain concept of decadence that I've been trying to describe in my work. I cannot contradict myself to such a degree. I thought I'd be able to disregard your lifestyle, your friends, I thought I could be patient and help you to avoid a few pitfalls, but I haven't got the strength anymore. I remember that afternoon when we were walking through the Jardin du Luxembourg and you were trembling from the cold, you were hardly wearing a thing. It began to rain so I put my coat over your shoulders—sure, it was a romantic sort of gesture, but the moment seemed to call for it. You pouted and made a face, then you pushed me away and exclaimed, *You don't actually believe I'm going to wear your old overcoat?* I hadn't realized how much your life revolves around what other people think. You live off their regard, and because of it and for it, and you would die without it."

It was no longer a time for confrontation but for cold realization, so Mia let him finish without protesting, without even feeling hurt. Now that she was relieved of the tension that had been building for several days, she waited for her turn to voice her conclusions.

"You don't live among your contemporaries any more than I do, and you have no idea who your *man in the street* is, the one you refer to so often. You bend reality so that it fits your ideas and not the other way around, and that's your brand of secondary rationalization. You're in love with your own reasoning, and what you call real has no reality whatsoever. You're part psychologist, part philosopher, part sociologist, and the role you like best of all is that of prophet, because you dream of predicting a global catastrophe and then watching it come. You'd die along with everyone else but at least you'd take with you the satisfaction of having foreseen what was invisible to the rest of us."

They sat in silence for a long time, relieved it had taken only a few words to sum up everything that had been brewing over the last few days.

"Only people who truly love one another can ordain when

they want the outside world to cease to exist," he added. "We can't."

"You're right, we can't."

Two planets located light years from each other had met, and according to astral logic, the instant of their meeting should end in an eclipse. In the very near future, one of them would cause the other's light to vanish.

A new silence, no doubt their last, left them motionless, their expressions lost in the darkness.

But beneath that silence was the rumbling of an incipient tumult, heavy with telluric forces, rousing fauna and flora, a rumbling that human beings could not yet detect. Mia and Philippe thought they were hearing the final murmurs of their lost idyll. They were both mistaken. The threat was very real indeed.

Yves had insisted Sylvie postpone an appointment with another client to spend the afternoon with him. He dreaded some sort of unpleasant disruption but nothing came to disturb their delightful encounter, a ritual they had perfected over the months, and which obtained the desired results. After they made love, Sylvie wrapped her hips in a beige silk shawl, like a loincloth, which emphasized her swaying curves as she walked by. She wandered around the apartment looking to see what had changed, then came back and lay down in a pose worthy of one of Maillol's models and held her hand out toward a plate of plump pears, which she then savored, allowing the juice to pearl at the corner of her lips. Typically, she interrupted their long silences to say something out of the blue: *What a pity you can't find any of those winter pears after April.* Or: *I really wish I liked reading.* But that Saturday, once she had assumed her odalisque pose, Sylvie asked, "Would you still fancy me if I were thin?"

Yves joined her on the bed to knead her body and reassure

her of her beauty. Then he stretched out next to her and closed his eyes, nestling peacefully against her curves. She roused him from his reverie by grabbing hold of his cock, wanking him with great delicacy, and starting up a conversation to see how long he would be able to stay with her.

"What will you do when you run out of money to pay for girls?"

" . . . I don't know. That day is drawing near . . . "

"It won't take you long to find yourself a wife."

"I've become . . . become . . . hard . . . to please."

"You'd be the perfect little hubby!"

Sylvie did not know that her client had come very near to fulfilling that destiny. Yves almost muttered a few words about his former life, but it was too late by then to mutter anything.

"You'd treat her well, you'd surprise her all the time, and I'm sure you'd never cheat on her."

"I . . . I . . . uh . . . "

As the desired effect of her hand movement was imminent, she stopped; he tore the wrapper off a condom with his teeth, then penetrated her urgently, which caused her to burst out laughing.

At the end of the afternoon, fresh and dressed again from head to toe, she left the apartment, saying, "If one day you find your sweetheart, try to stay in touch all the same. We'll go to tearooms together."

He went back to bed and buried himself in the sheets to prolong the languor for a moment. That evening he would go have dinner at Denis's brasserie, the guy had invited him so often. Between Agnieszka's tears and Céline's ramblings, Yves had not attended the previous Thursday session, and the ludicrous idea that he might have missed out on a testimony of major significance did cross his mind. He owed it to himself to respect his commitment to the Thursday meeting for as long as his journey through the land of streetwalkers lasted. On that day in the future that Sylvie had just mentioned, he would once again be a man like any other, but he'd be reconciled with himself, enriched by everything these women had brought to him.

He slung his leather jacket over his shoulders, and with his helmet in his hand he left his apartment, then went through the glass door into the hall, failing to notice a figure seated on the three steps leading down into the garage.

Suddenly he felt someone grab him by the collar, pull him backwards and fling him to the ground.

The aggressor knelt with all his weight on Yves's torso, taking his breath away. With a violent burst of threats and insults he hammered his face until the blood was spurting from his mouth.

Then he stood up, spat on Yves, kicked him one last time in the ribs and, before leaving the premises, forbade him ever to see his wife again.

They were sleeping in the same bed, sharing their sustenance, communing in good faith. And yet nothing enabled Denis to penetrate the eternal mystery of an intruder who was determined to remain an intruder, nor that of her imminent departure. Tired of resisting, he had to resume his exhausting labors of speculation, now tinged with fear: Marie-Jeanne was no angel from heaven, but most certainly the exact opposite: a succubus assigned to the forces of evil.

Denis had been tempted to believe there was a magnanimous God who would reward his creatures after he'd subjected them to a trial. If someone like Marie-Jeanne Pereyres had been sent to him, then no doubt it was so that she would be taken from him again, sooner or later.

And only the devil in person was known to give human beings the very thing they were most in need of, only to confiscate it so that they could buy their souls for next to nothing.

Yves spent the evening in the emergency room, knocked out by powerful analgesics. As soon as she got his message Sylvie came to see him, her face swollen with shame and sadness.

"Some little fucker went berserk and told me not to see you anymore."

"It was a mistake."

"You mean I got my face smashed in by mistake?"

"He thought you were Grégoire."

" . . . Who thought I was who?"

"The one who hit you was my guy. He may be a filthy bastard, a miserable wretch, a tool, and the cause of all my woe, but he's mine."

Yves just looked at her.

"He went through my diary and saw, *2:00 P.M. Grégoire, his place.* But in the meantime you called and I postponed my appointment. The bastard followed me to your place thinking it was Grégoire's."

Yves was then treated to the detailed account of a modern tragedy which, although it had its charge of intensity, was far less tangible than the pain in his ribs that made it impossible to breathe.

"Grégoire is my dietician client who's ashamed he fell madly in love with the only woman who isn't begging him to show her how to lose weight. My Greg goes crazy at the thought I'm seeing other clients. He wants me all to himself, but up until now he's always been afraid everyone will laugh at him."

Yves hesitated to let her go on; he refused to get caught, even fortuitously, between a small-time pimp and a guy who was building a global business on the back of a medical practice. Yves's only crime in the story had been to buy an assortment of frosted cream puffs to keep Sylvie happy.

"And just lately Grégoire made a decision . . . "

To live his love for her out in the open, in spite of his fear of being seen arm-in-arm with a living counter-publicity. Even if it meant he'd become the prey of living room psychoanalysts.

"A sort of coming out, basically. Display in public his penchant for voluptuous women. *I'm sleeping with a Rubens and you can just lump it.*"

Dazed with pain, Yves tried to feel sorry for the man's inner turmoil. While the pimp might be a real piece of shit, he nevertheless belonged to a well-known prototype and, in spite of his boundless scorn, Yves could easily imagine the guy's pathetic thought process. Grégoire, on the other hand, who dreaded being seen with a woman not because she was a prostitute but because she was fat, seemed to be the exemplar of a decadent era where it was not morality that decreed what was taboo or forbidden, but the imperatives of profit and the universal fear of media derision.

"And my pimp found out. He's such a coward but he wanted to play tough guy. And it landed on you."

Yves closed his eyes for a moment, just long enough to wonder what perverse God was hounding him like this. He had a sudden urge to scream and only just stopped himself, then felt tears of fatigue welling up. At around one o'clock in the morning they let him leave, with bandages on his face and a strap around his thorax. Sylvie had waited until the last minute to beg him not to file a complaint.

"He's terrified that he might get called in. He's been carrying this little suspended sentence, and if they send him down they'll give him a harder time than anyone, his nerves won't take it. What would become of him without me? He's too dumb. I'll do whatever you like, I'll come as soon as you call. I'll obey."

Yves went home in a cab, then with one hand on his ribs he walked painfully across the hall of his building, like the little old man he would be someday. He lay down but could not sleep, hindered by the pain that was just waiting to flare up, and by the memory of the attack, which would haunt him for several days to come. To dodge these thoughts he dreamt about that other Lehaleur, the one he might have become if, once upon a time, his betrothed had not cheated on him. For the very first time he wondered if he wouldn't have been better off had he stayed on that clearly marked path. How far along would he be by now, with his beautiful future?

In all likelihood, he'd be in that house in the suburbs, sitting outside on this summer night.

The baby, upstairs, would be sound asleep, and he and Pauline would be enjoying peace and quiet at last, after a day or errands, housework, and diapers.

They'd treat themselves to a little after dinner drink and discuss their next vacation.

Then they would go to bed, and maybe caress each other.

When they woke up it would be Sunday.

Back in his bed, after projecting himself into a future he would never know, Yves felt his physical pain taking on an entirely new meaning. It reminded him of yet another, purely psychological, pain that was just as violent and unfair, the one Pauline had inflicted upon him. And that pain had not been overcome in vain: it had made him stronger, and put him back on the right path. The pain that was shooting through him at present would take far less time to heal, and it was already delivering its message: every time a body or a soul felt pain, it marked the end of one cycle and the beginning of a new one.

Night drawing to a close, the suffocating heat mingling with the fever of bad dreams. The faraway rumbling seemed to signal the end of a dark voyage in limbo; in fact it was merely the very real echo of a nightmare still to come. The congested bowels of the earth had split open to eject their surplus into the ocean. Woken by the hoarse cries of a cloud of birds, Philippe glimpsed a murky, dirty sky, deserted by the sun. He got to his knees, lifted his hands to his temples to try and banish hideous visions, then looked up: a gray wall was rolling toward him, obstructing the horizon, crashing against the hill. Below him the beach was receding in a black ebb of sheet metal and hemp, bamboo and plastic, then was quickly covered again by another enormous wave. Mia groaned, her eyelids shut tight, refusing to confront the threat her body could already perceive, but she went to stand beside Philippe who was watching, unbelieving, as the island was destroyed. Another groundswell, more monstrous still, snapped the palm trees. Yielding to panic, Mia scrambled down the path toward the shore. Momentarily stunned by her absurd reflex, Philippe rushed after her. A wave rolled over the roof of the hotel and almost dragged Mia away in its wake. Philippe grabbed her arm, hoisted her forcefully before the following wave tore away the teak steps, leaving behind a shapeless muddy slope littered with upended deck chairs. When they reached the top of the hill they stood huddled together for an instant.

Below them the hotel had disappeared, the surging breakers seemed to want to swallow the entire earth. Mia refused point blank to believe what she was going through: no one abandoned Mia, this was unacceptable! Where had all the *people* gone? And the emergency services? When she sensed that Philippe was incapable of reassuring her, she pushed him away in a rage and rushed to her cell phone, forgotten on the corner of the bed. Beside himself with this new display of absurdity, Philippe went back out onto the terrace, where a wave crashed at his feet with incredible violence. Mia was desperately fiddling with her cell phone, the object that answered all her desires, all her concerns, all her questions; it was her only true connection to the world, to her family, to her agency; it provided her with the most intimate sensations and dispelled her secret fears. Always within reach, it also guaranteed her independence, her freedom: it would not let her down, not now. Philippe could hear her screaming again, helplessly this time, and he grabbed the phone from her, then slapped her to shock her out of her panic. *We are safe here!* he shouted, over the crashing of a giant roller. He held her close, and without really believing his own words, described the natural phenomenon that had been unleashed upon them, its violence only equaled by its brevity. Sleeping on top of the hill had been their misfortune, but from now on it would be their only chance of survival: at dawn, not long after the first earth tremor, the unusually strong waves had alarmed the guests and staff of the hotel, and they had all fled before the coast was devastated—two or three minutes had been enough to reach the beach, go around the hill, and take refuge inland. They were surely calling at that very moment to send rescue to those who were missing. Tempted by hopefulness, she held back her tears, but a wave that was higher than the hill crashed against the guardrail around the villa, smashing it to bits, ruining Philippe's fine words of hope at the same time. When he saw the water rushing in toward their bed, Philippe fell silent for good. What did he know, anyway, about natural phenomena and disasters? He had a few archival images in his mind, he vaguely remembered the testimony of a survivor, he had heard scientists on the news explaining the causes of earthquakes, cataclysms, typhoons, and cyclones, with supporting graphics, but he remembered nothing beyond the spectacle of absolute desolation, the hand of fate, planet Earth gleefully reminding man that she was all-powerful.

Mia fell to the ground, rolled up into a ball, whimpered long and loud like a battered child that refuses to accept she has been abandoned. She deserved better treatment than the ordinary tourist, and no one had the right to leave her to her own resources: she was the divine Mia, her effigy reproduced more often than any saint's. Mia, who was welcome among royalty, a goddess on three continents. Her whims were commands, her reproaches were death sentences. She was the center of attention, pampered like a toddler, protected to the extreme. She knew that wherever she went, someone was waiting for her; her time was worth a fortune; she took a helicopter the way others take the bus. Such cruel irony, all those helicopters she had chartered to go shopping or to show her face at a party in Monaco: not a single one would come now to save her life.

Philippe, too, was prey to the cruelest of ironies: for what obscene reason was he about to die in such a place? One week earlier, when he had first discovered the beach of Nusa Dua, he had entertained himself with a list of idealized images of the desert island: the indispensable palm trees rising above the fine sand, the turquoise waters, the lovers cast away, far from civilization, for eternity. The cliché returned now like a slap in the face, with the violence of a breaker; their villa alone was their desert island, and he and Mia were the forgotten castaways. Here was a man who never left his tiny study for fear of losing his train of thought, and now he would die from drowning in this caricature of an Eden, and because of Mia's fame the entire world would know about it. This was not at all how he had planned to bow out, it was not a death worthy of a philosopher, it was the death of a rich man, one who has always thought he was beyond reach, who's gone soft in his cocoon of luxury, macerating in his swimming pool. The news of his disappearance would make the headlines, in a garish, malevolent press, and he would go down in history as the man who had perished on the arm of a famous supermodel. An entire life devoted to research, note-taking, reading, writing, concepts, symposiums, and the courses he'd taken and given—and all that would remain, erasing the entire bulk of his work, would be a sensational gossip column item. So often, all through his life as a thinker, he had wondered what humanity would retain of his work: even if they went out of print and were never reprinted, his books would stay on library shelves for a long time, ready to recreate their author's ideas. But would his books suffice to preserve his place in the history of philosophy? What would these hundreds of pages represent, compared to a single concept throwing new light on the essential questions of the human condition? Had he ever had a single true idea, since he began peddling them? He still needed a few more years for his research—four, five, less than ten in any case—if he were to deliver his message in its most limpid form. He wouldn't have asked for more, he would even have agreed to be shown the door on condition that he could leave feeling that he had fulfilled his task. If he were to die here and now, what would they write in his entry in the major dictionary of universal thinkers? *Philippe Grosjean (aka Saint-Jean), French sociologist, author of an essay on the collective unconscious,* The Mirror-Memory. Now they would have to add: *Vanished in tidal wave in Southeast Asia.* The thought of it seemed worse than death itself.

The ebb had lost none of its magnitude. The waves seemed to be blocking out the sky. Mia lay on the ground, unmoving, and began to envisage the impossible: a world without Mia.

Waiting for the extreme wave to swallow her at last, she wondered if she ought to resist the strength of the current or, rather, let herself be borne away to a shore that might, miraculously, have been spared.

Then she wondered how to lessen the pain of drowning.

Philippe would not let go of his anger: he had not fought against the absurdity of things just to have it all end like this.

Stronger than fear, his indignation gave him the courage to confront the onslaught of the ocean. He grabbed Mia by the shoulder, dragged her to the wooden frame of the canopy where he had learned to isolate himself from the world, and forced her to climb up on top of it to gain eight or ten feet in height: the highest point on the hill. It was here, in this final refuge, that death would come for them, if it must.

At that very instant, the face of the only woman he had ever loved appeared before him, as the finest reason not to vanish on the far side of the globe.

9

On that September morning, a fine mist veiled a brief return of summer, and already the light heralded the chilly rhythms of winter, the short days, the silence. People returned quietly to work, to school, in a long series of little sacrifices that some would call autumn. To any gentle meandering, a citydweller would now prefer the quickest route; he would no longer hesitate over which way to go, or whether to take a sweater; he would be surprised to see tourists, still, lingering at crossroads to marvel over nothing.

Early one morning, Yves Lehaleur was riding his scooter at the speed limit along a deserted freeway. He was sensitive to the autumnal atmosphere; he too felt he was in a moment of *after*. The time had come to put an end to that strange phase of his life that he had lived through like some long summer, troubled by unexpected encounters and the frenzy of sleepless nights. In less than a year, he had had enough extravagant experiences for an entire lifetime, far beyond the scope of any ordinary window installer. As he no longer had the means or the inclination to continue his experiences, they must now take their proper place in his memory. He would create a mosaic of the moments when he'd seen how he could go to any extreme, a vast fresco that would always remind him—now that he'd taken all those women into his bed, and listened to the tales of all those men—of how he had come to love the human comedy. He had worked it out: a single day, planned down to the hour, would suffice to put an end to the last convulsions of his debauched life, before it was time to invent the future of the new Yves Lehaleur.

He left the freeway at Palaiseau, and sooner than he'd expected he found the dry cleaner's by the station with its orange sign, a relic of the 1970s. Through the tinted window he saw a woman in her sixties, wearing a dreary overall and waving a pole to reach the highest racks. He waited for the shop to empty, then went in and asked to see Annie—the real name of the villainous Maud, whose only known address, so hard to track down, was this shop in the outskirts of Paris.

"Who's asking for her?"

"Yves. I'm a friend."

How else could he introduce himself to a mother, whom Annie no doubt continued to call *Maman*?

"She's still asleep. Do you mind waiting for a while? I hesitate to wake her up, she came in late."

Madame Lemercier called to her husband, a little man bent over an ironing board, to introduce him to *a friend of Nanou's*, and she asked him to keep an eye on things while she went to make some coffee. Yves found himself stuck with a cup in his hand between a Formica table and laundry driers spinning at full capacity; an aroma of Arabica mingled with the warm smell of steam.

"Annie has so many friends but I don't know any of them."

For a moment Yves was afraid that this tranquil, tired lady might, by friends, mean precisely the very men who were hardly likely to be found in her daughter's company.

"With her job," she continued, "it must be so hard to choose."

He was equally fearful of what might be implied by the word *job*. She launched into a long summary of her lovely Nanou's activities, which were fascinating, but complicated. She still did not altogether understand what that job consisted of, nor its purpose, but it had thrust her daughter into a whirlwind of responsibilities. To be in touch with so many individuals, from many different milieus; to have to remember all those names, and keep track of their contact information, and recognize every single face. It was not surprising that she came home so late, exhausted. But despite everything, that is what she was cut out to do. A gift. Already as a little girl. She was the one who organized the parties, the soirées, the year-end festivities. And she'd kept on with it, but now she was employed by big companies and big bosses, to look after their public image. After a childhood spent in their modest shop, you had to wonder where she had learned so much class, so much know-how.

Public relations? Why not, after all. Literally, that's how you could sum up Maud's career. Yves was curious to hear about the various stages that had driven a girl called Nanou, a lively, joyful child, lacking nothing, born to devoted parents, to prostitute herself by creating Maud. From the little her mother had told him, he could imagine this Nanou, first prize in the friendship category, a socialite before the term was even invented, more attentive to her social calendar than to her school notebooks, aware that she was pretty, and popular, but bitterly ashamed to see other families' dirty laundry being washed by her own.

"I've become a specialist in cleaning cocktail dresses and Chanel suits. Sometimes I like to tell myself that if she always looks so impeccable, it's partly due to me."

Yves had to acknowledge his guilt for having crumpled not a few of those dresses himself, thus causing good Madame Lemercier to work overtime. Obviously she had to take care of numerous other household tasks, but looking after her little girl was, despite her age, a sweet obligation. And anyway, Annie paid her share, in her way; she may have had to spend recklessly at Hermès or Balenciaga—the job called for it—but she had plenty left over to give her parents presents.

"Sometimes she helps out in the shop."

Twenty years later, Maud and Nanou were sharing the same roof. After renting out her sex until late at night, Maud went back to the Pressing de la Gare in Palaiseau and straight to sleep, exhausted by her double life. Nanou woke up late, rested after the previous night's indiscretions, ready to reinvent the previous evening for her two greatest admirers. They were partial to names and details, and Nanou knew how to give them plenty. Their beloved daughter was on a first-name basis with television celebrities, and some of them invited her to their luxury hotel suites. Papa and Maman often wondered why, for all her Parisian high life, she had not met Mr. Right—they wanted so badly to have grandchildren. She was beginning to behave like an old maid averse to leaving her cocoon.

Yves understood by this that neither Nanou nor even Maud, despite her hundreds of lovers, had ever fallen in love.

Madame Lemercier sensed a faint trembling that would be inaudible to anyone else. *She* was about to appear. Yves saw Nanou coming down the stairs, her features still puffy with sleep, brown circles under her eyes, a smudge of mascara in the corner of her eyelid, her hair disheveled. Wearing a flannelette nightie so threadbare it was practically transparent, her feet in white mules she'd brought back from a luxury hotel, she closed her eyes with a final yawn. She opened them again on Yves Lehaleur and suddenly let go of the banister.

"Hello, Annie."

She was speechless.

He could have just left them there without even saying another word. Just savoring Maud's considerable discomfiture was revenge enough for Yves: she was ashamed to have been found out as Nanou, straight out of bed on top of it.

How many years of hiding had led to this moment, how many years of living life against the grain, patching makeup in nocturnal taxis, finding runs in her seamed stockings, stopping off at pharmacies after hours, so many sordid moments to overcome? She had managed so carefully to keep her dark secret from her parents, from the other neighborhood shop-keepers, and from her childhood girlfriends who still lived nearby. Now Yves had her at his mercy, in the palm of his hand; all he had to do was squeeze, and twenty years of depravity beyond suspicion would be reduced to nothing. He prolonged as best he could that spark of terror in her eyes, Maud the full-time whore and small-time thief.

And yet he had called her Annie. Maud would be able to negotiate.

Yves kissed her on both cheeks. *I was just passing through.* The mother served her daughter coffee in a cracked bowl with a yellow edge which probably dated back to childhood hot chocolates. Maud sought a reprieve during her short bitter sips, and managed to simulate the joy of seeing a friend again. *I'm glad you stopped by.* Yves did not seem to want to destroy anyone's life, but no doubt he was going to ask her to pay the price of her felony. And she would pay, no matter the price. To fill the silence, Madame Lemercier told a story about little Nanou, one of those stories that overwhelm a mother with nostalgia and a child with shame. Annie threw her a look that seemed to say, *Don't bother, Maman, he's not some chosen one I've been hiding from you, there is no chosen one.*

After she had quickly pulled on her jeans, a sweater, and a pair of espadrilles, Annie walked with Yves back to his scooter.

"Tell me what you want."

"I got what I wanted."

"To humiliate me?"

"Of all the superb whores I've met, you are the one whose other life I have most wanted to know about."

"Are you disappointed?"

"No, not at all. I'm glad to have met Nanou. Commonplace, to be sure, but so much more believable than Maud."

"We all play a part."

"And of all the whores I've known, you are the worst actress. You lie to your parents, you lie to your clients, but the one you're lying to the most is your own self. You dress up like a seductress, as if you'd been dreaming of some fairy costume. But you ought to know that the only mistress in you that anyone could enjoy is the schoolmistress. You think you can turn men's heads, but all you have are clients like me who like to get your satin bolero jackets dirty."

She did not answer.

"Make your peace with Nanou. Everything will go better after that. You'll avoid any more rough spots."

Yves put on his helmet, to ward off kisses as much as blows. He kick-started the scooter right away. Into the pocket of his jacket she slid Grandfather Horace's flask. He looked into her eyes to say goodbye then pulled out into the street, rode around the town for a short while, and found the road back to Paris. Time to deal with the next one.

At eleven o'clock, Denis was finishing up setting the tables for lunch when his boss stuck his head outside to decide whether to use the terrace or not. In early autumn it was still debatable. A faint ray of sunshine was threatening to break through the gray veil of mist. They set up a few tables on the sidewalk.

Most of the brigade congregated on the terrace to share either the beef with carrots or the salmon cooked on salt, which was the *plat du jour*. Denis was more talkative than usual, displaying a systematic, biting irony. As was usual before the noontime rush, he had drunk only water, and yet his joyful misanthropy seemed to stem from a sudden drunkenness. Nothing was spared: the chef's new menu, the bartender's stress, the boss's anal behavior, but above all the diners' moods, and by diners you were meant to infer all of humanity, that drearily predictable mob, that catalog of noxious creatures. Denis drew up a long list of daily oddities, ludicrous whims, bottomless pettiness. Don't even try to settle the score with people who are cantankerous or authoritarian, vulgar or bad-mannered; you can tell who they are the moment they sit down. Denis's condemnation was aimed, rather, at the devious types, whose courtesy was more strategic than sincere. Polite people were often hiding their condescension toward servants. The friendly ones betrayed how uncomfortable they were with class differences. If they were generous, they expected to be treated like royalty. In sum, any individual who went into a place in order to have food served to him was suspect. All the waiters could recall certain regular customers or typical phrases, and they added their personal touches to Denis's eloquent exposé. Yet Denis was not fooled by his own disingenuousness; as a good professional waiter working at a brasserie, he was no longer offended by the everyday lack of elegance. That morning, Denis Benitez's bitter loquaciousness, enough to make him despair of his peers, was aimed straight at Marie-Jeanne Pereyres.

Weary of blaming her for her stubborn refusal to share any of her plans, all that was left was to take it out on other people, on everyone he could.

Yves drove past the Montparnasse cemetery along the Boulevard Edgar-Quinet, and stopped his scooter outside a café where Jacek Kowalczyk was waiting for him. Ever since they had met on the construction site of a private villa in Saint-Cloud, Yves had been giving out Jacek's contact information to those in need of a good electrician; Jacek never failed to thank him, but the opportunities to do it in person were rare. Yves was relieved to see him there, sitting at a table, but surprised to see he was not alone. Jacek introduced a little blonde woman with curly shoulder-length hair, chubby cheeks, and a worried smile on her lips.

"This is my wife, Ewa."

Yves complimented Madame Kowalczyk, then shot a dark look at his colleague.

"I told you it was about a delicate matter."

"Exactly! I brought her along to help. Especially with this sort of business . . . "

Jacek's blunder was compounded by his wife's accusing expression: to be requisitioned for some sex scandal! Bound to be some crooked business, the way it always was. At opposite extremes from her concerns as a wife and mother and worker. Yves felt he was being judged by the woman's gaze, and as the conversation progressed he began to feel more and more uncomfortable, and it only got worse when Agnieszka walked through the door. Since their last meeting, the marks on her face from the attack had vanished, but an invisible veil had tarnished the bloom of her features, and the spark of naïveté in her eyes had disappeared. Yves, in French, invited her to sit down, then handed it over to Jacek.

"Explain to her that for once I'm going to need a translator. Two, as it happens."

Yves heard from Jacek's intonation that he was trying to be diplomatic, then saw the relief in Agnieszka's eyes, their shared delight at becoming acquainted in their native tongue. In Ewa's eyes he read a mixture of curiosity and reserve regarding a woman who had chosen prostitution to earn her living. Had the girl's obvious beauty had anything to do with it? Had both of them emigrated for the same reasons? Had Agnieszka suffered, as she had, during her childhood? What ties had she maintained with their country? Among their first words, Yves thought he recognized the word Kraków, then a few dates, and it all resembled a ritual between two immigrants from the same country: place of birth, date of arrival in France, profession. The dialogue quickly lapsed into easy chatter, and Yves no longer dared intervene. Ewa had let her guard down, and asked a question that made Agnieszka laugh.

"What are they saying?"

"Nothing," answered Jacek. "Ewa just made a joke, you can't translate."

Yves gave a faint smile to join in the sudden conviviality then, as if giving a discreet call to order, he placed an airplane ticket on the table.

"Round-trip for Warsaw. Tell her the return is open but she doesn't have to use it."

Ewa translated in Jacek's place, so mindful of accuracy that she even imitated Yves's intonation.

"I've added €2,000 to make up for loss of earnings. Tell her to use the trip as a vacation, more than anything. To make the most of it to see her family."

This time, after his wife had translated, Jacek added a detail that his wife immediately questioned, and which gave rise to controversy. Jacek was trying to get Agnieszka's consent about a precise detail but Ewa would not let go, for that particular point required a sense of nuance that was lost on her husband. Yves wondered what he was doing there.

"Can you explain what is going on?"

"It's nothing," said Jacek, "but my wife wants to know how long it takes Agnieszka to earn €2,000."

"What on earth!" exclaimed Ewa. "He doesn't know how to translate 'loss of earnings.'"

Yves began to feel a tug of annoyance; he had hoped, in a way, despite the strangeness of the situation, to keep it solemn. Now he was sorry he'd called on others; never, before now, had he needed anyone to convey even the most subtle argument to Agnieszka.

"Listen, you two. This girl has been having a rough time ever since she got to Paris—she may be brave but she's in constant fear. Of the police, of being attacked, of her family finding out what she does for a living, and worse yet, she's afraid her family might forget all about her. She takes it because she's learned to take it, but sooner or later something pretty awful will happen to her."

After what she'd been through, wasn't it time for Agnieszka, who was still in shock and beset by doubt, to seize this chance to start over? Once she recovered from this attack, nothing—not the next attack, or the one after that, or any of the psychological or physical attacks to come—would stop her from following a destiny that was all mapped out. Now was the time to transform her misfortune into an opportunity, before her delicate skin grew tough as leather and her heart hardened until she no longer felt a thing.

"I get the impression your wife just asked her something, but I didn't ask any questions!"

"Ewa asked Agnieszka if she had many clients who gave her gifts like this."

"And what did she say?"

"That you were the first."

Yves's instinct had been right, his fair lady was homesick, and this joyful impromptu encounter with people *from back there* was ample confirmation of the fact. Ewa, vested with a solemn mission, wanted to be a loyal spokeswoman, but she could not help but exaggerate: she was burning with solidarity, mixing her story up with Agnieszka's in a flood of words she could not contain. Soon the two women forgot their surroundings, an anecdote seemed to lead to a confession, a digression, and a host of childhood memories, for one in Lublin, for the other in Kraków. Yves looked at his watch again and fidgeted with impatience, worried he would not have his say.

"Now what are they saying?"

"Agnieszka has a sister who is studying in Kraków, in a neighborhood not far from where Ewa was born. They have found a place they both know, a little neighborhood bistro where they serve an onion salami. But they are wondering whether they might have met at the Christmas mass at the Polish Catholic Mission on the Rue Saint-Honoré."

Yves was speechless.

Jacek took the opportunity, while the two women were lost in conversation, to lower his voice and ask, "Out of curiosity, how much do you pay for an hour with a girl like her?"

Even if he had wanted to, Yves did not have time to reply. As if she sensed her husband had said something appalling, Ewa rebuked him for never surprising her with a trip—thus, without realizing it, suggesting a much better way for him to spend his money.

"Why don't you send me on vacation? Why not me?"

Yves gave Agnieszka one last look, and slid her ticket across the table to her. She leaned forward to kiss him, for the very first time, on the lips.

Then he left the table. Someone was waiting, clear across Paris.

Denis Benitez did not calm down, far from it; his spite intensified when it came in contact with thirty or more customers all smiling at his sardonic witticisms. Over half of them were women, and Denis did not neglect a single one, whether they were on their own or in pairs, and his preference was for tables of four or five, for that was where things were really difficult: how to make each one feel she was his favorite? With the help of his talent for deciphering, Denis pinned them like butterflies in an endless collection, wings spread wide, caught in full flight.

That one by the bar, *a chic sixtysomething, a former beauty who would give anything for one last ride on the merry-go-round.*

And that one, *the arrogance of the woman who has never loved, she's finally learning to lower her guard, but it's surely too late.*

Or that one, *with her voice of a former smoker, still likes her drink, laugh lines, no regrets.*

And then *that strange little person, nearsighted, curly hair, enormous patience toward life, she'll only ever love one man, not necessarily the right one.*

Oh, if only he could have used this same power over the only woman who was undecipherable in his eyes. Afraid she might get fed up, he had foregone the basic questions—*Who is Marie-Jeanne Pereyres? Where does she come from? What does she want from me?*—to keep only one: *When is she going to leave me?* Every night he was burning to ask her, and every night he merely told her about his day and fell asleep at her side. The next morning, she was still there, a book in her hands, a mug of hot coffee on the night table. They would resume their exploration of each other's body, trying to surprise each other before they returned to the motifs they both were fond of. Then Denis left for work, and the week went by without the slightest variation. On Sundays they might go for some fresh air by a canal, have a drink at a sidewalk café, talk about the past, but never the future, then Denis would suggest they head back so he could get some rest for his accumulated fatigue. The next morning it was back to his frenzied existence, his mind was nimble once again, he spoke to his female customers in a singularly casual manner, delivered his witticisms as if they were lines in a vaudeville comedy, and like a magician he performed the tricks he had learned in his twenty years as a waiter. Through the dozens of women he encountered day after day, it was Marie-Jeanne Pereyres he was seeking to entertain, tease, shock, and seduce. And, above all, to prevent from leaving.

As he was clearing the table before his break, he found a paper napkin next to a cup with the following handwritten message: *The pudding was sweet, and the waiter even more so,* followed by a phone number. Denis crumpled it up instinctively. Then smoothed it out again. Hesitated for a long time. And crumpled it up again.

Whenever Yves Lehaleur happened to enter the paved courtyard of a very old building, he liked to picture the way it was in bygone eras—the clothes people wore, and all the life that had been lived there and which gave the place its charm. In this quiet quartier of the Porte Dorée, in southwest Paris, an old stable from the 1700s had been home for over a century to various craftsmen who, when it came time to retire, transferred their lease to younger colleagues, who were ambitious, care-free, and ready to forge ahead with their careers while respect-ing tradition. The rectangular courtyard, where a gigantic cedar tree spread its branches over an uneven paving, gave onto the workshops of an upholsterer, a varnisher, a cabinet-maker, and a framer. Between the smell of varnish and the crackling of a transistor radio, Yves wandered aimlessly past the doors and glassed-in workshops looking for the space that had been recently vacated.

"You're one of the very first to see it," said a neighbor who had the keys. "It used to be a print shop, with a lithography press."

Yves entered a large empty room with peeling plastered walls and a Godin woodstove right in the middle of the room, old-fashioned but still functioning, and its odor of burning wood could not hide the lingering, persistent smell of ink. Once he was alone, he imagined once again the many artists who had visited this place over time, moved to see their work reborn in the lithographer's expert hands. He could feel the walls vibrating to the rolling of the press, heard the clicking of its intricate workings, even pictured the prints as they came fresh and colorful from the bowels of the machine. Céline roused him from his daydreaming with a prosaic, *What the hell are we doing here?*

Yves let her imagine the most extravagant replies, but none would be as extravagant as the real one.

"Don't tell me you wanted me to meet you here so we could fuck. Some fantasy you got into your head. A quickie behind a carriage entrance? Something like that. Because if so, I'm all for it. Let's start right away and then we head home."

"Commercial lease. There's some key money to pay, but then the rent is very affordable."

"What on earth are you talking about?"

"I'll write the check for the key money. You pay me back when you can. That will allow you to invest in supplies."

She went on acting surprised when, in fact, she knew very well what he was getting at, and in such a perverse way. From the moment she entered the room, the space had seemed so familiar, so right. She could already see where to put a six cubic foot kiln, and a potter's wheel, near the water source, opposite the enameling kiln, right near the light fixture. The workbench? Over there, against the wall, and above it she could install a rack to stock her clay and her tools. Near the entrance she could have a shelf display for her products, and it would all fit in five hundred square feet, in this dream of a courtyard.

"I'm not ready. I'll never be ready."

After she'd worked the stoneware, lava, porcelain, or kaolin, she'd design small objects to begin with—cups, bowls, bud vases, and a teapot she had designed years earlier and never produced. She'd go back and forth between simple shapes with sophisticated motifs and sophisticated shapes with simple motifs. Every item would be unique.

"You have to decide by six o'clock tonight."

Then she could get back in touch with her old contacts, she'd do the rounds of the boutiques, visit the pottery markets and crafts fairs, she'd make a name for herself with her range and they would recognize her style, even in the most discreet of her objects.

"Say yes, and I'll go with you to a business start-up center. You give them your information and they take care of the rest, and before the day is done you're no longer a whore, you're a ceramist."

Twenty minutes later, as the scooter wove in and out of the streets of the twelfth arrondissement, Céline, clinging to Yves's torso, her chin on his shoulder, whispered in his ear that she was not pregnant. Even if he had never thought she was, Yves was relieved.

"I'll pay you back, I'll take the time I need. I can even offer you a deal."

"What would that be?"

"You call me whenever you want me. You'll be my last client from my former life."

"Are you joking?"

"It wouldn't be hustling, I'd be paying you back!"

A moment later he dropped her off outside a building, took her in his arms, and promised he'd consider her proposal. Of all the women, Céline was the only one Yves would remember as a *fille de joie*.

When the time came to take the checks around to the last diners, Denis Benitez and his colleagues savored the moment when they could remove their aprons and decompress. That meant either smoking a cigarette out on the terrace, or counting tips, or chatting at the bar while they waited for the most stubborn clients to leave. Denis went behind the bar to make himself the cocktail he'd been craving all through his service. David and Remo, the *chefs de rang*, were perched on barstools wondering what to do with the rest of their evening, when they heard two young women giggling as they finished their white wine.

"Who's on fourteen?"

Denis nodded, then sipped the bitter sweetness of a proper mix of gin and Campari.

"They look cooked, medium rare," said Remo.

"They're looking our way, but who at?" asked David.

Denis didn't join in the conversation, but made himself a second, even stronger drink, to rid himself of the melancholy that had been getting stronger since nightfall. With the help of the alcohol, his obsessions, like his colleagues' voices, began to fade.

"The one in red is hot," said Remo.

"I prefer the other one, with her back to us."

"If she has her back to us, how can you tell?"

"She's classier, you can tell, even from behind. That's what class is all about."

"I figure they're single."

"No, they're having one of those 'girls-only' dinners. They're debriefing."

"Debriefing or catching up?"

"What's the difference?"

"Two chicks who haven't seen each other for a while, they catch up. But if one of them has something important going on in her life, then they debrief."

"Shall we do the digestif on the house thing?"

"They've had enough to drink."

"I figure they're bourgeois. Not the sort who go in for waiters. We're out of luck. What did they order?"

Remo grabbed the check from the saucer that Denis had prepared.

"Two chanterelles, one *carpaccio de Saint-Jacques,* tuna *a la plancha,* two *mi-cuits au chocolat.*"

"Shit, intellectuals."

"Intellectuals, but hot."

"Hot intellectuals, but married to senior executives."

Glass in hand, Denis felt himself entering a peaceful zone; he was no longer waiting or in limbo, and he no longer feared the intruder's logic: if she persisted in remaining undecipherable, that was her tough luck. A sudden impulse drove him to put an end to the absurd conversation he'd been listening to for long enough.

"The one in red is called Myriam, she works as a book-keeper at a TV station. She takes classes in modern dance. She's just left her guy, he's the 'dull heavy type' according to her, and she can't stop telling people she's free, she wants everyone to know. The other is called Charlotte, she lives in Montrouge, she's a PA, she's having an affair with a guy in marketing from her company but she claims she's 'too much of a flirt to be faithful.'"

"Bah, at least now we know who they've been looking at," said Remo.

"Denis! See if they want to go somewhere for a drink. Do it for our sake! The time it'll take us for the introductions you can sneak off."

"Sneak off? Why would I do that?"

Sylvie was not one to wear black to try and hide her curves; she wore bright colors to trumpet them in broad daylight. Most of the time she had a smile on her face, even when things were serious, even at work; this smile disconcerted a number of her clients, who thought she might be making fun of them, which would be unthinkably detached behavior for a whore; her smile helped her to withstand the psychological hardship, to elude the traps of ordinary ugliness, and nothing could wipe it off her face, not even her tears.

"I don't know how to thank you for not filing a complaint. Ask me for whatever you want."

"Anything I want?"

"You can't surprise me."

Yves had invited her to a café on the Place du Châtelet at an hour when theatres were emptying out and bars were filling up. Normally at that time of day, she would be wringing out her last client to the point of exultation, and if need be she would console him in his post-coital sadness, then back she'd go to her pimp. In front of the TV, his dirty plate still lying around, he would ask, all excited, *How'd your day go?* Which she translated as meaning, *How much did you make?* On a good evening, after they'd added it up, he would gratify her with a *Well done, honeybun,* and off he'd go somewhere, who knows where, with the money in his pocket.

"Leave that stupid fuck."

"What?"

"Forget the bastard. If you want to go on being a whore, do it for yourself, not for that asshole."

"You don't understand."

"At a push if you were hooked on a real hood, a public enemy, an honorable bandit, a prison escapee—apparently there are women who go in for that sort of guy—then I wouldn't want to get involved, but that guy of yours is a yellow-bellied punk. His little eyes shine when he watches gangster movies, but he needs to break your arm to feel like a man. And you're not even in love with him anymore, if you ever were. You just feel sorry for him."

Like a man in love, Yves sang Sylvie's praises—told her how she was so much more courageous and generous than that retard who only knew how to flatter her sense of sacrifice. Yves left her no time to argue, but tried to make her dizzy with words, to push her, to force her into the only decision she could make.

"Leave him. Leave him tonight."

"He'll go crazy."

"He's a coward. What do you think he'll do? The only strength he has is the strength you give him."

"I know."

"Don't go home. Go away, far away from Paris. Have you got an address? Someone he doesn't know?"

She didn't answer.

"Think, damn it!"

"My girlfriend Maïté . . . "

"Where?"

"In Biarritz."

Yves consulted his watch, grabbed the telephone. Since he had anticipated this conversation and known what it might lead to, Yves had told Sylvie to meet him in the center of Paris. From there he could reach any train station in less time than it would take to convince her. He took her by the hand, dragged her outside, and with considerable authority placed a helmet on her head.

"Gare d'Austerlitz, we'll just make it."

"What?"

"The last train is at 23:11, you'll be there at 6:53 A.M."

"But . . . I can't just leave like that, with nothing, without letting anyone know!"

"Above all, without letting anyone know."

Unable to run away, she watched as he maneuvered his scooter in the direction of the riverbank. He ordered her to climb on, and she obeyed, paralyzed by this authoritarian manner which was completely new to her. She straddled the scooter as best she could, clinging to the strap and almost losing her balance the moment he accelerated. As they were crossing the Pont de Bercy, he suddenly stopped, but left the motor on and asked Sylvie to hand him her cell phone.

"What for?"

"Give it to me, I said."

The moment he had the telephone in his hand, Yves tossed it into the Seine.

"That way, you won't be tempted to answer him or call him."

Sylvie's cries of outrage stuck in her throat. They continued on their way to the station, parked on the sidewalk, went tearing over to the ticket office where he bought her a one-way ticket. With one minute until departure, they ran headlong to the last train still on the platform. On the run like this she felt light, proud, a fugitive, as if wind-borne, already out of reach.

"When you get there, go straight to your friend's, and let some time go by. You know how to do that better than anybody."

"And what if Grégoire is trying to reach me?"

"If he's as in love as he says he is, if he's ready to assume the terrible shame of being seen with you, let him stew, he'll wait. Better yet, he'll find you."

Breathless, she said, "I didn't . . . I didn't know . . . that I could even run anymore."

To keep from bursting into tears, she burst out laughing, then climbed into the carriage. Once the door was closed, she put the palm of her hand against the window. Yves placed his on the same spot. She said a long sentence that he could not hear.

All too soon he was alone on the deserted platform.

Couples had formed around a vodka bottle in an ice bucket. Remo filled Myriam's glass, feigning a lively interest in her job with a television channel. She told him repeatedly that there was nothing exciting about it, but at the same time she went along with the pretence of being interviewed. On the dance floor, David moved closer to Charlotte; both of them liked nightclubs not so much for the people you could meet there as for the state of spontaneous combustion sparked off by the earsplitting music and molten bodies all around; their bodies were drawn together like magnets, swaying in harmony, creating an intimate bond. Denis, on a red leatherette couch, his hand glued to his glass, was listening distractedly to the confessions of a certain Mélanie who'd let him buy her a drink. There had been a time when he was well-accustomed to this nocturnal atmosphere, but nowadays he thought this form of commu-

nication was paradoxical to say the least, when complete
strangers, uninhibited by alcohol, shared moments of great sincerity screaming in each other's ears. At around three o'clock in
the morning, Mélanie was trying to convince her interlocutor
how perfectly unjust the diploma equivalencies were for admis-
sion into the prestigious École Nationale d'Administration.
Denis, whose eardrums were being hammered, nodded his
head to show he was listening, but in fact his fuddled mind was
transporting him to Marie-Jeanne's bedside; perhaps she was
awake, waiting for him. He tossed back another shot of vodka
to maintain his drunkenness and calm his anger; that woman
whom he'd never stopped calling *the intruder* persisted in refusing to reveal any of the reasons for her presence in his place, nor
had she reassured him in any way as to their future together. To
be sure, she gave him her body and her love of life, but had
Denis even asked for them? She had finagled her way past his
door then into his life, without the slightest permission, without
a single explanation. Tired of hypotheses and speculation, he
wanted to get to the bottom of it, that very night. He now knew
how to make her confess her hidden intentions, and to get her
with her back to the wall, how to pressure her, torment her if it
came to that. Without a doubt, Marie-Jeanne Pereyres was also
waiting for this ultimate confrontation.

"You see, a degree in management doesn't give me any particular advantage, so if I want to take the—"

"Shall we go to my place?"

In the roar of decibels, she thought she'd misheard. Denis
looped his hand behind her neck, placed his lips by her ear,
and with disturbing firmness said, "We're going to my place."

It was no longer even a rhetorical question.

The time of the taxi ride was hardly enough to sober up.
Mélanie, too preoccupied with her descriptions of the ins and
outs of her future career, suddenly noticed she had forgotten
to ask Denis: "And what do you do?"

In another era, Denis would have sidestepped the question with humor, but now he answered, *waiter in a brasserie.* Finding nothing better, she said, *That's cool,* and in the hall of his building she let him take her hand. Stunned by alcohol, he almost stumbled on his way up the stairs, and suppressed a peal of laughter. Outside his door he hunted for his key, and leaned down to kiss Mélanie on the neck.

Whether she was humiliated, disappointed, or panicked at the thought of losing him, the time had come for Marie-Jeanne to put aside her fine reserve and either burst into tears or spit in his face.

He went in first, turned on all the lights in the living room, made as much noise as he could, found a bottle of vodka in the freezer, put on some jazz, clinked glasses with Mélanie then put his arms around her.

Probably he hadn't made enough noise; the door to the bedroom remained firmly shut. Marie-Jeanne was sound asleep, he was going to have to wake her up and fling some nasty drunken comment in her face, the worst thing he could think of, and while he was at it he'd introduce his casual acquaintance.

He went into the room, turned on the overhead light, and saw the bed was empty.

On the night table was a folded note.

I think you're repaired now. Be happy, you deserve it.
                                                    Marie-Jeanne

Mélanie hesitated to follow him so soon into the bedroom. She called out, "Why don't we get to know one another first?"

At six o'clock in the morning Yves Lehaleur awoke from a heavy, calm sleep, more than well-deserved, he thought. The women who had been a part of his life were now all gone from it, as of yesterday, and life, with its strokes of luck and misfortune, could get back to normal. He thought he'd take a long reprieve to give his senses a rest, dulled as they were by so many restless nights, by the inflation of pleasure, by his exhausting commerce with all his women.

In the semi-darkness he saw the red flashing of his answering machine, and curiosity drove him out of bed. He listened to a courteous but sententious message from one Mademoiselle Perrine Le Bihan, a counselor at his bank branch, and the only woman in the world who was questioning her client's lifestyle. For several months she had been trying to get in touch with him, to explain the principle of life insurance to him and inquire tactfully why his insurance had been dwindling away. It was a losing battle, by now; in her message she informed him that his balance, once €87,000, now amounted to a credit of €26.45. Yves congratulated himself on such a fine job managing his debauchery budget. He put on a jacket and a pair of trousers, went down into the street, and took a long stroll to enjoy the cool morning air. He wondered how he should spend his last savings, with the weekend beginning. He stopped outside a fancy hotel that was offering a continental brunch for €22—he would not find better than this.

A few tables over on the deserted terrace, a very young couple, visibly the worse for wear after a sleepless night, were hunting in their pockets for enough change for a coffee. While they smoked their Camels, they commented with the arrogance of their age on the night's indiscretions. Then they kissed, immodestly. Passionately. Radiant with their exclusive love. Convinced that Paris was at their feet. That the world had better watch out. That their future would never end.

As he gazed tenderly and discreetly at them, Yves Lehaleur told himself that, despite his best efforts, he was not safe from a future love.

"I think the last time we saw each other was that night at the Crillon."

"Before that we ran into each other on the Rue de Tournon."

"Or maybe it was the Rue Mazarine?"

"It doesn't matter, it was also by chance. I don't know if it's a very good idea to let chance decide when we meet."

"That's why I called you."

"I couldn't believe it at first when I heard your message. To be honest, I thought, *Juliette is inviting me out for a meal, what's behind it*?"

"It's not every day you get to have lunch with a miraculous survivor."

"Ah . . . you heard about all that, as well."

"How could I avoid it? It was all over the papers, even on the evening news."

"Something I could have done without."

"The villa looked fabulous, even wrecked like it was. Is the version I heard the right one?"

"Which version?"

"You got left behind on the hill, had to fend for your-selves, etc."

"I can hear the irony in your voice, but when you're actually there and the ocean is starting to lick at your feet, you gradually lose your sense of irony. Once the hurricane had passed, there was so much destruction on the hill that we couldn't even get down to the shore. We had to wait for the rescue team."

"How long was it they took? Twenty-four hours?"

"That's what they said, but it felt like twenty-four days. And the worst of it was that if it hadn't been the world-famous Mia they were rescuing, I think I'd be there still."

"Oh, right, the disappearance of Philippe Saint-Jean might have brought a tear to the eyes of, let's say . . . one or two stu-dents hanging around the Sorbonne? And your older sister of course, and maybe your publisher."

"Yeah, really; he was delighted. He had the nerve to ask me to dash off a little book about those twenty-four hours. All the ingredients were there: a natural disaster, a celebrity in distress, and a philosopher asking his final questions as he is surrounded by Nature's fury. With already a heap of publicity before the book even came out. What could be better."

"What did you tell him?"

"To go fuck himself."

In fact, Philippe had started on a sociological essay, describing how contemporary man was harassed by demands of all sorts, and in his effort to keep up with his era, he could no longer keep up with himself. In the midst of this twenty-first century information overload, he was being instructed to be happy, forced to find pleasure, shackled to beauty, condemned to what was right; so many standards were being defined for him that he feared if he didn't comply he'd be left out. If Philippe ever finished his study, he'd dedicate it to Mia.

"With hindsight, the most unpleasant part of the whole thing was the rescue operation. The minute she had a hemp blanket over her head and her very first sandwich in her mouth, Mia regained the composure befitting a star. First camera she saw and she put on a survivor's persona worthy of *The Raft of the Medusa.*"

"I heard you on France Info. You sounded less inspired than she did."

"That was the worst. Because I have this status as an intellectual, they asked me to put it all into words. They figured I had enough distance to be able to pontificate on what I'd been through; they wanted some sort of eloquent pathos. And I sat there like a dork in front of their microphones, still stunned to be alive, obliged to act solemn, to come up with something meaningful, when all I really wanted was a steak and a very very very long night's sleep."

"Well, you're the one who went looking for that image as a media-friendly thinker, a prime-time philosopher, so you shouldn't complain. There you are now, on YouTube."

"The most absurd thing is that just before the disaster I had already decided to leave the island, and I was praying that no one would ever find out about my escapade beneath the coconut trees!"

"You have to hand it to that girl, though. To drag you, *you,* all the way to Indonesia. When you and I were living together, I could never have managed a feat like that."

"I'm not with her anymore."

Juliette looked at him.

"Are you surprised?" he said.

"To be honest, no. The two of you, it was sort of like a marriage between a carp and a rabbit."

"Who was the carp and who was the rabbit?"

"All I hope is that this odd episode has taught you something."

He would never answer that question; the tidal wave had carried away with it the very foundations of his thought. Why had the principle of reality, which he had invoked all through his career, been driven home to him there, of all places, with such brutality? How could he not see it as a lesson in humility, taught by Nature, how could he not question all his beliefs about chance, how could he not accept, in the end, the exceeding vanity of all things—his own little career as a sententious thinker to begin with? He who had always refused to see human beings as the playthings of superior forces, and now he found himself staring at a Pandora's box he would never dare to open, for fear of seeing his last remaining certainties explode in his face. Until he breathed his last, he would keep that box buried deep inside him, like the treasure of a future life, if peradventure there was one.

Today there was only one moral he wished to append to this

incredible fable: the return of Juliette, more luminous than ever.

"What did you do after they brought you home?"

"I reassured my parents, then I barricaded myself at home until the circus was over. You are the first person to get me out."

"Me? I'm flattered."

"I felt like seeing all six foot one and a hundred and thirty-nine pounds of you. Actually, is that still right?"

"With age, I fear it might be six foot and a hundred and forty-four pounds."

"What are you doing this afternoon?"

Juliette would never confess how afraid she had been of losing him when she heard he had disappeared. How sorry she had been, in that moment, for having abandoned him, without leaving him an infinity of second chances. How relieved she had been to see him brought back to life, with or without that girl on his arm. How she was looking forward, from now on, to knowing he was no longer so full of himself, after his misadventure.

"Nothing, and you?"

EPILOGUE

In an elegant building on the Rue d'Assas in the sixth arrondissement there was an immense apartment on the fifth floor which the owner lent out once a week—in general on a Thursday evening, between seven and nine o'clock— to some sort of association, whose bylaws she was not really acquainted with. It would seem to be a group of women who'd had a rough time of it in life, and who felt the need to talk: that brief explanation had sufficed. In the main salon a hundred or so chairs had been set up, and they could stay there as long as the mistress of the house, treating her rheumatism in the South, did not return to her Parisian quarters.

That particular Thursday there were a few new faces. It was easy to spot them, with their anxious expressions, their false air of schoolgirls on their first day, their desire to be ignored. One of them, however, did not seem to be as ill at ease as the others; of medium height, shoulder-length light brown hair, wearing jeans and a woolen cardigan, she sat down in the first row with the firm intention not to stay for long. And in fact, right at the beginning of the session, as soon as they had closed the double doors, she raised her hand to volunteer. She was invited to go and sit in a large armchair there in front of the others.

"This is the first time I've come, and in all likelihood it will be the last. After I've told you my story, I'll disappear, that's something I'm very good at."

Marie-Jeanne, pleased with the way she had started off, suddenly understood why she had come.

"I'm thirty-seven. I live alone. I haven't suffered from love. I have no causes for complaint. But I recently had an experience that is worth describing here. For your information, I should point out that I haven't had children, in spite of sustained efforts on the part of my companion and me. We pictured ourselves as perfect parents and lovers but, after an interminable ordeal, where we tried everything that science had to offer, it began to look as if this was not a role we would be asked to play. The companion in question got fed up and went to have children elsewhere, and for a long time I saw myself the way some people saw me: a dry sort of person who would never be truly a woman if she did not become a mother. In the long run I convinced myself that not all women are destined to be mothers, and I have spent ten years in a state of relative detachment, prepared to experience whatever life throws my way. In particular, the episode I am about to relate to you, because while it did not give me the opportunity to create a life, I managed nevertheless to save one."

Having set out her basic premise, she paused before launching into the story, like a good storyteller who knows how to reel in her audience.

"One day I happened to hear—I say happened for the lack of a better word—someone telling their story, a story I should never have heard. This man was complaining. A man like so many others, not stupid but not particularly brilliant, rather funny, but often without intending to be, a man that some of you would have found charming, and others would not even have noticed, in short, the kind of man we have all known at some point. This one did have something exceptional about him, however: he had a grudge against every woman on the planet, because he was sure he was their chosen scapegoat, that they were taking their revenge on him for the age-old villainy of men."

Where had she heard this story? Who had told it to her?

Was it on that memorable evening when, before a hundred or more witnesses, the man had complained of such terrible injustice, with such cruel precision? Had she found her way into that secret society? And if so, how had she managed to deceive the congregation, who had never mingled with any women? Or had some tactless member relayed the story to her, thus betraying all his fellows? One thing seemed certain: Marie-Jeanne Pereyres had *heard* Denis Benitez.

"I knocked on the man's door, and I found him in such a state of confusion, of inner turmoil, that his last remnants of resistance could not stop me from moving in. My time was my own, I had enough savings to last for several months, why not give this unique adventure a try?"

The only one in the audience who wondered how such a thing could be possible was, as it happened, one of the new visitors. Pauline found that the speaker was skipping too quickly over some essential points: what words had she used to convince the man to let her invade his space? Had she ever questioned her true reasons for setting herself such an unbelievable challenge? Was this sudden devotion to a stranger not rather suspicious? Pauline was forced to admit that the story she had to tell would seem quite banal in comparison with what she was hearing.

For a time in the recent past, her name had been Madame Lehaleur, until one sad morning when, without even realizing it, she had become Pauline Revel once again. Because of a night's escapade, she had been repudiated like a sinner, without the slightest chance to make amends, and to see herself through her husband's eyes had left her feeling sullied. Henceforth, she needed to know how other women would react to her, women who would not judge her, the way the man she had once loved had judged her. Nowadays, she no longer felt guilty over the tragic end of their relationship, but she needed, for once, just once, to tell her version of the truth.

"The experiment lasted several months, with its rules and its constraints, but also its joy and sadness and excess."

Another newcomer seemed to be devastated by what she was hearing. To interfere like that in a man's life, without the slightest connection, the slightest obligation, and above all, without the slightest thing to gain, other than a vague moral satisfaction? Christelle had to admit that the notion of a gratuitous gesture put her ill at ease, particularly where men were concerned. When, during her work hours, she slipped on her uniform as Kris, and went to clients' homes so that they could gorge themselves on her body, she did it solely for money and nothing else. And it was, no doubt, this "nothing else" that she would speak of to these women, hiding nothing about her profession, even if it meant she was the first sex worker who had ever crossed the threshold of this room.

"If you are interested in this story, I can tell it to you in detail."

That Thursday evening, there would be time for only one testimony. Christelle, Pauline, and the others encouraged her with a simple silence.

ABOUT THE AUTHOR

Tonino Benacquista was born in France in 1961. He is a screenwriter, cartoonist, dramaturge, and the author of four crime novels published by Bitter Lemon Press, among them *Holy Smoke*. Benacquista won a César (French Oscar) in 2006 for the script of Jacques Audiard's *The Beat that My Heart Skipped*. He lives in France.

EUROPA EDITIONS BACKLIST
(alphabetical by author)

Fiction

Carmine Abate
Between Two Seas • 978-1-933372-40-2 • Territories: World
The Homecoming Party • 978-1-933372-83-9 • Territories: World

Milena Agus
From the Land of the Moon • 978-1-60945-001-4 • Ebook • Territories:
World (excl. ANZ)

Salwa Al Neimi
The Proof of the Honey • 978-1-933372-68-6 • Ebook • Territories: World
(excl UK)

Simonetta Agnello Hornby
The Nun • 978-1-60945-062-5 • Territories: World

Daniel Arsand
Lovers • 978-1-60945-071-7 • Ebook • Territories: World

Jenn Ashworth
A Kind of Intimacy • 978-1-933372-86-0 • Territories: US & Can

Beryl Bainbridge
The Girl in the Polka Dot Dress • 978-1-60945-056-4 • Ebook •
Territories: US

Muriel Barbery
The Elegance of the Hedgehog • 978-1-933372-60-0 • Ebook • Territories:
World (excl. UK & EU)
Gourmet Rhapsody • 978-1-933372-95-2 • Ebook • Territories: World
(excl. UK & EU)

Stefano Benni
Margherita Dolce Vita • 978-1-933372-20-4 • Territories: World
Timeskipper • 978-1-933372-44-0 • Territories: World

Romano Bilenchi
The Chill • 978-1-933372-90-7 • Territories: World

Kazimierz Brandys
Rondo • 978-1-60945-004-5 • Territories: World

Alina Bronsky
Broken Glass Park • 978-1-933372-96-9 • Ebook • Territories: World
The Hottest Dishes of the Tartar Cuisine • 978-1-60945-006-9 • Ebook •
Territories: World

Jesse Browner
Everything Happens Today • 978-1-60945-051-9 • Ebook • Territories:
World (excl. UK & EU)

Francisco Coloane
Tierra del Fuego • 978-1-933372-63-1 • Ebook • Territories: World

Rebecca Connell
The Art of Losing • 978-1-933372-78-5 • Territories: US

Laurence Cossé
A Novel Bookstore • 978-1-933372-82-2 • Ebook • Territories: World
An Accident in August • 978-1-60945-049-6 • Territories: World (excl. UK)

Diego De Silva
I Hadn't Understood • 978-1-60945-065-6 • Territories: World

Shashi Deshpande
The Dark Holds No Terrors • 978-1-933372-67-9 • Territories: US

Steve Erickson
Zeroville • 978-1-933372-39-6 • Territories: US & Can
These Dreams of You • 978-1-60945-063-2 • Territories: US & Can

Elena Ferrante
The Days of Abandonment • 978-1-933372-00-6 • Ebook • Territories: World
Troubling Love • 978-1-933372-16-7 • Territories: World
The Lost Daughter • 978-1-933372-42-6 • Territories: World

Linda Ferri
Cecilia • 978-1-933372-87-7 • Territories: World

Damon Galgut
In a Strange Room • 978-1-60945-011-3 • Ebook • Territories: USA

Santiago Gamboa
Necropolis • 978-1-60945-073-1 • Ebook • Territories: World

Jane Gardam
Old Filth • 978-1-933372-13-6 • Ebook • Territories: US
The Queen of the Tambourine • 978-1-933372-36-5 • Ebook • Territories: US
The People on Privilege Hill • 978-1-933372-56-3 • Ebook • Territories: US
The Man in the Wooden Hat • 978-1-933372-89-1 • Ebook • Territories: US
God on the Rocks • 978-1-933372-76-1 • Ebook • Territories: US
Crusoe's Daughter • 978-1-60945-069-4 • Ebook • Territories: US

Anna Gavalda
French Leave • 978-1-60945-005-2 • Ebook • Territories: US & Can

Seth Greenland
The Angry Buddhist • 978-1-60945-068-7 • Ebook • Territories: World

Katharina Hacker
The Have-Nots • 978-1-933372-41-9 • Territories: World (excl. India)

Patrick Hamilton
Hangover Square • 978-1-933372-06-8 • Territories: US & Can

James Hamilton-Paterson
Cooking with Fernet Branca • 978-1-933372-01-3 • Territories: US
Amazing Disgrace • 978-1-933372-19-8 • Territories: US
Rancid Pansies • 978-1-933372-62-4 • Territories: USA

Alfred Hayes
The Girl on the Via Flaminia • 978-1-933372-24-2 • Ebook •
Territories: World

Jean-Claude Izzo
The Lost Sailors • 978-1-933372-35-8 • Territories: World
A Sun for the Dying • 978-1-933372-59-4 • Territories: World

Gail Jones
Sorry • 978-1-933372-55-6 • Territories: US & Can

Ioanna Karystiani
The Jasmine Isle • 978-1-933372-10-5 • Territories: World
Swell • 978-1-933372-98-3 • Territories: World

Peter Kocan
Fresh Fields • 978-1-933372-29-7 • Territories: US, EU & Can
The Treatment and the Cure • 978-1-933372-45-7 • Territories: US, EU & Can

Helmut Krausser
Eros • 978-1-933372-58-7 • Territories: World

Amara Lakhous
Clash of Civilizations Over an Elevator in Piazza Vittorio •
978-1-933372-61-7 • Ebook • Territories: World
Divorce Islamic Style • 978-1-60945-066-3 • Ebook • Territories: World

Lia Levi
The Jewish Husband • 978-1-933372-93-8 • Territories: World

Valerio Massimo Manfredi
The Ides of March • 978-1-933372-99-0 • Territories: US

Leïla Marouane
The Sexual Life of an Islamist in Paris • 978-1-933372-85-3 •
Territories: World

Lorenzo Mediano
The Frost on His Shoulders • 978-1-60945-072-4 • Ebook •
Territories: World

Sélim Nassib
I Loved You for Your Voice • 978-1-933372-07-5 • Territories: World
The Palestinian Lover • 978-1-933372-23-5 • Territories: World

Amélie Nothomb
Tokyo Fiancée • 978-1-933372-64-8 • Territories: US & Can
Hygiene and the Assassin • 978-1-933372-77-8 • Ebook • Territories: US & Can

Valeria Parrella
For Grace Received • 978-1-933372-94-5 • Territories: World

Alessandro Piperno
The Worst Intentions • 978-1-933372-33-4 • Territories: World
Persecution • 978-1-60945-074-8 • Ebook • Territories: World

Lorcan Roche
The Companion • 978-1-933372-84-6 • Territories: World

Boualem Sansal
The German Mujahid • 978-1-933372-92-1 • Ebook • Territories: US & Can

www.europaeditions.com

Eric-Emmanuel Schmitt
The Most Beautiful Book in the World • 978-1-933372-74-7 • Ebook •
Territories: World
The Woman with the Bouquet • 978-1-933372-81-5 • Ebook • Territories:
US & Can

Angelika Schrobsdorff
You Are Not Like Other Mothers • 978-1-60945-075-5 • Ebook •
Territories: World

Audrey Schulman
Three Weeks in December • 978-1-60945-064-9 • Ebook • Territories: US
& Can

James Scudamore
Heliopolis • 978-1-933372-73-0 • Ebook • Territories: US

Luis Sepúlveda
The Shadow of What We Were • 978-1-60945-002-1 • Ebook • Territories:
World

Paolo Sorrentino
Everybody's Right • 978-1-60945-052-6 • Ebook • Territories: US & Can

Domenico Starnone
First Execution • 978-1-933372-66-2 • Territories: World

Henry Sutton
Get Me out of Here • 978-1-60945-007-6 • Ebook • Territories: US & Can

Chad Taylor
Departure Lounge • 978-1-933372-09-9 • Territories: US, EU & Can

•

Roma Tearne
Mosquito • 978-1-933372-57-0 • Territories: US & Can
Bone China • 978-1-933372-75-4 • Territories: US

André Carl van der Merwe
Moffie • 978-1-60945-050-2 • Ebook • Territories: World
(excl. S. Africa)

Fay Weldon
Chalcot Crescent • 978-1-933372-79-2 • Territories: US

Anne Wiazemsky
My Berlin Child • 978-1-60945-003-8 • Territories: US & Can

Jonathan Yardley
Second Reading • 978-1-60945-008-3 • Ebook • Territories: US & Can

Edwin M. Yoder Jr.
Lions at Lamb House • 978-1-933372-34-1 • Territories: World

Michele Zackheim
Broken Colors • 978-1-933372-37-2 • Territories: World

Alice Zeniter
Take This Man • 978-1-60945-053-3 • Territories: World

Tonga Books

Ian Holding
Of Beasts and Beings • 978-1-60945-054-0 • Ebook • Territories: US & Can

Sara Levine
Treasure Island!!! • 978-0-14043-768-3 • Ebook • Territories: World

Alexander Maksik
You Deserve Nothing • 978-1-60945-048-9 • Ebook • Territories: US, Can & EU (excl. UK)

Thad Ziolkowski
Wichita • 978-1-60945-070-0 • Ebook • Territories: World

Crime/Noir

Massimo Carlotto
The Goodbye Kiss • 978-1-933372-05-1 • Ebook • Territories: World
Death's Dark Abyss • 978-1-933372-18-1 • Ebook • Territories: World
The Fugitive • 978-1-933372-25-9 • Ebook • Territories: World
Bandit Love • 978-1-933372-80-8 • Ebook • Territories: World
Poisonville • 978-1-933372-91-4 • Ebook • Territories: World

Giancarlo De Cataldo
The Father and the Foreigner • 978-1-933372-72-3 • Territories: World

Caryl Férey
Zulu • 978-1-933372-88-4 • Ebook • Territories: World (excl. UK & EU)
Utu • 978-1-60945-055-7 • Ebook • Territories: World (excl. UK & EU)

Alicia Giménez-Bartlett
Dog Day • 978-1-933372-14-3 • Territories: US & Can
Prime Time Suspect • 978-1-933372-31-0 • Territories: US & Can
Death Rites • 978-1-933372-54-9 • Territories: US & Can

Jean-Claude Izzo
Total Chaos • 978-1-933372-04-4 • Territories: US & Can
Chourmo • 978-1-933372-17-4 • Territories: US & Can
Solea • 978-1-933372-30-3 • Territories: US & Can

www.europaeditions.com

Matthew F. Jones
Boot Tracks • 978-1-933372-11-2 • Territories: US & Can

Gene Kerrigan
The Midnight Choir • 978-1-933372-26-6 • Territories: US & Can
Little Criminals • 978-1-933372-43-3 • Territories: US & Can

Carlo Lucarelli
Carte Blanche • 978-1-933372-15-0 • Territories: World
The Damned Season • 978-1-933372-27-3 • Territories: World
Via delle Oche • 978-1-933372-53-2 • Territories: World

Edna Mazya
Love Burns • 978-1-933372-08-2 • Territories: World (excl. ANZ)

Yishai Sarid
Limassol • 978-1-60945-000-7 • Ebook • Territories: World (excl. UK, AUS & India)

Joel Stone
The Jerusalem File • 978-1-933372-65-5 • Ebook • Territories: World

Benjamin Tammuz
Minotaur • 978-1-933372-02-0 • Ebook • Territories: World

Non-fiction

Alberto Angela
A Day in the Life of Ancient Rome • 978-1-933372-71-6 • Territories: World • History

Helmut Dubiel
Deep In the Brain: Living with Parkinson's Disease • 978-1-933372-70-9 •
Ebook • Territories: World • Medicine/Memoir

James Hamilton-Paterson
Seven-Tenths: The Sea and Its Thresholds • 978-1-933372-69-3 • Territories:
USA • Nature/Essays

Daniele Mastrogiacomo
Days of Fear • 978-1-933372-97-6 • Ebook • Territories: World • Current
affairs/Memoir/Afghanistan/Journalism

Valery Panyushkin
Twelve Who Don't Agree • 978-1-60945-010-6 • Ebook • Territories:
World • Current affairs/Memoir/Russia/Journalism

Christa Wolf
One Day a Year: 1960-2000 • 978-1-933372-22-8 • Territories: World •
Memoir/History/20th Century

Children's Illustrated Fiction

Altan
Here Comes Timpa • 978-1-933372-28-0 • Territories: World (excl. Italy)
Timpa Goes to the Sea • 978-1-933372-32-7 • Territories: World (excl. Italy)
Fairy Tale Timpa • 978-1-933372-38-9 • Territories: World (excl. Italy)

Wolf Erlbruch
The Big Question • 978-1-933372-03-7 • Territories: US & Can
The Miracle of the Bears • 978-1-933372-21-1 • Territories: US & Can
(with **Gioconda Belli**) *The Butterfly Workshop* • 978-1-933372-12-9 •
Territories: US & Can